Vanished From Budapest

D.J. Maughan

Hulyeseg Publishing

For you, Dad. Your love of reading inspired me. I miss you.

Prologue

My teeth feel like they might rattle out of my mouth. Am I cold, or is someone shaking me? Something's not right. A fog is floating in my head. Am I awake? My eyes are open, but I see nothing but blackness. As I stare into the darkness, remembrance comes to me. Last night, as my husband sat on the bed next to me, he wore a mask. His face was blank, completely void of emotion as I lied to him. Never in our marriage has he ever raised a hand to me. That's why I didn't flinch as he doubled his fist and punched me full in the face.

The fog in my head begins to clear. My arms are throbbing. I try in vain to move them. Panic rises in my chest as I lie on my side, my face resting against something cold and hard. The smell of stale dirt fills my nostrils. The floor shifts and moves. I'm in a vehicle.

Almost on cue, the bumping slows then stops. I hold my breath, listening intently to the silence. Through gritted teeth, I turn from my side onto my back. The movement awakens an eruption of pain in my wrist. I press my hips to the floor, limiting the pressure on my wrist.

Listening closely, I hear footsteps then scraping metal as light bursts through the swinging door. I force my eyes closed, avoiding the light and fearing whoever may come through the door.

"Get up."

The voice is unfamiliar. I'm surprised. I expected to hear my husband, not this nasally, coarse male. I push my eyelids open, blinking against the burning light.

My mouth is stuffed, gagged. My eyes are adjusting to the light, focusing on the stranger standing in front of me. He reaches out, and I wince as he grips my foot, pulling me to him. He drags my body along the floor of the dirty box truck. I press against the gag, trying to scream, but my cry is swallowed. He roughly grabs me by the shoulders, pulling me up into a sitting position. My head spins and my arms throb. My stomach turns and I worry I may vomit into my gag.

"Do you need to pee?" he asks me.

I can't respond and only nod my head. The man stares at me, warning me with his eyes. Finally, he bends over and unties the rope around my ankles.

The stench of tobacco and body odor waft over me.

"I'm going to allow you out of this truck so you can pee. But I warn you, no funny business. I'll be watching you the whole time. And if you try to run," he holds up a shiny pistol, "you better be faster than a bullet. I don't miss. Understand me?"

Without thinking, I bend one knee and bring it up and forward. My aim is true as I connect my knee to the man's balls. Immediately, he drops to the ground. I bend the other knee extending my foot and connecting with his face. Blood springs from his nose.

I leap down from the truck and I take off running. The sun is blinding. *Where am I?*

I momentarily stop, looking around wildly. In front of me stands a forest. Behind me, a dirt road, and Andras's delivery truck. I head toward the forest. An explosion sounds behind me, and I feel the whiz of a bullet before it slams into the bark of the tree in front of me.

I stop, turning to look back.

"The next one will be in your head," the gunman says, walking toward me.

Chapter One

Peter

B udapest – October 2000

Peter is late. A part of him hopes Stephen—the young man he is meant to meet—won't show and it won't matter. Stephen claimed his 22-year-old girlfriend had disappeared, and he seemed to think Peter, a private investigator, was the only man to help him. Looking out the window, he becomes increasingly aware of the dread growing in the pit of his stomach. Cases like these are precisely why he left the New York City Police and returned home to Budapest. Images of an NYC alleyway flash in his head.

The streetcar stops and Peter rushes to exit. In his haste, he catches his foot on one of the steps. His reflexes aren't what they used to be, but as he falls, he is able to slow his descent by grasping the railing. Unfortunately, his hand slips and he bounces off the bottom step, rolling onto the platform in front of several waiting passengers. As he lies on the concrete, he closes his eyes, imagining he were a magician making his audience disappear.

"Are you okay?" a young man asks as he leans down to extend his hand.

Peter opens his eyes and grasps it. "Yes, I'm fine thank you." As he stands, he realizes his hat has fallen off.

The youth leans down, picking it up, and extends it to him. "Maybe you should take one step at a time, Pops."

"Thank you. At least I'm not behind the wheel of a car, right?" Before the younger man can reply, Peter crosses the street and begins striding down the sidewalk.

He's grateful for the young man's help but senses the not too subtle jab at his age. At 54, Peter isn't necessarily old, but he isn't young either. Lately, he has begun to feel out of touch with the ever-increasing impact technology was having on society. Three months of no cases will do that to you. Several short months ago people had been afraid the world would stop, computers would no longer work, it would be the end of the world simply because the year flipped from 1999 to 2000. Now, the internet was becoming bigger and bigger. The World Wide Web was the way to interact, to market, even to investigate. Peter never used a computer and felt intimidated by them. He had contemplated changing careers. But to what? Investigation was all he knew. He hated the prospect of reinventing himself. *Maybe coming back to Budapest was a mistake?* No, he shook his head. He was being dramatic. In the last week, he had been called three times and was close to solving one of the cases. He was now headed to a new client meeting. Things would be okay.

As Peter enters the near-deserted café, he immediately recognizes Stephen. There are five or six small tables and only a few people scattered among them. Only one with a young man in his early twenties dressed like an American—Nikes and Levi Strauss jeans. Hungary had been behind the Soviet Iron Curtain as recently as nine years ago, and although advances were being made, they were far behind Western Europe and America in commerce. Clothing, hairstyle, health, and dental care were some of the most obvious signs. Westerners just looked different. Peter walks over and sits down in front of him without speaking. This is part of his method. Upon meeting new people, he forces them to speak first. It gives him insight into their personality. Stephen looks at him anxiously, seeming unsteady. Peter sits waiting.

"Peter?" the young man asks.

Peter leans back and nods as he appraises the young man. Stephen seems ordinary, average in height with a lean build. His hair is light brown with eyes that match. His face is symmetrical with well-defined features. He guesses women might find him handsome if not for his timidness. He melts under Peter's gaze, squirming in his chair.

Peter decides to take pity on him. "So, Tom told you to call me, huh?" Peter keeps his face impassive. As a detective in New York, he developed a reputation. The other cops called him the "truth seer" and "Sauron," a nod to the Dark Lord in *The Lord of the Rings*, "the all-seeing eye."

"Yep," Stephen replies.

"How long has it been since you saw your girlfriend?"

"Five days."

"What do you think happened to her?" Peter likes asking pointed questions. He finds it keeps the potential client or witness off balance. They begin to respond emotionally which leads to more candor. Uncomfortable people divulge information they intend to keep secret.

Stephen takes his hands off the table and wipes them on his jeans. "I don't know. She's not coming to class anymore."

"Maybe she's sick?"

Stephen shakes his head and sits forward in his chair. "No, something happened to her."

"What happened to her?"

Stephen shrugs. "She either went back home to England or something bad happened."

Peter taps his fingers on the table and stares back at him. "You think something bad happened to her?"

"Yep."

Peter crosses his arms over his chest. "Like what?"

Stephen shifts in his chair again. "I think someone might have taken her."

"Taken her where? Who?"

"I don't know. I guess that's why I'm contacting you. I'm worried about her."

"Why did you contact me? Why not the police?"

"I don't speak much Hungarian. I mean, my family is Hungarian, but I grew up in Cleveland, Ohio. I'm only here for school. I wouldn't know who to contact."

Peter puts his right index finger to his chin. Although he's calm on the outside, he's fighting the growing sense of uneasiness on the inside. Cases involving violence toward women are precisely why he left the NYC Police and returned home to Budapest. "Tell me everything you can about her. Start from the beginning. Don't worry about repeating things."

"Where do I start?"

Peter shrugs. "How about her name?"

"Her name was Samantha."

"What do you mean was?"

Stephen takes a short breath and corrects himself. "I mean her name is Samantha."

"Samantha what?"

Stephen hesitates. "I actually don't know her last name."

"She's your girlfriend and you don't know her last name?"

Stephen shifts in his chair. "I only met her a couple weeks ago. It never came up. I don't know if she's actually my girlfriend."

"Why do you say that?"

"I don't know, we never talked about it."

Peter rubs the beard on his chin. "How did you meet?"

Again, the kid shifts around in his chair. "We met in school. We are both students at the International Business School in Northern Buda."

Peter had never been to the school but had heard about it. "Where is she from in England?"

"Preston."

"And you are from Cleveland, Ohio?"

"Yeah."

Peter leans back again and stares at Stephen. He needs the money this case would bring, but he dreads the result. Relying on his many years of interrogation experience he keeps his tone low and calm. "What does Samantha look like?"

"She's really pretty."

Peter shakes his head. *This again?* How many times had he told clients or witnesses that he needs detail? A detective without detail is like a painter without paint.

He leans forward and speaks forcefully to Stephen. "Look, young man, I need you to be as detailed as possible; the more detail you give me, the better. *She's really pretty* doesn't work. I need to know why she's pretty. I need to know her height, the type of clothing she wears, the way she wears her hair, makeup, etc. The more detail, the better chance I have of finding her. Understand me?"

Stephen swallows hard but agrees.

"I want you to tell me how you met her. Give me all the details. It isn't up to you to determine what is and isn't important. I need everything."

Stephen raises his hands, extending his palms to Peter. "Okay...okay." He takes a deep breath. "As I got off the plane here in Budapest, I nearly turned around and got back on, begging for them to take me home. I've only been to Budapest once in my life. I was thirteen, and I came with my grandma, who is Hungarian. My mom had just died; Grandma brought me in an attempt to distract me. Returning as an adult brought a lot of those memories flooding back. I arrived on a Friday and school was due to start on Monday. I spent the weekend attempting to acclimate to a completely foreign language and environment. I broke my toilet the first time I used it, lit my hair on fire from the water heater below the shower, and was terrified when leaving the apartment fearing I was going to be accosted by an elderly woman looking like Mrs. Doubtfire."

Peter smirks but says nothing. A cute woman around Stephen's age is sitting at the table across from them and keeps looking in Stephen's direction.

"By the time Monday came along, I was beginning to wonder what else could go wrong," Stephen continues. "I was sure I would get lost and never make it to school. I knew the streetcar ride would be about twenty minutes. I was anxious as I got on, I had never ridden public transportation and I worried someone would speak to me and I wouldn't know what to say back. Eventually, I heard my stop announced and got off the streetcar. The school was across the street. As I walked up the steps, I felt like a five-year-old going to their first day of kindergarten. I was certainly excited but also very nervous. This was my fifth school."

"What do you mean, your fifth school?" Peter asks.

"I mean including grade school, middle school, high school, and college."

"Oh...okay. Get to the point. How did you meet her?"

Stephen hesitates. "The school was vastly different from Ohio State or high school; there weren't a thousand kids walking around. I barely saw anyone. It looked more like an office building. To my right, I saw a room which looked like a main office. I walked over and opened the door and was greeted by a gorgeous blonde woman in her early twenties. Immediately, I felt my face flush and my hands sweat. I've never been good with beautiful women."

Finally. The young woman sitting in the café across from them, picks up her purse, and walks past them. As she does, she makes eye contact with Stephen and smiles. He turns away, looking back at Peter, and continues with his story.

"The striking blonde smiled at me and said, 'Hello, are you a student?' I was relieved to hear English.

"'I am. My name is Stephen Nagy,' I said and extended my hand to her. She stood and came around the desk. She was one of the prettiest women I had ever seen. She had long wavy blonde hair and electric-blue eyes. She wore professional clothing. Her handshake was firm but feminine. She was about five foot six but with her heels, a couple inches taller than that. 'I'm Gretchen. Welcome to IBS! Are you American?'"

Peter holds up his hand. "Wait. I thought you said her name is Samantha?"

Stephen looks incredulous. "Yes, her name is Samantha."

"Then who is this Gretchen?"

"She's the first girl I met in the school."

Peter starts shaking his extended hand and rises out of his chair. The kid gave him the out he was seeking. "No, this isn't going to work."

Stephen remains seated in his chair looking up at Peter. "What? Why?"

"I've been sitting here," Peter pauses and looks at his watch, "for ten minutes. All I have from you is her first name." He begins shaking his head. "Oh, and she's from Preston, England. I asked you to tell me about her and you start telling me about your first few days in Hungary and the first girl you met?" Peter holds up both hands. "Sorry, Stephen. You would drive me crazy as a client. I wish you the best of luck in finding her, but that help won't be from me."

Stephen stands and his voice rises in pitch. "Peter. Please don't leave. I'm sorry."

He seems genuine and Peter hesitates. He pushes aside the growing sense of guilt and embraces the relief.

"I know people, Stephen. I know when they are lying to me. You are intentionally withholding information from me. I can't work with clients like that." He leans forward and pats Stephen on the shoulder. "Sorry, I'm already late to another appointment." With that, he turns and walks out the door leaving Stephen staring after him.

Chapter Two

Peter

As Peter exits the small café, he looks at his watch. Fifteen minutes to reach Memento Park. Even in the best of traffic, arriving on time would be tight. It's now rush hour. Peter can only hope for a miracle at this point. A week ago, he was contacted by a man who had been robbed. The robbery included several old communist relics which had sentimental value to him. Yesterday, he learned a thief was planning to sell them to Ferenc, the proprietor of the memorabilia shop in Memento Park. The thief promised to return at five pm. Peter's client would pay a premium for the return of the property, but he was going to miss his chance. The thief would come, Ferenc would turn down the opportunity to buy, the thief would know someone had tipped him off, and he would disappear. Peter would lose him.

He walks briskly now, almost running. The sidewalk is full of people, and he has to dodge and weave as he makes his way from the café to Móricz Zsigmond Square. The square is close, maybe only a hundred meters away. Peter knows he can find a taxicab parked in front of the grocery store, Tesco. As Peter rounds the corner and enters the square, he looks to his right and sees two yellow taxi cabs parked on the corner. He runs to one, opens the car door, and slides into the seat, slamming the door behind him. "Memento Park" he tells the driver. "And I'll give you an extra five hundred forint if you can make it there by five p.m." That seems to be the right amount of motivation for the driver. He never even turns around to look at Peter. Instead, he pulls out from the curb and guns it, cutting in front of several cars and winning himself a chorus of honks and extended middle fingers.

Fifteen minutes later, Peter pays his driver and gets out at the most unique spot in all of Budapest. After the fall of the Soviet Union, Hungary tried to erase any memories of those oppressive forty years. They began to rename, or in some cases, revert back to former street names and buildings. They removed communist statues from all across Hungary and created this park. The park includes a photo exhibition and storage showroom. Today it is the storage showroom Peter is interested in. The showroom displays loads of old communist memorabilia for purchase. As Peter enters the showroom, he is pleased to see Ferenc behind the desk. He is a small man with large glasses and gray, almost white, hair. His face shows the wear of a longtime business owner. He looks at Peter and his eyes widen as recognition dawns.

Peter walks over to him while looking at his watch. "It's five past five. Have you seen my guy yet?"

"No not yet. He said he would be here around five p.m."

"Alright. I meant to be here earlier. I'm going to look around your shop. When he comes in, tap on the desk, okay?"

Ferenc shrugs. "Sure. But I don't want any trouble. I have a lot of irreplaceable things that could be broken."

Peter assures him nothing will be broken. He doesn't mind having a few minutes to look around. He heard about this place after coming back to Hungary but hadn't had occasion to visit. Now is his opportunity. He walks over to one of the glass display cases and opens it. Inside are several trinkets from the communist days. Peter picks up a watch. It has a large red star in the middle. Next to the watch is a pass issued to someone to travel outside of Hungary in 1977. Peter begins to wonder how much of this stuff Ferenc sells and who buys it. He never had much interest in collectibles. Off to his right, looking through one of the other display cases, stands a group of four boys dressed in white shirts and ties. They are speaking English. Each wears a black tag on his shirt pocket. Peter overhears one of them say, "My dad would love this." He's holding up a pocket watch.

Peter approaches them curiously. "Where are you guys from?"

The tallest one, with dark brown hair, turns to Peter. "What?"

Peter repeats the question. "Where are you guys from?" speaking English to them.

"Oh, I'm from Ogden, Utah."

Peter looks at the next one. He is shorter with a muscular build. "I'm from Fresno, California." The other two tell him they're from the US also.

"What are you doing in Budapest?" Peter asks.

The tall one seems accustomed to the question. "We came on missions for our church." He holds up his name tag for Peter to see. The tag reads Elder Chambers Az Utolsó Napok Szentjeinek Jézus Krisztus Egyháza.

"So, your name is Elder Chambers?"

"Yeah, well, Elder is a name used in our church when you're on a mission. My real name is Maury."

"Why is the name of your church in Hungarian?"

Chambers shrugs. "We come here and learn Hungarian so we can teach the people in their native language."

"Hungarian is a difficult language. One of the hardest in the world. How long have you been here?"

"Two years. I'm headed home tomorrow. I'm just doing a little shopping. My dad would love to have something from the communist days." Chambers frowns. "Hey, how do you speak such good English? You sound like you're from America."

"I'm Hungarian but lived in New York City for many years where I worked in the police force." Behind him, Peter hears the door open and a man in his early twenties walks in carrying a couple bags and a large, framed picture. Ferenc begins tapping his hand on his desk.

"Have you heard of our church?" Elder Chambers is looking at Peter, but Peter is distracted.

The man begins placing his items on the desk in front of Ferenc. Ferenc keeps glancing back and forth from the young man to Peter.

Peter turns back to Chambers. "How would you like to perform one last act of service to a Hungarian?" Chambers looks at his companions and they all agree. "I want you guys to stand close to that door." Peter points to where Ferenc is. "I'm an investigator and that guy there is trying to sell stolen property. I need to confront him. And I have a feeling it will go much easier with some backup. I don't want you to do anything. Just look like you're here with me."

The boys get big grins on their faces, nodding. As Peter walks toward the young man and Ferenc, the American boys hang around the back by the door. Four of them together is a daunting obstacle. When he had been a police officer in New York City, he almost always had a partner to accompany him. Since moving to private practice, he had to find clever methods of improvisation.

As he reaches the young man and Ferenc, he overhears their conversation.

"As I told you, my grandfather recently died." The man is pulling several different items from his bag including a sheet of rare stamps, several procommunist pamphlets, and a vintage communist poster.

Peter feels his pulse quicken as he recognizes the figure in the framed photo. It's Rákosi Mátyás, the ruthless leader of the Hungarian Communist party during the 1956 revolution. This framed photo is one of his client's prized possessions. Peter looks at Ferenc who is standing as rigid as a flagpole and keeps looking at Peter. The thief turns to see what has distracted the shop owner.

"Is that Rákosi?" Peter asks, feigning interest and distracting the thief.

"Uh...yeah it is," the young man replies and steps closer to the picture. He isn't tall. Peter has him by several inches. He's older than Peter guessed when he first saw him. He wears a scruffy beard that hasn't filled in and his teeth are overcrowded and crooked. He wears a T-shirt and a pair of shorts. The smell of tobacco wafts off his hair and clothing.

Peter steps to the desk. As he does, he reaches out and hands a note to Ferenc. The shop owner turns the note over, looking back at Peter. Peter scowls at him before turning back to the young man. "That's a valuable picture. Where did you get it?" The thief looks from Peter to the shopkeeper and back to Peter. As he does, he begins to place the memorabilia back into his bag. Ferenc holds up his finger and interrupts them nervously, saying he must go to the restroom.

The young man has moved in front of the stolen property now, shielding it from Peter with his body. "My grandfather recently died. He had all of this stuff."

"Well, I'm a collector. I've been looking for some of these things for a long time. Do you mind if I look at them more closely?"

He hesitates then finally says, "Not at all."

Peter begins examining the memorabilia. He is deliberate in his movements. "How much are you selling all this for?" Peter asks him.

"Twenty thousand forint."

Peter lets out a low whistle. "That's steep. I don't think I'd go anything more than ten thousand."

"Sorry. It's worth more than ten thousand." The thief looks to the door and notices the four American boys for the first time. They seem to spook him, and he resumes stuffing all the relics back in his bag.

"Wait a second," Peter reassures. "I could do more than ten thousand." But it's no use. The thief has finished packing the bag and is turning away. Peter reaches out and grabs him by the shoulder in an effort to turn him back. Without warning, the thief whips around and pushes Peter with both hands. Peter falls back a step but as the thief turns to flee, he is immediately seized by Elder Chambers. Chambers being a head taller grabs the thief in a bear hug while his companions wrestle the bag away and assist. They slam the thief to the ground and hold him, giving Peter time to come over.

"Looks like you won't be selling anything today," he tells the thief.

The shopkeeper comes around the corner after hearing all the commotion. He turns to Peter. "What are you doing?"

"Did you call the police?" Peter asks. Ferenc nods. Just then, two police officers enter the shop followed by detective Kovacs Lajos. Peter turns back to Chambers. "Boy, am I glad you guys were here."

Ten minutes later Peter finds his opportunity to speak with Detective Kovacs. Before he does, he thanks the young Americans and pays for the stopwatch Chambers picked out. He is impressed by the dedication they showed in leaving their country for two years and studying Hungarian. When Peter finds Kovacs in the gravel parking lot, the detective is giving final instructions to the police officers as they escort the thief away in handcuffs.

"It took you long enough." Kovacs turns to Peter and shakes his head. It is now early evening in Budapest and shadows are extending east from the buildings and statues.

"We got here as soon as we could. It's not like we were just around the corner. You could have given me a heads-up."

"I wasn't sure it was the guy I was looking for, but once I saw the photo of Rákosi, I knew he was my guy."

"Your client will be happy, huh? And so will some other people." Kovacs kicks a pebble in the parking lot as they stand in front of the shop. "Nice work on this one. It sounds like the kid has a lot more stolen property. He already admitted to that, hoping we'll go easy on him if he cooperates."

"Well, you know, sometimes you get lucky. I figured there were only a few places he'd be able to sell old communist crap. This was one of those places." Kovacs nods. "So, how long should I tell my client it will be until he can reclaim his property?"

Kovacs puckers his lips, and a line appears in his forehead. "Probably not long. Give me a week, then have him come to the office. I should be able to release it to him by then, provided I don't have any other days like today." Kovacs takes out a pack of cigarettes and presses one to his lips.

"Why, what happened today?"

Kovacs grimaces. "I had several cases come in. One was particularly troubling." Peter waits for him to say more but Kovacs seems lost in the memory.

"What was that one?"

"What? Oh...I got a call from a woman in Greece. Her daughter came here a couple weeks ago and never returned home. Nobody has seen her. She just seems to have vanished." Kovacs shakes his head and kicks another pebble with his scuffed shoe. "I don't know what's going on but that's the third call like that in the last couple months."

"All of them from Greece?"

Kovacs frowns. "No. But each has been foreign." He extends his hand holding the cigarette and flicks it away with his middle finger.

"Funny you should say that. Today I met an American kid. He's here studying at the international business school. He contacted me because his girlfriend, another student in the school from England, has disappeared."

Kovacs looks at Peter sharply. "You're kidding?"

"I'm not. I was going to be contacting you to see if you wanted to take over the investigation."

Kovacs shakes his head. "It would only be added to my already large stack of files. We're overrun with cases like these and other criminal matters. I think hiring you is a better solution for him right now. I'll get to it when I can, but if you could help, I'd appreciate it. I just don't have any time." That isn't what Peter is hoping to hear. He needs the work and the money but violence toward women is exactly the type of case he is trying to avoid. The type he fears.

Chapter Three

Peter

P eter leaves his apartment early Thursday morning. It's October now, and the early mornings are beginning to feel cool. He came to Budapest almost a year ago. His second time running to the city, although the first time was forced. He was raised in a town three hours south of Budapest called Pecs. Pecs is known to be one of the most picturesque cities in Hungary. It lies near the border with Croatia, so it feels warmer than most of Hungary, but it also has charming green hills that surround the city. He spent his childhood living in a home on those hills.

"*Kezét csókolom.*"

Peter is roused from his thoughts as he heads down the stairs of his apartment building. To his right he sees his spunky little neighbor, Judith, looking at him. The phrase *kezét csókolom* is used primarily by children to greet an elder while showing respect.

"*Szia!* Good morning," Peter replies smiling.

She waves and goes back in her apartment. The smile lingers on his lips. Judith is so friendly and outgoing. She must sense his loneliness because she always tries to greet him. Descending the remaining flight of stairs, a line creases his forehead. Although he loves to see her, she also reminds him of the loss in his own life. *How old would Catherine be now? Twelve.*

Pushing those thoughts aside, he lets his mind consider the day he has before him. He's grateful for the busy schedule. It will keep his mind occupied.

He reaches the bottom of the stairs and walks out the door. As he does, he pulls his jacket tight. The sun is beginning to rise, illuminating the sky, but the tall buildings block its rays. The street is engulfed in shadow and only the bright sky above indicates the sun is rising. Peter lives on the Pest side of the river near the main walking street in Budapest called Váci utca. He turns north heading up the street. Two days ago, he received a call from a woman. She wanted to hire him and he set up a meeting. She called herself Dobo Kata. In Hungarian, surname comes first so her given name is Kata. She contacted him wanting her husband followed.

"What types of cases do you specialize in?" she asked after he answered the phone and they exchanged pleasantries.

Peter hates this question, and he gets it a lot. People want to feel like they are hiring the best and always believe their case is more complicated than most. Rarely is that ever true.

"Why don't you first tell me why you're contacting me?"

"I think my husband is cheating on me," she responded flatly with little emotion. *No surprise there.* Nearly every woman contacting him believes their husband is cheating. Peter took a moment to choose his words carefully.

"Why do you suspect him?"

"Because he travels for work now and never used to before. And he has a difficult time looking me in the eye when I ask him things. Something feels wrong."

Peter told her he could probably help her and quoted his going rate. After hearing his fee wouldn't be a problem, he suggested they meet.

He knew several coffee shops along the street and suggested Kata meet him in one of them. Walking along now, he considers how interesting the world of private investigation is. Just a couple weeks ago, he was sure he would need to find a new form of employment. The world seemed to be more and more sinister, but he just wasn't being hired to investigate. He didn't have a website and really didn't have much interest in advertising on the internet. It's a young man's game; just look at all the Hollywood movies.

Then he got a job finding stolen property, Stephen called about his girlfriend, and Kata about her husband. Evidently, he was wrong, the PI world hadn't passed him by just yet.

He enters the coffee shop a few minutes before eight and immediately smells the roasting beans. They agreed to meet at eight and nobody else is in the shop other than one gentleman who stands looking at the menu board. Peter walks to the counter and orders a tea and sits down. He had never been a coffee fan. He preferred the smell and taste of tea.

He finds a table and sits down, breathing the smell of his lemon tea as he watches the foot traffic on the street. A few minutes after eight, a woman comes through the door. This has to be Kata. *Why is it always the gorgeous women who get cheated on?* She has long, elegant, dark brown hair, and striking facial features. She takes a moment to look around the café until her eyes land on Peter. She gives him a slight nod then strides to the counter. She wears black heels, a gray skirt, and a frilly red blouse. Her black bra is visible through the sheer fabric.

After ordering, she makes her way to Peter. He stands and motions for her to take a seat. She places her coffee on the table, puts her purse on the seat next to her, and sits crossing her legs. Peter guesses she's in her late thirties or early forties based on her choice of clothing. But she could easily pass for ten years younger. Her skin is flawless, no wrinkles around her eyes or neck.

"Peter, I assume?"

He meets her gaze. "Yes, Kata, I'm Peter."

They sit there, neither speaking, appraising each other.

"So, what do you want to know?" Kata finally asks. She's folding her arms in front of her.

Is she cold or protecting herself?

"Tell me about your husband." She leans back in her chair and looks out the window placing her hands flat on the table.

"Well, his name is Dobo Andras. He's tall, he's put on a little weight in recent years but he's athletic. He played handball when he was younger. He has dark hair that is now turning gray at the temples. He's forty-four. He and I have been married for nine years. He owns a restaurant here in Budapest called Szép Ilona's on the Buda side of the city. Have you heard of it?"

Peter nods.

A man walks into the café. Kata's back is to him. She turns to look at him, then looks back at Peter. She unfolds her arms and begins clicking her long fingernails on the table between them. Her voice drops to nearly a whisper.

"We both grew up here in Budapest. We met at a club ten years ago. He was so handsome and confident, and I think I was in love with him from the start. We dated for a few months, then lived together for a while, then married. For about five years, we were blissfully happy. He was all I thought about and I could tell he felt the same about me. He's a chef." Kata goes back to folding her arms and turns a bit in her chair so she can more easily look out the window. "Before we met, when he was younger, he spent a couple years in Paris attending culinary school. He's so talented; he can cook anything. His restaurant is primarily Hungarian cuisine, but he loves to include French, German, and Spanish fare in his menu as well." Kata rubs her arms and Peter has his answer. She's cold, not closed off.

"So, why do you suspect him of cheating on you?"

She looks around the café, checking to see if people are listening. Eventually, she looks back out the window. She watches the people scurry by as she speaks, and Peter has to lean forward to hear her. "Several reasons really, but I feel stupid. I may be overanalyzing things."

This is something said by nearly every woman being cheated on. They all seem to know but hate to face it. She pauses, looking for him to support the idea that it might be nothing. He simply stares back at her; telling clients what they want to hear isn't him.

"He goes out of town a lot. In our first five years of marriage, he was home every night. Working in a restaurant often meant he would get home late, but he would always come home." She shakes her head. "But lately, he's gone a few times a month. He just recently opened a new restaurant in Zagreb. He says he needs to spend a lot of time there training the staff and learning the market."

"But you don't believe him."

Kata uncrosses her legs and recrosses them with the other leg now forward.

"It's not that I don't believe him," she sighs and looks back out the window, "it's that...I don't know." She shakes her head again. "He seems different with me. It's hard for me to explain why." She looks back at Peter, and he can see the emotion in her eyes.

"It would help me if you could explain it to me," he tells her.

She squirms again in her seat and looks out the window before looking back at him. "It's in the way he kisses me, it's in the way he holds me; it's the lack of excitement I see when he comes home; it's the look in his eyes." She looks down at her trembling hands and moves them to her lap underneath the table, hiding them from view. "I'm sure it sounds stupid to you. I'm probably reading the whole situation wrong, but I've been telling myself that for a few months now and I continue to feel something is not right."

Peter moves for the first time in the conversation, leaning back in his chair.

"So, what would you like me to do?" he asks her.

This time, Kata doesn't look away and sits forward in her chair. Her response is forceful and direct.

"Find out. Tell me if I'm being crazy or if he is really cheating on me."

Five minutes later, Peter says goodbye to Kata and exits the café, he looks at his watch. The motion transports him back to ten years ago. He sat across from his wife, Karen, at his favorite steakhouse in NYC. They were celebrating their tenth wedding anniversary. Karen's eyes twinkled as she slid a gift across the table. He could still see the blue wrapping paper and silver ribbon. Little did he know the gift inside would match the paper. As he opened the box, he was shocked to see a Breitling Chrono mat stainless steel watch. It was beautiful. He had always adored planes and longed for the chance to fly. The watch delighted him. But as much as he loved the watch, he had adored the smile beaming at him from across the table. How he missed that smile. Today would have been their twentieth anniversary and his heart broke knowing he would never see that smile again. Knowing that he was responsible for her death.

It's now almost nine thirty in the morning. At ten thirty, he would be meeting the client who had hired him to find his missing communist memorabilia. This would be a pleasant meeting. Rarely were the closing meetings with clients joyful. Take Kata for instance, even if he did his job and found Andras, her husband, was cheating, she wouldn't be happy. In the case of the stolen memorabilia, the client would get back all his cherished relics.

He decides he is going to do a little shopping, since his fridge resembles an empty cavern. It would be tight, but he should be able to shop, take it home, then head to the client meeting.

Chapter Four

Stephen

I hope this is the right building. Tom gave me this address. I look down at the note again, squinting to read Tom's handwriting. I look back up at the building number. Yep, this is it.

It's a bright day and the thoroughfare is hopping. There must be hundreds of people shopping and walking on the street. I rang the bell at least five times with no answer. He's probably looking out the window at me, waiting for me to leave. Who can blame him? I was so stupid yesterday. No wonder he didn't take the case. I'd walk away and leave him alone, but I can't. He's my only hope of finding her.

I look down the street and see a tall man with broad shoulders carrying a couple grocery bags. He's walking toward me. It's him. He hasn't noticed me yet. I'd never guess he's Hungarian. He looks American to me. Like any middle-aged man I'd see back home. He looks up and our eyes lock. He sees me now, angling toward me.

"I thought we concluded our business in the café?" Peter says, eyeing me.

I shrug. "You're my only hope."

Peter closes the remaining distance between us and stands looking at me. He doesn't look pleased to see me. "I wish I could help you. But

I can't. You don't have enough information for me to work from, and I just took another case this morning."

I look past him down the street at shoppers mingling around the stores. This street doesn't allow any cars, only pedestrians. My hands are in my pockets, and I feel myself subconsciously rocking back and forth from heel to toe. I've got to win him over. "I'm sorry, Peter. I promise to be better and answer your questions more succinctly. I thought about our meeting all night. I couldn't sleep."

Peter's eyes narrow, and I know he's considering it. He's looking in my eyes and I wonder if he can tell I had been crying.

"How did you find me?"

I duck my head. "I found Tom this morning and badgered him into telling me where you live."

Peter looks up and I can see he's annoyed.

I take my hands from my pockets now. I'm going to need every bit of persuasion to convince him. "Please, Peter? I might be the reason she's gone. Help me."

"Wait here," Peter commands and turns and walks to the apartment building. Without a word he enters. Should I follow him? He told me to wait. I guess I better stay. After a couple minutes he comes back out.

"I'm late to another client meeting. You can come with me. We'll talk on the way."

My face breaks into a huge grin. I think he's going to do it.

"I'm not saying I'm going to take this case," Peter says. "In fact...I still don't think I will. But some of that will depend on how you answer my questions."

I nod my head at him. "I understand."

"Good." Peter begins striding down the street and I hurry to catch up. "I'm going to ask you the same question I asked you yesterday.

Let's see if you do a little better with it. Tell me about the first time you met Samantha."

"She was in my first class with me. But I don't remember seeing her until after school that day."

We were at the end of the street now, and without a word Peter walks to the bus stop. I follow him, unsure where we are going.

"What do you mean?" Peter asks. "You didn't see her in the class?"

"No, I was nervous. I hadn't ever been to a class in a foreign country before. I also have a fear of being asked to speak in public. I really don't remember much from that day."

"Okay, so you were in the same class, but you didn't notice her. After school you saw her?"

"Yeah, I had just walked out the doors into the courtyard. I wasn't feeling well. I hit my head on one of the desks in the first class and felt sick to my stomach."

He stops and stands at the bus stop turning to face me. He holds up his hand as he looks at me. "Come again? How did you hit your head on a desk?"

"During that first class, with Samantha in it, the professor made us all stand up and introduce ourselves. When I stood up, I hit my notebook and knocked it on the floor. I rushed to pick it up and slammed my head on the desk. I saw stars."

Peter raises an eyebrow at me but says nothing. The bus has arrived. I'm grateful I have a comprehensive public transportation pass, otherwise I don't know what I'd do. As is, I follow Peter onto the bus and sit right next to him on the seat.

"How's your head now?" Peter asks me.

I reach up and absently rub the spot where I hit it. "Oh, it's fine. I threw up a couple times after I got home that day, but otherwise, I was fine."

Peter frowns. We're seated side by side and the girth of his shoulders makes the seat feel crowded.

"Sounds like you had a concussion. You should have gone to a doctor."

"How? I don't speak enough Hungarian for that. Plus, I don't even know where a hospital is."

Peter grimaces, looking at me out of the corner of his eye. "I'm sure your school has a nurse on staff."

"Maybe."

"Okay, so you walked out into the courtyard. Then what happened? You still haven't told me anything about Samantha."

I feel my face flush. I can't have him lose patience with me again. "I didn't see anyone in the courtyard. I thought it was deserted then I heard a woman's voice ask me if my head was okay. I looked around and saw this pretty girl staring at me. There's a lot of beautiful women here, but she was different. For starters, she was a redhead, probably the only one I can remember seeing since I arrived. I've always believed there are no mediocre redheads. They are either gorgeous or plain. She was gorgeous. But it wasn't her hair that intoxicated me, it was her eyes. They were green, but not just ordinary green, they were a bright green with a touch of blue."

I can see Peter is intrigued by my description of her. "How tall is she?"

"Not tall. Maybe five-two. I never saw her in anything other than heels. She admitted to me that she hated being short."

Peter falls silent and it gives me a chance to look out the window. We are crossing the Elizabeth Bridge heading to the Buda side of the city. Budapest, years ago, had been two different cities. The Pest side, where Peter lives, had been more industrial and commercial. The Buda side, where we head now, was where the royals and wealthy landowners lived. The Buda side features beautiful hills. The Danube River splits the city in half.

"So, she asked you how your head was... And?"

I had kind of zoned out there. "Oh...yeah right. I was embarrassed and asked her if she had seen me hit it which she clearly had." I can't help but shake my head at the memory. "Dumb question. Anyway, that's when I noticed she had an accent. I pointed it out and she laughed and said I was the one with the accent. She told me she was from Preston, England." We are now on the other side of the river and Peter pulls down on the red wire indicating he wants to get off.

"This is my stop," he tells me and nudges me with his shoulder. We stand and I make my way off the bus with Peter trailing me.

After we walk a few paces, Peter stops and turns to me. "Look, Stephen. I know you want to find Samantha. But I just don't think I'm going to be able to help you. You still haven't given me anything to work with. I'm not even sure where I would start looking. Have you mentioned your concerns to the school? If she just disappeared, they must know something."

My face falls. I thought he had already agreed to take the case. "No. I didn't think they would talk to me. I'm sure they aren't going to tell me anything."

Peter puts his hand to his chin. I think he can see my point. Schools are typically careful about student privacy.

"Peter, I'll pay you double your rate. Please help me."

My pulse is rapid, this is it. I must look like a concentration camp victim asking for my last meal. Looking at me, Peter's face begins to soften.

"Stephen, it's not just the money. I don't have anything to work with. I have nothing to investigate."

"What kind of information do you need?"

Peter looks at his watch. His appointment is at ten thirty. "I'm sorry. I'm already late. I've got to go."

I'm undeterred. "What would help you? What kind of information?"

"I don't know. Obviously, her last name. Her address here. Her address back home. Contact information for her family back home. Whether she had roommates. What other classes she had here. If anything unusual had been happening to her. Anyone who scared her or was following her." We were walking again, and Peter reaches an apartment building and stops. He points to the building. "This is it. Sorry, Stephen. I have to go." He moves to reach for the buzzer at the intercom station.

I grab his arm and stop him. "She did tell me about someone following her. She described him as creepy."

Peter's eyebrows furrow and a line appears in his forehead. "Don't you think you should have led with that information? Come on, Stephen. Who was following her?"

I can feel my cheeks fill with heat, and my lip begins to tremble. "I didn't say anything because I didn't think it was important. I didn't want to make an accusation without anything to confirm it."

Peter blows out the air from his lungs. He's frustrated with me again. "When she went missing that kind of information becomes very important. Who was this person that was following her?"

"Mr. Hodges. The professor from school."

"The one from the class you both were in?"

"Yeah."

Peter looks at his watch. He is late. "Look, Stephen, I need to go inside and talk to this other client. What's your schedule like today?"

I hold up my hands feeling a great sense of relief. "I don't have anything. Just some homework."

"Wait here. I won't be longer than about thirty minutes."

Chapter Five

Peter

P eter walks down the steps of the old apartment building following the client meeting. The landlord would never get away with this in America—no way ADA compliance is being met. No elevator or ramp. Something about the building reminds him of being sixteen again. He came to Budapest for the first time after being kicked out of his family home. Having nowhere to go, he snuck onto a train headed for Budapest. When he arrived, he had no idea where he would go. Luckily, it was summer, and the weather was warm. He marveled at the size of the buildings and the number of people on the streets. The year was 1962, and although Budapest looked very different now with the number of cars, trains, buses, and billboards, most of the buildings hadn't changed. Unfortunately, any new buildings that were built since 1962 were primarily built by the communists. Communism didn't encourage artistic design. Peter could remember reaching the Margit Bridge and looking out over the Danube River. What an amazing sight it had been for a kid who grew up in a little town in southern Hungary. With the castle up on the hill, the Buda Hills behind it, the river in front, and the Parliament building to the south, he had been captivated.

Budapest in 1962, not unlike today, was an interesting place. It had been on the wrong side of WWII. The war ended several years earlier, and Hungary became part of the USSR. The Russians claimed to be freeing the Hungarians from Nazi oppression but simply installed their own.

After living on the streets for a few nights, Peter was picked up by the police. Upon learning he had come from Pecs, they forced him to go to work in a factory. While he worked in the factory, he became friends with an 18-year-old, David, who was infatuated by the west. He described America as the "land of opportunity." Peter had dreamed Budapest would be that for him, but after only a few days, he had his doubts. David told Peter he had been planning to leave Hungary and head to America.

"You should come with me," he told him. "You don't have anything holding you here in Hungary."

Peter was easily convinced and a few weeks later, Peter boarded a train with him to Sopron, a city on the western edge of Hungary bordering Austria. He and David snuck across the border to Austria.

"Where are we going to go?" Peter asked him.

"To Vienna," David responded.

Peter had nothing other than a few apples and potatoes for food. They walked the seventy-five kilometers to Vienna over three days, sleeping in fields out under the stars. After arriving in Vienna, they found a refugee camp with other Hungarians. David was able to obtain papers allowing him to go to America, but Peter wasn't so lucky. He knew nobody in America and the United States government already had enough people entering the country. A kind woman in the American Embassy took pity on him and helped him. David had already left by the time Peter obtained his papers. Peter was completely alone as he boarded the train headed to Paris and then a ship to New

York City. He was beyond scared. He was headed to a foreign country where he knew nobody and didn't speak the language.

Something about that experience and memory was now pulling him closer to Stephen. He can relate to the kid. It was scary to be in a foreign country not knowing the language. His first months in New York City were terrifying.

Peter reaches the bottom of the stairs now. The client meeting went great. Better than expected. Not only had he received payment from the client on the balance owed, but he was also given a 5,000-forint bonus. As he opens the outside door to the building, he immediately blinks his eyes. The light from the sun is blinding in comparison to the dark apartment building. He is expecting to see Stephen as he opens his eyes, but he is nowhere to be found. He looks up and down the street without any sign of him. *Maybe the kid gave up?* Peter's conflicted at the thought. He's both disappointed and relieved. Halfway up the block, Peter notices a bus stop with several people lined up around it. With no Stephen, he can focus a hundred percent of his time on Kata's case of the philandering husband.

As Peter begins to walk toward the bus stop, he recognizes the figure sitting on the bench. The man sits staring out at the street, unaware of anyone around him. He is staring so intently; Peter looks out to the street wondering what has captivated his attention. There's nothing unusual. Cars continue to flash by as Stephen stares straight ahead. Peter moves right next to him now but still Stephen stares almost transfixed.

"Stephen," Peter says.

He doesn't move. Peter walks around him so he is standing right in front of him. Still, Stephen doesn't react. "Hey, Stephen. Can you hear me?" Peter sees no reaction from him. *Is he possessed?* Stephen continues to gaze straight ahead, looking right through Peter's body. Finally, Peter reaches out and pats him on the shoulder.

Stephen startles and looks up. "Oh, hi, Peter. I didn't see you come out."

"Yeah, I could tell." Peter says. The bus pulls up now and Peter turns to look at it. It's northbound. "Why don't we get on this bus?" Stephen stands and follows Peter as they climb aboard. They find a seat near the back, again side by side. Once they are seated, Peter is anxious to hear more about what Stephen told him prior to entering the building. "You said Samantha had been followed by your professor Hodges."

Stephen looks back at Peter. "Yeah, that's right."

"How do you know that?"

Stephen hesitates. "She told me."

"What did she tell you?"

Stephen places his hand on the seat in front of him and looks down. He hesitates again and Peter wonders if it's because he is trying to remember.

"On the last date we went on, she asked me what I thought of him. I told her I liked him. That's when she said he had been following her."

"How did she know he was following her?"

"She said she saw him in the library."

Peter frowns at him. "It's not unusual for a professor to be in the library."

Stephen agrees. "But it wasn't just that. She said she saw him another time following her on the streetcar."

Peter leans his head to the side as he considers this. "Again, that could just be coincidence."

"But she said he was creepy." Now Peter begins to rub his chin. The bus driver announces they are reaching Moszkva tér. Moszkva tér is the major transportation hub for the Buda side of the city. From there, you could transfer to a bus, streetcar, train, or subway tube.

Peter stands and nearly falls as the bus bumps. "Let's get off here."

Peter patiently waits for other passengers to file off before climbing down himself, followed by Stephen. As they walk a few paces to create distance between them and other passengers, Peter can't stop thinking about his wife. Does Stephen share the same regrets about Samantha?

He turns back to Stephen. "Do you have any pictures of her?"

Stephen shakes his head. But after seeing the look on Peter's face snaps his fingers.

"Actually, yes, I do. When we went and toured around the city, we took some pictures together. I just haven't developed the film yet. I have several of us together at Heroes Square in Pest."

"Go and do that right now. I'll talk with this Mr. Hodges."

Stephen smiles and his face lights up with excitement. "Does that mean you will help me?"

Peter holds up a hand, trying to deflect some of that excitement. "Before I answer that, I want you to tell me why you think you are responsible for her being missing. Why did you say that?"

Stephen looks down, placing his hands in his pockets. He shifts side to side. "I didn't take her warning seriously. She needed help and I didn't hear her." Stephen looks back up.

As Peter gazes in his eyes, he sees the same regret he has been harboring. Not long ago his wife had expressed fears of being followed. He had dismissed it as paranoia. Now he'd never absolve himself of the blame. Something in Stephen's eyes touches his heart.

"Will you help me, Peter?"

"I don't think I have a choice. I can't stand the thought of this girl being taken and nobody looking for her." Peter begins to leave but another thought strikes him. He turns back to Stephen. "What about roommates? Did she have any?"

Stephen pauses to think. "She said her roommate was Italian. But I don't know her. I don't think I've ever seen her."

"See what you can do to find out who she is. I'll call you tonight."

Chapter Six

Peter

Peter reaches the school and goes through the front door. As he enters the lobby, he notices several students standing around talking and flirting. Ah, young love, he thinks to himself. Being in his fifties now, he sees teens and those in their early twenties flirting back and forth and wonders if he was as obvious when he was their age. Sometimes he wants to go up to them, shake them by the shoulders, and implore them to simply express their interest in the other person. Just say it straight out. But of course, he wouldn't, and frankly he doubted it would do any good. When he was twenty, he was the same way. He worried so much about what others thought of him, it was easier to hide his feelings than to be rejected. Nothing is as personal as being rejected by a crush.

Peter came to the school to seek out and talk with Mr. Hodges, the shared professor of both Samantha and Stephen. After walking around the school to get the lay of the land, he locates and enters the Strategic International Management building. The building is seemingly void of light in comparison to the bright day outside. The entrance hallway has no windows, only fluorescent lighting, but the floor is a pleasing white marble that softens the area. *I wonder what other classes Samantha has?* Stephen said he had four classes for the semester and Peter assumes the same is true of Samantha. He knows his best chance is to locate Hodges. According to Stephen, he is a tall man, with wire-rim glasses, blond hair, and a lean body type. He came to Hungary from Florida.

The first classroom he looks in has a female teacher. The next classroom has a man that looks to be about the same age as Peter. He has a large belly and gray beard with a balding head. *That's not him either.* After a few more classrooms, he finds who he thinks is Mr. Hodges. The man matches the description Stephen gave. Peter does a double take as he looks more closely at him. He looks almost identical to a man Peter had met in Switzerland years ago. Peter and the Swiss man shared a train car from Zurich to Paris. The man was a thief and had tried to pick Peter's pocket on the train. Peter, being a detective, was wise to his move and turned him over to the authorities when they arrived in Paris.

Hodges is now deep into a lecture. Peter steps back, positioning himself behind the door where he is out of eyesight. He watches Hodges pace around the room. Hodges seems energized by the topic of the conversation.

"So, what made Microsoft so successful?" Hodges asks the class. "This year is the first year of the new millennium. Bill Gates has more money than anyone throughout history. More money than God. Why? What made him so successful?"

One of the boys in the center of the room raises his hand. "He created Windows. Windows made the personal computer possible. As computers grew in popularity, almost all of them ran Windows."

Hodges continues to pace back in forth in front of the class. "Yes, that's true," Hodges responds, "but why him? And by the way, you could argue his partner, Paul Allen, actually had more to do with the creation of Windows than Bill Gates. But I digress, what made Bill Gates the household name he is today? It certainly wasn't his looks. I mean, thin, nerdy-looking American men are a dime a dozen." Hodges stops pacing, and with a goofy smile, points at himself. Most of the kids look blankly back at him.

Hodges, seeing his joke fell flat, goes on. "Bill Gates had a fair amount of luck on his side. When he was in eighth grade, his school purchased a computer along with blocks of processing time. That was in the year 1969. You can imagine how rare that was." Hodges turns and faces the class, pointing his index finger to the ceiling while tapping it against his chin. "But that wasn't all. The school eventually ran out of money to buy additional blocks of processing time. Gates and his friend, Paul Allen, found a way to exploit the system and use the computer for free. By the time he was fourteen, he was already writing code for companies. At seventeen, he was admitted to Harvard but dropped out after one year to pursue his computer dreams with Paul Allen." Hodges resumes his pacing, occasionally looking back at the class but mostly looking down and using his hands to express his thoughts. "Several years later in 1980, Gates negotiated a deal to license the DOS operating system to IBM for fifty thousand dollars but didn't transfer the copyright. Because he didn't transfer the copyright, which was the norm at the time, Microsoft was then able to go out and sell the software to other customers, exploiting their profits."

Hodges turns back to the class. "I put this question to all of you. Is Bill Gates a truly great leader? Or was he just lucky? Was this just the case of being in the right place at the right time?" Hodges is standing at the front of the room looking over the class, almost daring someone to have an opinion.

Finally, a dark-haired girl in a cute blue dress raises her hand. "Yes, he was lucky," she replies matter-of-factly, "but there was more to it than that. How many other people were in that same school as him and didn't end up co-founding Microsoft? They had the same opportunity to use the computer lab."

Hodges bobs his head. "That's true." He extends his index finger again. "Just one more thought before we dismiss class. He and a guy named Steve Jobs with Apple, are both known for being tyrants as bosses. I want you to study what you can about both men. Next week, I'd like you to turn in an essay choosing which one you would prefer to work for and why."

With that, Hodges dismisses the class and immediately goes over to talk with one of the girls on the front row. Peter waits in the hallway, allowing the students to file out. Hodges and the girl continue to talk, smiling and laughing far more often than necessary. The flirtation is obvious on both sides. Finally, she waves goodbye and walks out passing Peter in the hall. As Peter enters the classroom, he finds Hodges is standing by the blackboard erasing something he wrote. His back is to Peter, but he catches Peter's movement out of the corner of his eye.

He turns and looks in Peter's direction, immediately raising his eyebrows. "Can I help you?" he asks.

"Um...I'm not sure," Peter stammers, "I'm seeking my niece." Peter exaggerates a London accent. He worked to develop it back in NYC. For a time, he had a British man as his partner. Being partners with a Londoner had helped him hone the accent. He wishes he could demonstrate a Preston accent, but he figures Hodges won't know the difference.

"Oh, maybe I can help you," Hodges responds. "I don't know a lot of students here, I'm new, but maybe she's in my class. My name is Niles Hodges."

Hodges extends his hand to Peter, and Peter takes it, eyeing him closely.

"What's your nieces' name?"

"Samantha," Peter responds, never taking his eyes off Hodges.

Hodges becomes visibly nervous. He holds his breath and swallows hard; his Adam's apple bobs up and down. He turns away from Peter and begins walking toward the window, tapping his finger to his lips. "Hmm, I don't think I have a Samantha in my classes, but I admit, I don't know all the students; it's only been a few weeks since classes started."

He turns back to Peter, seeming to right himself.

Peter continues to watch him before he speaks again. "Samantha is missing."

Hodges pulls back his head and raises his eyebrows. "Missing?"

"We haven't been able to reach her, her mother and me. We've grown concerned so I decided to come and see if I could find her."

Hodges furrows his brow and begins shaking his head as he walks closer to Peter. "Well, I wish I could help you, but I don't have a Samantha in my classes. I really hope you find her." Hodges smiles at Peter, dismissing him.

Peter thanks him and they shake hands before Peter turns to leave. As he walks to the door, he decides to ask one more question to test Hodges. He turns back, watching Hodges closely. "May I ask? Why would an American professor choose to come to Hungary to teach?"

Hodges was watching him go and seems nervous again from the question. "Uh, well," he stammers, "it seemed like a new adventure. I really hadn't been out of the United States much."

Peter raises an eyebrow and tells him he hopes he will enjoy it and walks out.

Chapter Seven

Peter

Peter sits on the park bench outside the Strategic International Management building, waiting. Hodges is his best lead to finding Samantha and his behavior when questioned by Peter was odd. Something isn't right with the professor. He clearly knew the name "Samantha." Why would he try to hide it? He also never offered to review his class rolls. *Wouldn't he have at least checked the rolls?* It's plausible Hodges doesn't know every student by name. Based on the class Peter witnessed, Hodges would have forty to fifty students. If you figure he teaches five to six classes, that could mean up to three hundred students. When you also consider classes had only begun a month ago, it makes sense that Hodges might not know her. But the recognition Peter saw in his face was impossible to miss. Hodges is hiding something.

Peter waits almost thirty minutes, checking his watch occasionally. He selected a bench with a view of the front door, surrounded by shadows. Finally, Niles Hodges emerges from the school. As he begins to move across the courtyard, Peter stands and follows him. After spending about five minutes in the head office, Hodges leaves the school and heads toward the streetcar. Peter keeps his distance, remaining within seeing distance but never close enough for Hodges to notice him. The streetcar stop is tricky. It isn't particularly big and there are only four or five people waiting. Peter notices a taxi waiting to his left and decides that's going to be a safer way to keep out of sight.

Peter approaches the taxi, instructs the driver to follow the streetcar, and sits in the back. After five minutes, the streetcar pulls up. At each stop, Peter watches anxiously, waiting for Hodges to step off. Finally, six stops later, at Moszkva tér, Hodges emerges. Peter pays the driver and exits the taxi. Moszkva isn't the ideal spot for trailing someone who would recognize you. Certainly, Moszkva has its advantages because of the traffic and number of people, but it also makes it extremely easy to lose someone in the crowd. Hodges enters the square and heads west toward the train station. Peter keeps his distance, trying to maintain line of sight. For a moment, Peter thinks Hodges might be headed for the train, but he veers off to the north toward the bus stop. He walks right up and climbs on a bus.

Peter stands and debates his options; no taxicabs are nearby. If he chooses to ride on the bus, there's a great chance Hodges will notice him. But if he doesn't, he must let Hodges go, choosing to pick up the trail another time. Every moment he stands debating means another chance for the bus to pull away. Finally, he decides to take the risk and climb on. As he does, he chooses a spot right at the front hoping it means Hodges won't notice him. The drawback is Peter no longer has eyes on him. Losing sight of Hodges could mean his exit without Peter's knowledge. The bus has two exits, one in the front and one at the back. Peter can only see the front.

After a couple stops, the bus turns onto Hűvösvölgyi út and they head west into the Buda Hills. This had always been one of Peter's favorite parts of the city. He loves the wide street that includes a streetcar track right down the middle. It always scared him when he saw vehicles driving right in front or to the side of the streetcar. But his favorite part are the large trees that line either side. Being October, the leaves on the trees are beginning to turn orange and brown but haven't begun to fall. They create a canopy of color. He had always believed this street belonged in a movie somewhere. After a couple more stops, he hears the chime of a stop request and catches movement out of the corner of his eye. It's Hodges, he's near the back of the bus standing at the door waiting to get off. *Perfect.* Peter can stay seated until Hodges begins descending the stairs, then hustle to the front and get off. Unless he looks back, he won't know Peter is behind him.

After the bus stops, Hodges climbs down the stairs and Peter rushes to the front exit. Unfortunately, they are the only two people who get off and Hodges almost immediately looks behind him, spotting Peter. Not only had he seen him, but he also recognizes him. Hodges scowls and walks back to him. As he approaches, he shakes his head at Peter.

"Are you following me?" he asks.

Peter considers his options. If he admits he is, he can get more pointed with his questioning of Hodges. He decides to answer the question with another question. "Why did you lie to me in your classroom?"

Hodges rears back. "Lie to you? What makes you think I was lying to you?"

It appears that neither of them can say anything without it being a question. Peter isn't about to let Hodges have the upper hand. "Why did you turn away from me when I mentioned Samantha?"

"I did?"

That's not an answer and Peter waits for a response.

"I don't know why," Hodges says. "I guess I was just surprised to hear her name."

"Why did her name surprise you?" Peter is watching him closely, trying to detect any untruth.

"Samantha's my wife's name." Hodges shakes his head and looks up before looking back at Peter. "Was my wife's name. I lost her to an accident."

Peter searches Hodges's face and he appears to be telling the truth. He's void of any of the nervousness he exhibited before. Peter knows this is his opportunity with Hodges. If he has any hope of finding Samantha, the clock is ticking, and every hour allows the trail to grow colder. "So, you are telling me you don't know Samantha?"

"I don't think I do. I don't recognize that being the name of any of my students, and that is a name I would remember."

Peter has to concede that point. You don't forget your wife's name. Anniversary maybe, not name. "Why didn't you review your class rolls? It would've been easy for you to verify whether she was a student?"

Again, Hodges shrugs but continues to meet Peter's gaze. "I don't know. I should have; I just didn't think about it."

Peter concedes it's possible, but lame. Hodges's expression and body language indicate he's being truthful. *Time to bluff.* "Why did you lie to me about the reason for coming to Hungary? You didn't really come for, quote, 'a new adventure?'" Peter hits home with this one and he knows it.

Hodges can't meet Peter's eyes and looks away. He brings his hand up to wipe the sweat forming on his forehead. "That's really not any of your business. I answered your questions about Samantha. I hope you find your niece, but I don't have anything more to discuss with you." With that, Hodges turns and walks away.

Chapter Eight

Stephen

That was not very smart. I can't believe I did that. I was planning to get to work on my term project but instead I rode the streetcar two miles too far and had to walk back. I was daydreaming again, about Samantha as usual. I was thinking about our first date together. She called me out of the blue and asked if I wanted to join her sightseeing. When we met, she expected me to be her guide. I guess she had the impression I knew all about Budapest because my family is Hungarian. Seizing the opportunity to impress her, I took her to see Heroes Square, the Parliament Building, the Castle, and Fisherman's Bastion. It was magical. The best date I could remember. As we stood looking at the city, Samantha expected me to kiss her, but I chickened out. She abruptly left and I had to work hard to get her to agree to another date.

As I reach my building and begin climbing the stairs to the entry doors, my heart sinks as I hear someone shout my name. I turn around slowly, and notice Tom sitting on the park bench. I met him the second day after arriving in Budapest and have chatted with him on several occasions. He speaks excellent English having lived in England for some years. I think he likes practicing English and talking with an

American. He was the one who recommended Peter to me. I'm not in the mood for chit-chat, but Tom is waving me over and I don't want to be rude. I walk down the steps and head over to him.

"Are you more comfortable in Budapest yet? How many times have you been lost?" Tom smiles and laughs as he says it. It's a low gravelly laugh, reminiscent of a John Deere tractor.

"No, I haven't been lost," I tell him. "But I did have a little adventure with the streetcar ticket agents during my first week."

Tom turns to me in surprise. "What happened with them?"

I proceed to tell him about forgetting the need for tickets and trying to play it off as a stupid American. They were buying it also until I accidentally spoke Hungarian to the kind elderly man who helped me. After that they threw me off the streetcar and I had to walk home. Tom starts to laugh loudly at this, and I can't help but laugh also. More at Tom than at the situation. The old man has an infectious laugh, and I can feel my mood improving after the two-mile walk of today.

"They were just playing with you," Tom tells me. "The most they would have done is give you a ticket. I've seen that kind of thing happen a thousand times. How has school been? Have you liked it so far?" Tom pulls a pack of cigarettes from his pocket and puts one between his lips.

"Yeah, it's been pretty good. It's kind of cool to be in a school with so many students from all over the world. I'm sure they all have interesting backgrounds."

"What do you mean? Haven't you talked with any of them?" Tom gets out his lighter and begins puffing on the cigarette until it starts to glow.

"Not really. Well...other than Samantha."

"Did you convince Peter to take the case?"

"He's at the school investigating Mr. Hodges right now." Tom nods and takes a drag of his cigarette. I've never been a fan of cigarette smoke. My grandfather smoked until the day he died. He was a grumpy old man. The cigarettes are what killed him. I've never understood why people smoke. Tom turns and stares into my eyes now.

"And what are you doing to help him?"

"What do you mean?"

"Just because Peter took the case doesn't mean you just sit and wait. Peter's smart and experienced, but from what you've told me, he doesn't have a lot to work with. What are you doing to help him?" I haven't thought about it like this. I was singularly focused on getting Peter to take the case. Once he had agreed, I kind of figured I should just let him handle it. "Can I be an old man giving a young man advice for a few minutes?" Tom takes another drag on his cigarette and turns his head away from me before blowing out the smoke.

"Do I have a choice?"

Tom smiles but ignores the jab. "When I was in London, I was close to your age, I met a woman named Angelica. She was my dream woman. She was cute, smart, pleasant, kind, and caring. We dated for several months, and I was in love with her. I thought about her all the time." Tom gets a distant look in his eye, and I sense there is lingering pain in the memory. "I had to come back to Hungary. My father got sick and was near death. I thought about asking her to marry me—we had talked about it—but she was hesitant to come home with me. She wanted to stay in London. Well, I left London thinking I would be back in six months. Then that lunatic Hitler invaded Poland. Before long, England declared war on Germany and Hungary became a German ally. I was a Jew living in a country aligned with Germany. I couldn't leave or communicate with anyone in England. Before long,

Nazis came into Budapest. They started rounding up Jews and placing them in ghettos." Tom takes a long drag on his cigarette.

"After a few months, I was sent to Auschwitz. You've heard of it?" Tom is looking at me with such intensity, it frightens me. All I can do is shake my head. Tom turns and stares forward, barely moving as he talks. "We were packed on a train so tight we couldn't move for eleven hours. There were no stops. No bathroom breaks. No food or water. Some people died and we were so crowded together that they didn't fall. Instead, they stayed there, stuck to the people next to them. There was nothing you could do. You can't imagine the smell." Tom turns his head back to me and I can see the emotion in his eyes. "Finally, we arrived at the camp. They separated us. Separated children from parents, siblings, friends, everyone. I watched as my family and friends were marched off. They were stripped of their clothes and ushered into large showers. Toxic gas was pumped into the showers and all my family was killed. I was forced to clean them from the showers and burn their bodies. I had to separate their clothes for the Nazis. I was a slave and given barely any food for over a year. I was marked with a number." Tom pulls up the sleeve of his shirt to expose the tattooed number. A couple kids are playing in the park next to us, but I barely notice. I had heard about Jewish concentration camps in school but never met anyone who had been in one. "When we were finally liberated, I was so thin I could barely walk. They had to limit the amount of food and water they gave us so that we wouldn't overeat and die. Finally, after three months, I was able to come back to Hungary. But to what? I had lost my family and friends. Not only that, the Soviets and communists controlled Hungary. They wouldn't allow foreign travel to the west."

Tom puts his hand on my shoulder. "Do you know what got me through those days?"

"I don't."

"I had an image of Angelica in my mind. I had an image of the last time I had seen her." Tom takes his hand off my shoulder and looks away. "I told myself I would see her when the war was over. I imagined the kids we would have." Tom pauses and I think he is done talking. "I never saw her again. I came back to Hungary and couldn't leave. I've sent a few letters through back channels but never had a reply." Tom turns back to me. "Why do you think I told you this story?"

What do you say to someone who has experienced such horrible things? I sit in silence unsure what to say.

"Don't live a life of regrets," Tom says. "If I could go back in time, I never would have left Angelica. I would have done whatever was necessary to stay. I would grab her, kiss her, and never let go. Do the same for Samantha. Do everything you can to get her back."

Chapter Nine

Peter

"Are you eating alone?" the cute hostess asks Peter as he enters Szép Ilona Bisztro. He's come to learn more about Andras, Kata's husband. The hostess has light brown hair, a warm smile, and striking gray eyes. Peter has noticed after living out of the country for so many years that many native Hungarians have a distinct eye color. The color and brightness resemble those of a Husky dog, not really a blue, more a bright gray. This girl has those same eyes. She's wearing a teal blouse and black skirt with black tights. Peter guesses her age at nineteen or twenty.

"Yes, just me," he answers her. She doesn't seem disappointed. Sure, they would love to have more people joining him, but it's four p.m. during the week. They'll take any business they can get. Peter counts himself lucky they are open, some restaurants only open for dinner. The restaurant sits up in the Buda Hills in an almost exclusively residential area.

Peter follows the young hostess to a table along the side of the dining hall near the window. She motions with her hand as if she's presenting some grand arrangement to him and he sits down.

She smiles again, handing him the menu, saying, "*Jó étvágyat.*" *Jó étvágyat* is the Hungarian equivalent of *bon appétit*.

Before he opens the menu, he looks around the room. It's pretty quiet. There's a couple, both in their mid-forties, sitting side-by-side in a booth. They seem enraptured with each other, so much so, he doubts they know anyone else is in the room. At the table to the left, a woman in her mid-fifties sits with another woman he presumes to be her daughter. Whatever they are discussing, the younger woman doesn't seem happy.

Peter moves his gaze to the bar. The bartender is a blonde woman, older than the hostess but younger than Peter. She's wearing a tight-fitting black tank top, low cut with a fair amount of cleavage. She's pretty and has certainly figured out her tips are bigger when she dresses provocatively. Behind the bar is the kitchen, and to the side of the bar, a secluded office. Peter wonders if this might be where Dobo Kata's husband, Andras, typically works. Maybe he's there right now. The bartender is someone he is going to want to talk with.

Peter walks to the bar. "Hi there, do you mind if I sit here?"

She smiles at him. Her teeth are a little overcrowded on the bottom but, aside from that, a nice smile.

"Of course! Sit! What would you like to drink?"

"What do you have on tap?"

He has a particular beer in mind. He loves the malt and caramel taste of the dark beer.

After rattling off a few different options she mentions Dreher, and he points to her, indicating that's the one.

"Great choice!"

This woman is good at her job. Not only does she dress for attention, but she compliments her customers. She clearly knows how to push men's buttons and Peter can bet she has a lot of regulars. He looks down at the menu he brought with him from the table. Immediately, he confirms what Kata had told him. The cuisine choices are indeed diverse. The menu includes several different regional cuisines including German, Spanish, Italian, French, and Hungarian.

After a few minutes, the bartender comes back to take his order. "What would you like to eat?" she asks.

Peter had placed the menu on the bar and now picks it back up. "How's the Wiener schnitzel?"

She smiles. "Decent if you like Wiener schnitzel. I'm not a big fan so I haven't tried it, but I've been told it's good."

Peter frowns and looks back down at his menu. After taking a few more seconds, he looks up. "What would you recommend?"

She has a dish rag in her left hand and begins absently wiping the bar "Uh, well..." she ponders, "it depends on what mood I'm in, but today..." she pauses and looks away furrowing her brow, "I'd order the stroganoff."

Peter shrugs. "That was actually my second choice. I'll take that." She reaches out for his menu and Peter hands it to her. In a few minutes, she comes back and begins washing glasses and cups. Peter gets the impression it's to pass the time because they look to be clean.

"I'm Peter," he says to her.

She looks up and smiles at him. "Hi Peter, I'm Zsuzsa."

"How do you like bartending?"

She smiles and Peter wonders if she thinks he's hitting on her. He's sure this is a common occurrence but based on her looks, attire, and occupation, she can't be surprised.

"Most days I like it, but I really should grow up and do something else at some point."

Peter looks at her without breaking expression. "What does growing up look like to you?"

Zsuzsa stops washing the glass in her hand and comes over to stand closer to him. "When I was younger, I always wanted to be a detective. You know, someone who caught all the bad guys?" She smiles and shakes her head. "But that ship has sailed."

Peter smiles and shrugs. "Why aren't you Detective Zsuzsa now?"

She giggles. "Because I'm not a very disciplined person." She turns and starts cleaning the glasses again.

"Why do you say that?" Peter takes a drink from his beer. It's a little warmer than he would like but still delicious.

Zsuzsa presses her lips together. "I liked to party too much when I was younger. I started bartending and liked the money I was making and decided I didn't need to go to school anymore." She stops washing and shakes her head. "No, it wasn't that I didn't think I needed to go to school anymore." She leans her head to one side. "I thought I would take a little time off and go back. Then I was making pretty good money and just kept putting it off. Now it's been ten years."

"Have you always worked here? I mean in the last ten years?"

"No. I worked in a couple spots in Pest where there was a younger crowd, but I got tired of it. Maybe I'm getting a little too old for that now. I came here about three years ago." She leaves and when she comes back, she's carrying Peter's food. She places it before him, gets him some utensils, and refills his beer. She's back to washing the cups. "I like the feel here better. I'm not as young as I used to be. I like a little quieter place and the owner treats me pretty well."

Peter loves when someone independently guides the conversation. This allowed him the opportunity to ask about the owner without being the person to bring him up. He takes a bite of his stroganoff. *Wow! That's amazing.* Between bites, he asks, "So, who owns this place?"

Zsuzsa doesn't look up from her washing. "Andras. He owns this restaurant and another one in Croatia. He's owned this one for a while; the one in Zagreb is new."

Peter nods. "You must like working for him if you've stayed for three years?"

Zsuzsa studies him. She seems to be wondering whether Peter is simply making conversation, or he has another motive. Peter knows he needs to be careful.

"Yeah, I like him. He's been good to me."

Peter was hoping for more, but she seems to be guarded when it comes to her boss. He better move to safer ground. "This stroganoff is excellent," he tells her. "Thank you for the recommendation."

She brightens, seemingly relieved to be moving off the subject of her boss. "I'm glad you like it! It's one of my favorites."

"Honestly, this was my best meal in a long time. The food is superb, the beer tasty, and the conversation pleasant, and the beauty of the bartender was intoxicating."

Zsuzsa blushes and looks down. "Thank you."

Peter hands her enough forint to easily pay for the meal and provide a nice tip. "You can keep the change," he tells her.

She smiles again as she cleans up his dishes. "Again, thank you."

Peter stands and starts away from the bar but only takes a few steps before he turns back to her. "I'd like to come back again soon. May I ask when you are usually here?"

Zsuzsa smiles and blushes again. "I typically work afternoon and evenings Tuesday, Thursday, Friday, and Saturday."

"Excellent! I'll see you soon."

Chapter Ten

Director Toth

It's ringing again! I can feel my temper flare. It's 6:00 p.m. and I'm still sitting behind my desk in the headquarters of the Hungarian National Police. You'd think being director of the entire country's police force would give me a little more flexibility. I had planned to leave an hour ago but nothing about today has gone as planned. The phone seems to buzz endlessly, and I'm coerced into several bureaucratic meetings all promising to improve efficiency and make my job easier with no concrete plans to do so. I have a feeling this call will be just another request for me to sign or authorize something. I pick up the phone. "Yes? What is it?" It comes out more harshly than I intend but maybe that's a good thing at this point.

"Director?"

I'm not expecting to hear this voice on the other end of the phone although I immediately recognize the raspy tone of my agent. "Yes, this is Director Toth."

There's a momentary pause before the voice speaks again. "I think I'm getting closer. He's beginning to trust me more."

I sit forward in my chair. If that's true, this would be significant to our investigation. "Why do you say that? What happened?"

"I was allowed to stay in the room this time," Tibor responds.

I feel my pulse quicken and I grip the phone harder. "What did you see?"

The agent briefly describes what he had witnessed. When he finishes, I stand from the desk and walk to the floor-to-ceiling window overlooking Göncz Árpád City Center. The long spiral telephone cord stretches from my desk to my ear as I stand looking out over the city from my eighth-story view. The National Police Headquarters sits in the heart of the city directly across from the subway station.

"Listen to me. Whatever you are doing, keep doing it. Change nothing. We need hard evidence. We need to know who else he's working with. How far this goes." I hear nothing on the other end, and I fear the line has gone dead.

I hear a sharp intake of breath and what sounds like a stifled sob. I wait, listening closely, as the agent fights for control. When he finally composes himself enough to speak, there is obvious emotion in his voice. "I don't know if I can do this. I can't watch this happen over and over and do nothing."

This is arguably the hardest part of my job: convincing undercover agents to witness things or, in some cases, even do things that hurt people in order to uncover the real criminals. For five minutes I reassure and encourage him. I feel more like a high school football coach giving a halftime speech than a national police director. Eventually, the agent's speech becomes less emotional and more direct. I've convinced him to remain embedded, the only acceptable outcome. We've been working for months to place him. If we had to go back now and start again, we'd lose a year. How many more victims could that mean?

After hanging up the phone, I turn and walk back to the window. Night has fallen over the city and millions of lights twinkle back at me. My thoughts are on the agent. Tibor is one of our veteran agents. A big burly man, tough and rough. What could cause him to break down in tears? Whatever it is, will be very difficult to stop.

Chapter Eleven

Stephen

I sit at my apartment's kitchen table pretending to do homework but thinking about the advice I received from Tom. I believed once I got Peter onboard, my work was done. I realize Tom's right; I need to help him. I haven't given him much information and need to help him. *But how?* As I sat thinking about where to go next, my phone starts ringing. *Who could that be?* I answer and I'm surprised to hear the voice on the line.

"Stephen?"

"Dad?" I respond.

"How are you doing, son?" It's nice to hear his voice albeit a bit crackly. A subtle reminder of how far away I am from home.

"I'm fine. How are you, Dad?"

"How's school? Have you had any trouble there?"

"School's fine. No real trouble."

Dad is quiet on the other end of the phone, considering where to go with the conversation. "What time is it over there?"

I look at the alarm clock next to my bed. "It's six p.m."

"I forget how different the time is over there."

Again, we sit, neither of us knowing what to say next. Finally, Dad breaks the awkward silence. "How's your Magyarul coming?"

"You know I don't speak much Hungarian. Plus, what Hungarian I do know revolves mostly around food."

Dad laughs. "You know that's part of why I didn't want you to go."

I feel my temper flare. When I told him about the idea of coming to Hungary for school, he laughed at me. I expected him to be supportive. I'd be going back to his parents' home. "Dad—" I fight to control my voice. "I don't want to hear it."

There's a pause and I sense he's deciding how far he wants to push. "Steve, this is a stupid idea and it's about time you acknowledge it. Your grandpa and grandma left Hungary for a reason. The country has some major flaws and it's not exactly safe, especially for an American kid who hasn't ever left Ohio. After the revolution in '56 your grandparents had to crawl through barbed wire fences to cross to the Austrian border. They had to leave everything behind, and all their possessions were stolen. You can get a way better education back home."

What control I had over my anger now flies away. I grip the phone tightly, letting loose on him. "Dad, it's not just about school. It's about experience. Forcing myself to go to a place where I know very little and needing to figure it out on my own will teach me way more than classroom discussions." This was the same argument we shared over and over since I decided to come. "Is this why you called me?"

Again, Dad pauses on the other end. "Come home, Steve. You aren't ready for this."

I slam the phone down. Not again. I'm not going to hear this again from him. I walk back to the kitchen and slam my hand on the table, bouncing the empty cup high into the air. I fight to control my breathing wanting to smash something. To hurt something.

I slump into a chair at the table. Well, there goes my homework. No way I'm going to be able to concentrate now. As I sit fuming over the conversation, I look for something to distract my mind. Something that will buoy my spirits. I think about Samantha.

On Monday, the last week I saw her, she told me she would think about my dinner date request. I walked into class Wednesday knowing today I would get my answer. She was already there when I arrived. She was reading and didn't see me as I passed her on my way to my normal seat. Eventually, she looked up and smiled at me. I thought that must be a good sign. Before, she wasn't even looking at me. I considered walking over and striking up a conversation when Mr. Hodges appeared and stood before the class.

"Who invented the automobile?" Mr. Hodges asked, looking around. As was typical, we stared back at him.

Finally, someone raised their hand, "Ford, I think."

Hodges smiled. "You might be right. Then again you might be wrong. It depends on how you define 'invented.' Henry Ford is probably most credited with the concept, but several people have the right to a claim on that credit. Leonardo da Vinci actually created a concept for a car, but it was only a concept." Mr. Hodges walked to the other side of the room. "Nicholas-Joseph Cugnot was the first to build a vehicle resembling an automobile a couple centuries later. Ford was the first to build the Model T, which most closely resembles our current automobiles."

Mr. Hodges used his hands as he talked. He looked like an Italian chef making a pizza. "Henry Ford shouldn't be remembered for inventing the automobile. In my opinion, he did far greater things. Can anyone tell me what those things were?" He let his gaze float from person to person.

Completely out of character, I raised my hand. "He pioneered the concept of the assembly line."

Hodges started walking toward me down the aisle, his palm extended. When he reached me, I raised my hand and he slapped it. "Yes!" he exclaimed. "Not only did he pioneer the assembly line, but he was also responsible for finding a cost-effective method of producing cars, paying his workers more, and creating the five-day work week, which we all appreciate today."

Hodges continued to talk about Henry Ford's leadership through the remainder of the class. I was only mostly paying attention. My eyes were drawn to Samantha. Occasionally she'd feel my eyes on her and she'd look up. Our eyes would lock, and I'd get this jolt of exhilaration.

As usual, by the time I reached the hallway after class, she was gone. The rest of my classes went painfully slow. As my final class ended and I made my way to the courtyard, devastation struck. I anticipated seeing her sitting on our bench, but she wasn't. Dejectedly, I sat down and waited, hoping she would come but knowing it wasn't likely. Before long, the courtyard emptied, and I sat there alone and brokenhearted. I had never met another girl like Samantha. She was everything I had ever wanted in a woman. After sitting alone for a while, I considered leaving but to what? Wherever I went, I'd be thinking of her. The sky was cloudy and I'd feel an occasional rain drop. It was like the sky understood my heartache. Finally, the door to the Strategic International Management building opened. Samantha came striding out. Immediately, she looked to the park bench and smiled.

"What are you doing?" she asked as she walked up.

I stood. "I was just enjoying some time outside."

She looked up at the sky and gave me a quizzical look. "In this? Are you sure you weren't waiting for me?"

"Well... I was hoping you'd be here."

She smiled that dazzling smile. "I'm sorry, I got caught talking to a professor longer than I expected. Are you headed home?"

"Yep, I think so. You?"

She nodded.

"Do you want to walk together to the streetcar?" I asked.

"Of course," she said.

We walked and talked about our day and the classes we had. Samantha was on a different track than I was. Her focus was on international marketing. She was hoping to work for an advertising firm with a large international client base. I was fascinated by arbitrage. I dreamed of a chance to travel the world buying and selling assets, including businesses. As she rattled on about class, I couldn't keep my eyes off her. She wore a blue button-up blouse with white pants she called trousers and matching blue shoes. She hadn't buttoned the top few buttons on the blouse revealing a silver locket hanging from her neck along with a slight amount of cleavage. I studied the locket but was careful about not looking too much. I remembered the episode of *Seinfeld* when Jerry Seinfeld told his friend George Costanza, "looking at cleavage is like looking at the sun. You don't stare at it. You glance at it, get a sense of it, then look away."

"What did you think of Mr. Hodges's discussion on Henry Ford today?" she asked.

She was staring up at me as we reached the streetcar stop. A woman was smoking a cigarette and we moved a few steps away from her.

"Oh, I thought it was interesting. What did you think?"

"I liked it also," she said. "I was impressed by your comment. You seem to know a lot about him. Is that something required in the States?" She smiled playfully.

"No, but he was from Michigan which is close to my hometown. When I was in high school, I wrote a report on him, so I had to learn all about him." As we stood waiting for the tram, I remember being unsure what to do with my hands. I flipped between putting them in my pockets and crossing them. I noticed the woman who had been smoking the cigarette occasionally shot glances over at us. Eventually she walked to the other end of the stop, seemingly annoyed by our English conversation.

"I heard about Henry Ford in England, but I didn't know much about him."

The streetcar arrived, and we got on, sitting side by side.

"What stood out to you most about Henry Ford?" I asked.

"Hmm, good question. Probably that not only did he have a revolutionary idea, the Model T, but that he recognized to make it a success he would need help. He would need to find ways to make his employees more efficient. He also seemed to care for them by paying them higher wages and creating the five-day work week. You would think that the man who invented the assembly line would see employees as merely a cog in the wheel, but he seemed, instead, to care about their wellbeing. I think that's rare." Once again, she amazed me; not only was she outwardly stunning, but she had a depth to her I found fascinating. She loved to learn, and she was insightful.

We were nearing Moszkva tér and Samantha still hadn't agreed to have dinner with me. *Had she forgotten?* She wouldn't forget something like that. *Maybe she's testing me.* She could be testing to see if I would ask again. I felt my heart rate quicken but I was running out of time.

"Are you going to allow me to make you dinner?" I looked at the seat in front of us, unable to make eye contact, fearing the answer.

"Yes," she replied, then laughed at the look of relief on my face, "but only if it's good."

I looked up at her and smiled. "Oh, it will be."

Just then the conductor announced we were arriving at Moszkva tér.

She giggled as she collected her bag, preparing to stand. "So, am I just supposed to know where and when? Or do I have to guess?"

I flushed. I was so relieved to hear her say yes, I forgot about the rest. "How about we meet here at Moszkva tér, say at six?"

"On Saturday?"

"Yes."

She got up and I stood back so she could pass. She let her hand slide along my arm as she went by. "It's a date then," she said.

After she walked off the tram, I watched her until she was out of view. As the streetcar pulled away, I smiled to myself. Quickly that smile faded when I realized I had no idea how to cook. I glanced around the streetcar and noticed several people look down as I caught their eye.

I look up now with a start. I'm still sitting at my kitchen table, but the room is completely dark. I wonder how long I've been out this time. I look at the alarm clock in my room and see that it says 8:00 p.m. I was so caught up in the memory of Samantha I had skipped dinner. For two hours I had been in memory land. Standing and walking to the fridge, I work to focus my mind. How am I going to get Samantha back?

Chapter Twelve

Peter

As Peter looks out the window of the streetcar toward the river and Margit Bridge, his thoughts focus on Samantha. Hodges certainly didn't look like a killer. But then again, he had investigated murders before, and the killer proved to be someone he hadn't expected. If Hodges had done something to her, what could it be? Had he gone so far as to kill her? If so, why? Had he made advances toward her, and she had rebuffed them? Was he hiding something, and she found it out?

"*Segíthet?*"

Peter looks up to see a boy, maybe fifteen or sixteen, asking for spare change. He has long dark hair and dark eyes. His clothes are worn and ragged.

"We came to visit family here in Budapest and now we don't have enough money to get home."

"Where's home?" Peter asks the boy.

"Transylvania, in Romania."

Peter reaches inside his jacket and finds a couple 10-forint coins, handing them to the boy.

"*Köszönöm,*" the boy says and moves on.

Transylvania is now part of Romania but had been in Hungary before. Prior to both World Wars, Hungary was much larger having lost a third of its size following WWII. Over a million native Hungarians now live in Transylvania. Between the bordering countries and migrations to the United States and Canada, almost more Hungarians live outside of Hungary than within.

After a transfer from the streetcar to the redline subway, Peter exits on the Pest side of the river at Kossuth Lajos tér. The redline is the only subway that runs under the Danube. All the other subway lines are exclusive to Pest. He had heard plans were being made for a Buda line, but that had yet to be completed. As Peter heads for home, he considers what he learned today. He met the elegant and lovely Dobo Kata and heard her suspicions about her husband. He went to the school and met Mr. Hodges—something was off about the man. He had also eaten at Szép Ilona's and confirmed some of what Kata told him by speaking with the bartender. Now the tough part of his job: where should he go next? As he strolls along Váci Street, he notices a sign he's walked past a thousand times. Internet café. Never has he entered, but he figures what could it hurt. Hesitantly he turns toward the door and walks inside. There's a counter near the front and multiple computer stations scattered throughout the room.

"Yes, can I help you?" the girl behind the counter asks. She's wearing all black and has a piercing in her nose. Her hair is dyed jet black, and Peter can see she has multiple tattoos.

"Yes, I was hoping to use one of the computers."

She scowls. "How much time do you want?"

Peter looks up at the sign overhead. Prior to that moment, he had no idea you must pay for the use of the computer by the minute.

"Thirty minutes," Peter tells her, not sure he can figure out how to turn the computer on in that time but unwilling to commit to more.

"Two hundred forint," she tells him.

She rolls her eyes as he fishes his wallet out of his pocket. He hands her two 100-forint bills.

"Okay, you get computer number four. Type in this password to access the browser." She hands him a slip of paper with a four-digit number.

Peter finds computer number four and sits down unsure what a browser is. The screen prompts for a password and he types the number on the sheet of paper. After hitting enter, the password prompt screen disappears, and he sees a blank blue screen with a large letter E icon. Using the mouse, he moves his cursor to hover over the E. Nothing happens. He clicks one of the two buttons on the mouse but still nothing happens. He looks around the room suddenly feeling very old. All the other computers are occupied by people he would consider kids; nobody over the age of twenty-five. A young girl, maybe eighteen, smiles at him from across the desk. She's on the computer closest to his.

Seeing the hopeless look on his face, she leans over and asks, "Do you need some help?"

He lets out a breath of relief. He was seconds away from standing and walking out. "Yes, I'm not good with computers," he admits.

"Have you ever used a computer before?"

"Does working next to them on a desk count?"

She giggles, stands, and comes over to him. "Okay," she says, "what are you wanting to do?"

He shrugs. "I was hoping to look up someone. A teacher."

"No problem. Just take your mouse and double click on the E on the home screen." He hovers his mouse over the E and clicks once then again. Nothing happens. He looks up at her and she fights to suppress a laugh but can't and bursts out laughing. "I'm sorry," she says putting her hand on his shoulder, "you have to double click fast, like this."

She takes control of the mouse, hovers over the E, and double clicks the button on the mouse quickly. A new window opens with "AltaVista" written over the top. Below the name, there's a search field box. "You can put your cursor inside that box then type what you want to search and hit enter. Options will come up and then you double click to read more."

Sensing his hesitance, she holds the mouse and says, "Here, I'll show you. What is the name of the teacher?"

"Niles Hodges," Peter responds.

"Oh, he isn't Hungarian. English?"

"No, actually he's American."

"Okay." She types Niles Hodges in the search field. "Does this look right?" she asks him. Peter nods and she hits enter. After a few seconds, several search options begin to populate, each with a short description of that entry. "If you hold down the left button on the mouse over here," she moves the cursor to the right side of the page, "on the scroll bar you can move through the entries."

Peter is astounded. He can't believe the number of options that come back after typing the name Niles Hodges. "Hmmm... Great," he says, rubbing his beard and gazing at the screen.

"My name is Ildiko. I'll just be back at my computer. Go ahead and give it a try. If you need me, just ask."

Peter takes the reigns from her and begins clicking and reading. What he had expected to be only fifteen minutes quickly turns into an hour. The more he reads about Hodges, the more convinced he becomes Hodges played a part in Samantha's disappearance. Now he just needs to prove it.

Chapter Thirteen

Peter

Peter walks into his apartment, anxious to place two phone calls. After a quick stop in the kitchen, he walks down the hall and sits down at his office desk. The room is sparsely decorated and feels cold. Only a desk, swivel chair, telephone, and notepad populate the room. All the furniture is worn and old, having been used when Peter bought it. He picks up the telephone and punches in the first phone number. After several rings Peter hears the familiar voice of Detective Kovacs.

"Good day. You have reached the desk of Kovacs Lajos. Unfortunately, I'm unavailable right now. Leave me a message and I'll call you back. If this is an emergency, please dial 112. Thank you."

"Yes, Lajos, this is Andrassy Peter. I need a couple favors from you. They shouldn't take long. I know how busy you are right now. Please give me a call when you get this message." Peter hangs up the phone. He checks his notepad for the next phone number, picks up the receiver, and dials the number. After three rings, Peter hears Stephen's voice. He has to smile; the kid is trying to speak Hungarian.

"*Jo estet kivanok. Stephen vagyok. Hogyan segithetek?*" (Good evening. This is Stephen. How can I help you?)

"Stephen? This is Peter."

"Yeah, Peter. Thanks for calling."

"Did you find out who Samantha's roommate is?" Peter hears hesitation on the other end of the phone.

"No, not yet. But I'll be in the school tomorrow. I have a couple Italians in my classes. I'm hoping one of them can help me."

"Okay."

"Did you talk to Mr. Hodges?" Stephen asks.

Peter tells him about going to the school and talking with Hodges. About Samantha and the strange way Hodges acted at the use of her name. He also tells him about following Hodges and confronting him.

"So, what does that mean? What do we do?"

Peter begins to tap his pen on the table. "Well, actually, there's more to the story than even that."

"What do you mean?"

Peter hesitates to tell him. "That man you know as Niles Hodges isn't really Niles Hodges."

Chapter Fourteen

Peter

P eter rarely sleeps well when working a case. He can't seem to turn off his brain and his mind keeps working even when he's exhausted. At 2:00 a.m. he wakes, and for the rest of the night, he lies in bed tossing and turning. Occasionally he dozes off but never into restful sleep.

At 6:00 a.m., he gives up and gets out of bed, takes a bath, and has some tea. While sitting in his kitchen, his phone rings.

"Good morning! How can I help you?"

"Peter, this is Kovacs Lajos, returning your call."

"Right, Lajos, thanks for calling me back. You remember the case I told you about? I need a little help." When Peter came back to Hungary, he knew one of the hardest parts would be not having a relationship with the local police department. In NYC, he knew several private investigators and the most successful leaned on the police department. They developed friendships that paid dividends. When Peter came back to Hungary, he made it a point to help the local police on a few different occasions without the expectation of getting anything back. Now Kovacs had learned to trust him.

"What do you need?" Kovacs asks.

"The British girl I was telling you about is still missing. Remember, the American kid who hired me?"

"Yeah, I remember. Unfortunately, as I told you, I'm spread thin. I'm not sure what's happening but these cases are coming up more often. I know it sounds horrible, but I just don't have the time. I added her to my file, but I haven't had a chance to do anything with it yet."

Peter was expecting this. "I understand. I'll keep working that case and I'll let you know if I get anything. But I do have one request. It won't take you long."

He hears Kovacs take a long breath then sigh on the other end of the phone, finally he asks, "What is it?"

"There's a teacher at the IBS school in Northern Buda who is teaching under an assumed name. I need you to do a background check on him. See if anything pops."

"How do you know he's teaching under an assumed name?"

"He lied to me a couple times, so I did some internet research. Turns out his name is Carson Fredrickson and he's from Orlando, Florida."

Kovacs lets out a low whistle "Well, I'll be. I would never have guessed you would be using the internet to help with cases. Did hell freeze over?"

Peter sighs loudly. "Just look into it will you?"

"Okay. I will."

"How generous are you feeling?"

"What do you mean?"

"I need one more background check. Have you heard of the Szép Ilona restaurant in Buda?"

"No, I'm not familiar with it."

Peter tells him about the owner Dobo Andras, about his wife hiring him.

"Sorry, Peter. You know I can't help you in an affair case. If I investigated every married person having an affair in Budapest, I would do nothing else. That's not against the law."

"No, I'm not asking you to help with that. I'm asking you to tell me if he has a criminal record."

"Why would you think he'd have a criminal record? And even if he does, how does that help you determine if the guy is having an affair?"

"It's just a hunch. Can you help me out?"

Kovacs agrees and tells him both searches might be done by the end of the day.

Chapter Fifteen

Stephen

It's still dark outside as I arrive at the school. I need internet time and know how busy the computer lab can be later in the day. Like most universities, students at IBS don't love the mornings. I don't either, but since talking with Peter last night about his findings on Mr. Hodges, I can't think of much else. As I walk through the hall and into the lab, I look around in relief. Only four of the six computer terminals are occupied. I walk over to the lab assistant, who's reading a textbook and hasn't acknowledged me.

"Hi, I'd like to use one of the computers."

The kid, at least three years younger than me, still doesn't look up from his book, he just points at the clipboard sitting on the desk.

So sorry to disturb you, I think and pick up the clipboard. What is this? Why do they need all this information? After feeling like they now have everything but my blood type, I drop the clipboard on the desk, it rattles to a stop. The lab assistant finally looks up.

"You can have number five," and points to the back of the room. He's already back in his book.

I can't help himself and exclaim with mock sincerity, "Thanks so much for all your help. You've been great!" I turn and walk to the number five computer.

I'm shaking my head as I sit down. I could have written anything on that clipboard. I should have. I should have said I'm Obi-Wan Kenobi and I'm here to meet Darth Vader.

After I've sat down at the computer, and entered my school ID, I pull up Internet Explorer. I have a computer in my apartment, but it doesn't have any internet access. I could get internet access, I brought an AOL disc from home, but then I'd need to install a modem, set up AOL, and dial in through the phone line. Even then it's far from painless. If anyone calls, it kicks you out and you have to restart the whole thing again. Each login takes five minutes. I don't think it's worth the hassle, and I really don't need it that much; I typically only use the internet to send email to family back in Cleveland.

This morning is different. I need to find all the information I can about Mr. Hodges, or should I say, Mr. Fredrickson. I still can't believe the bombshell Peter dropped on me last night. Turns out Mr. Hodges isn't really Niles Hodges at all. His name is Carson Fredrickson. He's a 38-year-old former business school professor at Central Florida University. Hodges is hiding something, and I'm going to find out what it is. Last night, Peter navigated to the IBS school website to read the profile written about Hodges. The profile mentioned Central Florida University and that Hodges had graduated from the University of Miami. Peter said he had a hunch that information was accurate. Peter said most good liars try and limit the amount they lie about; that way they have less they need to remember.

I am now on yahoo.com and run a search for "Carson Fredrickson Florida." After a few seconds, the search results begin to load. I'm surprised. There are pages and pages of results. That's pretty unusual. I click on several options but finding nothing interesting. Now I narrow the search to Carson Fredrickson Central Florida Business Professor. That's much better; only producing a couple pages this time. My eyes are drawn to one article from the *Orlando Sentinel* mentioning a fired Professor Fredrickson. The page loads and I immediately recognize the photo at the top of the page. It's Hodges. He's younger, and he isn't wearing his glasses, but it's definitely him. My pulse is racing as I read.

University of Central Florida business professor, Carson Fredrickson (33), was fired Friday for his alleged actions taking place at a Central Florida fraternity. According to a source, Fredrickson had been intoxicated and engaged in sexual misconduct with at least one female student. He had been a tenured professor at the University and was described by many students as "a lot of fun" and "really caring."

I look up at the clock with a pang of disappointment. Class is about to start. Not only that, but it's the class of the lying professor. I get up from the computer, never allowing my thoughts to wander from Hodges. Acting has never been my strong suit. How am I going to see the man in a couple minutes and not call him out on his lies?

As I walk down the hallway toward Hodges's classroom, my hands are sweating, and I can feel the blood coursing through my body when another thought hits me. What if his name isn't even Fredrickson? What if he's done this before and that isn't even his real name?

Chapter Sixteen

Stephen

"Has anyone here heard of a man by the name of Charles Ponzi?" Mr. Hodges has just begun his lecture for the day, and as is his customary lecture technique, he's asking a question to get things started.

I can hardly focus on anything he's saying. I'm now convinced, more than ever, he had something to do with Samantha's disappearance. Hodges begins pacing back and forth at the front of the class as he talks.

"Charles Ponzi was born in Italy in the 1880s. When he was nineteen years old, he decided to leave Italy for America, believing America would be a land of promise. When he arrived in America, he was destitute, having almost no money. Immediately, he went to work in some hard labor jobs in both the USA and Canada, and even spent some time in prison for forgery and smuggling." Hodges stops and turns to the class. "Is everyone clear on what forgery is?"

A girl in the front, Sandra, raises her hand. Sandra always sits near the front.

"Yes," Hodges points to her, "Sandra, go ahead and tell the class what forgery is."

I can see a bit of exasperation in Hodges. This is a common occurrence in class as Sandra raises her had whenever she knows the answer to anything, and sometimes when she doesn't. She turns around in her chair as she speaks, her air of superiority palpable.

"Forgery means you sign someone else's name on an official document without their consent." She turns back to Hodges.

Hodges smiles. "Yes, thank you, Sandra."

She smiles and bobs her head at him.

"Typically, you see cases of forgery in official documents like loan agreements, deeds, or even personal or business checks. Ponzi had stolen money by forging signatures and got caught." Hodges begins pacing back and forth again.

"But there were bigger infractions in Ponzi's future. In 1919, Ponzi was in Boston, in the United States, and opened a business promoting a scheme. He was calling it International Reply Coupon. These 'coupons,'" Hodges holds up his hands to mimic quotation marks, "could be used to buy postage stamps in different countries. His plan was to purchase these coupons in bulk in Europe and then redeem them in America where they could be sold at a higher price. He was going to make thousands, if not millions, from this scheme, which would have made him a very rich man."

Hodges stops pacing and turns back to the class.

"Ponzi had a problem though. What do you think that problem was?" I watch but nobody raises their hand, not even Sandra.

I know the answer, but I have no interest in talking directly with Hodges. No way would I keep the contempt I feel for the man from showing. Hodges waits but nobody volunteers.

"Come on," Hodges prods. "Nobody can see what the problem was with this plan?"

I can't take it any longer and begrudgingly raise my hand. Hodges smiles and points to me.

"Yes, Stephen, what was his problem?"

I keep my answer short and to the point, barely looking at him. "He didn't have the money to buy the coupons."

Hodges claps his hands. "Yes! Exactly! Ponzi could get the coupons, but he didn't have the money to buy them. He had planned to buy them in bulk, which would've taken a lot of money that he wouldn't earn back until he sold them."

Hodges resumes pacing.

"Ponzi began promising a fifty percent return on investment for anyone who gave him money. And not only did he promise an outrageous return, but he also promised to return people's money within forty-five days. So, Ponzi started bringing in loads of money. But he ran into a problem in getting the coupons and before he knew it, he ran out of his promised forty-five days for the original investors. What did he do?"

Hodges turns back to the class again. Sandra immediately raises her hand. She's so anxious I'm reminded of a four-year-old kid who just lost their helium balloon into the sky and tries to reach it before it flies away forever. Hodges notices Sandra, how could he not, but waits to call on her, hoping someone else will raise their hand. After a few excruciating seconds, he finally puts her out of her misery by pointing at her.

"Yes, Sandra, what do you think?"

She smiles and turns around to the class, sensing none of his exasperation. "Well," she smirks, "he probably just went back to those original investors and asked for a little more time. He explained to them that it was taking a little longer than expected but they would get their money." She turns back to Hodges expecting praise but finding him shaking his head.

"No, that's not what he did. It would have made sense for him to do that, but instead, he had another idea. He took the money invested by his more recent investors and paid off the original investors meeting his promise of a fifty percent gain and forty-five-day payback. Now, how many of you see a problem with this? On the one hand, he was meeting his obligations—he had promised a fifty percent return and to pay it within forty-five days—with this idea he was fulfilling his promise. But what wasn't fair about it?"

On cue, Sandra raises her hand. Hodges looks at her but doesn't have the heart to call on her.

"It looks like Sandra sees it. Does anyone else see anything wrong with this?"

Hodges begins looking around the room as Sandra continues to reach for her balloon. Finally, a boy in the middle of the class raises his hand. Hodges points to him with a look on his face like he's a Titanic passenger who just found a lifeboat.

"Well, it doesn't seem fair to the new investors. They are basically paying back the first investors with their money."

Hodges smiles. "Exactly!" he says while snapping his fingers. "Not only that, but the investors believed they were investing in a coupon business; not using their money to pay off a debt." Hodges begins slowly walking now while also shaking his finger. "But there's more to this. The company is supposed to be using the investment to operate the business. It's supposed to be making money. But it's not and if new investment stops, the whole thing falls apart. Those that have invested money now will be left with nothing." Hodges turns back to the class. "Ladies and gentlemen, the term for this is a Ponzi scheme, named after its most famous proponent.

"About a year later, reporters began looking into Ponzi's business and it didn't take long for them to find what was happening. They began writing about it and Ponzi was sunk. New investment stopped and Ponzi was arrested. He was then convicted and sent back to Italy in 1934. He died five years later in Brazil, in poverty. Since that time, Ponzi schemes have proliferated all over the world, many by former business school students like yourselves. My plea to you is for you not to be one of these people. Don't let your greed get in the way of your ethics. As leaders, you will have times of extreme pressure. You will have times when you are tempted to compromise your ethics. Fight the temptation."

That's it! I'm not going to sit here and let this man preach ethics to us. The blood is coursing through my body, and I let a laugh escape my lips. "Like you are someone that should be preaching ethics to us," I say loud enough for others to hear.

Hodges is about to say something else but stops short. Everyone in the class turns to look at me now, but for once, I don't care. I'm not about to stop now.

"What's in your past, Mr. Hodges?" I'm sneering at him as I say it. "Or should I call you Mr. Fredrickson?" The transformation is instantaneous. Hodges turns white as the whole class turns from me to him. I go on, "Why don't you share with the class who you really are?"

He's trying to collect himself now. "Stephen, I think you are mistaken. I don't know where you are getting your information but it's not accurate." Before I can respond, Hodges looks up at the clock on the wall. "We're just about out of time. I'm going to dismiss class a little early so Stephen and I can clear up this misunderstanding."

I make no move to say anything else. After watching us stare at one another, the other students get up and start to leave, looking over their shoulders. As Sandra leaves the room, she looks back and gives me a withering look.

Chapter Seventeen

Stephen

Once everyone leaves, Hodges sits down on one of the desks opposite me. I continue to look out the window, doing my best to ignore him.

"What was that all about?"

I turn and glare at him. "You know what it was about."

"No, I really don't. What brought that on?" Hodges is calm and looks at me as if I'm the liar.

I don't understand how he can be calm. Does he feel no guilt? Does he lack a conscience? He could have done something to Samantha and not even feel bad about it. I want to lash out at him. Say these things to him. But I know I need to keep my cool. I've got to be smart. I take a couple deep breaths and look him in the eye.

"I have a simple question for you, what's your name?"

He doesn't even blink as he responds, "My name is Carson Fredrickson."

He's caught me off guard. I was expecting a lie. "Why are you going by the name of Niles Hodges?"

He smiles at me and shakes his head. "Well, that's a bit more complicated." He leans back hugging one of his knees to his chest.

I shrug at him saying, "Let's hear it."

He stands and walks toward the window, looking out on the courtyard. "I used to work for the University of Central Florida in the Business Department. My wife also worked for the school in the English Department. I was absolutely in love with her. I had never met a woman more lovely, more genuine, more passionate than her. We were married three years and blissfully happy." He turns back to me now and I can see emotion in his eyes. "One day as I sat in my office after school, I received a phone call. I answered and didn't recognize the voice on the other end of the phone. The man told me he was Officer Purdy from the Campus Police. He told me my wife had been crossing the road in front of the English Department and was struck by a car. She was in an ambulance headed to the hospital."

Fredrickson comes and sits down across from me again. I can see he's having a difficult time with the memory, and I feel a pang of guilt. "When I arrived at the hospital, they wouldn't let me see her for a few hours. They said the accident was severe and that they were working to save her life." He shakes his head. "I was in a fog. I couldn't believe what I was hearing. That morning I held her in my arms. How could that person now be fighting for her life?" Fredrickson stands and walks back to the window. "After a few hours, the doctor came and explained she could no longer breathe on her own. They could no longer detect any brain activity. She was essentially a vegetable." I can see a tear form at the edge of his eye and it spills out, running down his cheek. He senses it and wipes it away.

"I went into the ICU to see her and couldn't believe what I saw. She was hooked up to a breathing machine and had all these other machines all around her. She was battered and bruised. But as disturbing as that was, the feel in the room was worse. She was gone. What I saw was a lifeless model of what my wife had been. That vibrant personality disappeared. My chest felt like someone had ripped it open and removed my heart." Now Fredrickson can't hold back the tears. They begin running down his cheeks. He walks to the desk at the front of the room and grabs a box of tissues. "I'm sorry. Obviously, this is still difficult to talk about."

After wiping his eyes and blowing his nose, he composes himself and walks back to me. "Even though her spirit was gone, I couldn't let go. It took a couple days for me to authorize removal of the machines. I sat holding her hand as her chest rose and fell for the last time." He sits down on the desk again looking at me with tear-stained cheeks. "I was placed on leave by the university, given a month to deal with my grief. I went through stages of depression, utter sadness, and anger. I considered taking my own life, reasoning a life without her wasn't worth living. After a few weeks, people told me I needed to get back to teaching; I needed to move on with life and eventually things would get better. So I went back. But I was just going through the motions. I began to drink heavily. I wanted an escape. I no longer wanted my life. I valued nothing, not my job, or any other aspect of my life." Fredrickson stands and walks back to the window. "Well, after a few months of continuing this way, a female student expressed concern for me as she had heard about my wife. She encouraged me to come to a student party at a frat house on campus. She convinced me I needed to have some fun." He turns back to me and shrugs. "Like an idiot, I believed her and went." He begins rubbing his forehead. "To tell you the truth, I remember almost nothing about the party; I was blackout drunk. The next morning, I woke up in jail. Apparently, the police had been called after a fight broke out. They found drugs in the house and a number of people were arrested, including me."

Again, he sits on the desk. "Well, the student that had convinced me to come to the party claimed we had sex. That I coerced her into it. Given my intoxicated state and presence at the party, I didn't have a leg to stand on and the university fired me. Not only that, but the local newspaper and TV stations picked up the story. Weeks later the student admitted we never actually had sex. She had made the whole thing up. But the damage was done." Fredrickson leans over and puts his face in his hands. "It was rock bottom for me. I had to decide: Was my life over? Or was I going to get some help?

"That night I checked myself into a treatment facility. I spent thirty days drying out and dealing with my grief. I talked to some very caring social workers and counselors and when I came out, I knew I was in a much better place." Now he stands and walks back to the window. "But I had a problem. I had lost my job in a very humiliating and public manner. It was a job I loved but, given the scope of the media attention my firing had garnered, I knew getting another job would be difficult. Especially in teaching." He turns back and looks at me. "It's funny, when you go through something like that, you see the best and worst in many people. There were some people I called friends who never spoke to me again. In fact, they wrote me some nasty letters saying some pretty awful things." He shrugs his shoulders. "But others were truly amazing. They reached out and helped. They looked at me with concern rather than judgment. They showed me love when I most needed it. It humbled me.

"One such friend was a fellow professor at Central Florida. He knew how much I loved teaching and resolved to help me find a new teaching job. He's the one that found the opportunity here. Somehow, he found IBS was hiring for different business school professors. He called and spoke with the Dean. He explained the situation but vouched for me and even gathered references from other professors I had worked with. It touched my heart that someone would do all that for me. I'll never forget that generosity." Now he leans back and exhales. "The Dean of the business school here called me and, after several conversations, became convinced that I was the right person for the job. He made me an offer and I moved halfway around the world to restart my life." He stops talking now and looks directly at me.

I think he's done and wants me to respond. I'm not sure what I'm supposed to say.

"Wow, that's a lot," I hear myself say.

Fredrickson smiles. "I suggested to the Dean that perhaps it made sense for me to teach under a different name. He liked the idea. We determined it would be less complicated and leave me a better chance at anonymity." Now he chuckles. "And it worked great. That is until you came along and found me somehow." Now he raises an eyebrow at me. "Speaking of, how did you find out?"

What can I say other than the truth? "I was investigating you."

"Why?"

I take a few seconds before answering. I consider several scenarios and decide better not to reveal too much. "One day in class you referred to yourself as Mr. Fredrickson not Mr. Hodges."

"I did?" he asks. "When was that?"

"It was last week during a lecture. When I heard that, I couldn't let it go. I had to know why. A little internet history confirmed much of what you just told me, at least about you being fired by Central Florida." I look at the clock on the wall. I'm very late to my next class. I stand and extend my hand to him. "Thanks for telling me that story. And I'm sorry for what you have been through."

Fredrickson takes my hand in his. "Thanks for listening."

I turn to leave the room, but before I do, I turn back around. "I guess you want me to keep calling you Hodges?"

He smiles. "If you wouldn't mind."

I shrug. "Sure. By the way, what was the name of that professor who did so much for you?"

Fredrickson cocks his head to the side. "Fred Carter. Why do you ask?"

Again I shrug. "Just curious." And I walk out the door. As I hurry to my next class, my thoughts remain on the story he just told me. He's either the best liar in the world, or that really happened. In either case, I've got to know which is true.

Chapter Eighteen

Peter

P eter does a double take as he enters the head office of the International Business School. This must be the blonde, Gretchen, Stephen mentioned when he first came to the school. His description of her beauty was lacking. The woman belongs on a model runway rather than sitting behind the desk of a school. She has soft long blonde hair that features a light curl. As he walks toward her desk she looks up and smiles a dazzling smile, her bright blue eyes sparkling.

"Can I help you?"

"Yes, well I hope you can. I don't know, I'm just so confused." Peter does his best to impersonate a helpless old British man. Knowing he's a decent-looking fella, he's used his charm to encourage women to help him in investigations. That's not going to work on Gretchen. She isn't going to succumb to his charms. His only chance is to play the hapless old fool and see if she will take pity on him.

"I hope I can too," she says, a look of concern in her eyes.

He slows his speech and adds a touch of desperation to his voice. "My niece goes to school here, and it's her birthday. I wanted to surprise her with flowers." Peter holds up cellophane wrap of flowers. Props always make a lie more believable.

The arresting blonde smiles. "Oh," she coos, "that's so sweet. What a lucky girl she is to have an uncle like you."

"That's nice of you to say. Thank you. But I'm embarrassed to admit, I don't know where to find her in this big school." Peter turns and makes a big sweeping motion with his left arm.

She smiles. "Well, maybe I can help you. What's your niece's name? I can look her up in our database."

He knew it would come to this, but he has a plan. "Her name is Samantha."

"Great! Samantha. What's her last name?"

"Hmm, well, our family name is Jones, but she may go by her stepfather's last name, which is Smith." He brings his hand to his chin and starts tapping it with his index finger. "But wait a second, she might even go by her natural father's name, which is Williams." He shakes his head. "Now that I say all that, I'm embarrassed. My sister has had a few different men in her life, and it certainly hasn't made things easy for Samantha. Maybe if I had been a better brother, she would have had better luck in the romance department."

Peter looks down and the pretty blonde stands and pats his hand. "I'm sure it isn't your fault. You seem like a very caring uncle and I'm sure you are a great brother."

He looks up and smiles. "You are so sweet. Thank you." He extends his hand. "My name is Peter Jones."

She takes it. "I'm Gretchen Wagner."

He smiles at her. "It's very nice to meet you, Gretchen."

"You too, Peter." Gretchen turns back to her computer. She enters a few keystrokes and frowns at the computer. "I don't see a Samantha listed."

He was afraid of this. "You mean you don't have any Samantha's in the school?"

She looks up. "No, we have a couple but none with the name of Jones, Smith, or Williams."

He considers how to play this with her. "I remember her mentioning a teacher she likes. She said he was from America." Peter rubs his chin like he's trying to come up with the name. "I think she said his name was...Hodges?"

Gretchen smiles. "Oh yes, we have a Niles Hodges teaching here. That's a good idea. Let me check his rolls." She begins typing again but after several seconds, she frowns. "I don't see a Samantha in any of his classes."

Peter looks down in disappointment. "Hmm, well, I guess I'm not delivering any flowers today. Gretchen, you have been very sweet. Thank you for helping an old man."

She smiles. "I'm sorry I couldn't help you more."

He turns to leave then turns back. "Gretchen, can I ask you one more question?"

"Of course!"

"If Samantha left school and quit, would she still show up in the database?"

She purses her lips as she thinks. "Well, that depends. If she chose to leave the school and not come back, basically unenroll, then, no, she wouldn't show up anywhere. But if she simply stopped coming to class, she would still show as enrolled."

He raises an eyebrow. "That makes sense. Thank you again." With that, he turns and leaves the office. As he walks out of the building and back to the streetcar stop, he thinks about Samantha. Only twenty percent of missing person cases are solved once the subject had been missing for five days. He's running out of time. Based on Gretchen's explanation and her inability to find Samantha in the database, she must have unenrolled in school. Either that or someone with access removed her.

Peter turns and walks back to the office. He needs to ask another question. As he enters the head office, Gretchen looks up with surprise.

"Peter? Did you forget something?"

He nods. "Sorry, Gretchen, I need to be honest with you. My name isn't really Peter Jones. My name is Andrassy Peter. I'm a private investigator, and I've been hired to find Samantha. She disappeared several days ago, and she was last seen here at the school."

Gretchen rears back and takes a sharp breath. As she does, she turns her computer monitor away from him.

"I'm sorry that I didn't tell you the truth before, but I need to ask you one more question. Who has access to your database? I mean, who could add a student or delete a student from the database?" Gretchen hesitates. "I promise, I'm not going to ask you anything else specifically about a student. I just want to know, could one of the teachers add or delete a student from the database?"

She thinks about that for a few seconds, still looking at him warily. Then she begins to shake her head. "No, a professor wouldn't be able to add a student to the database." If a light bulb could have appeared over her head in that moment, it would have, however. She drops her voice to a whisper and leans forward. "But I think they could delete a student if they knew how."

Peter smiles. "Thank you, Gretchen." He puts the flowers on her desk. "Again, I'm sorry for deceiving you before. Please accept these flowers as an apology."

Chapter Nineteen

Stephen

I'm lost in my thoughts as I sit waiting for the streetcar.

"Are you all done with school for the day?"

I look up and don't immediately recognize the man standing in front of me. He peers down at me, half smiling half frowning. He's tall, maybe six feet two inches with a muscular frame, especially considering his age, a balding head and salt and pepper beard. Recognition finally dawns. "Oh, Peter? I didn't recognize you."

"I didn't recognize you at first either. I was staring at you for quite a while."

Peter comes and sits down next to me. He reminds me so much of Sean Connery. Not James Bond Sean Connery. More *Indiana Jones and the Last Crusade* Connery. If only he'd turn to me and say something like, "Indiana was the dog's name." But he doesn't. Instead, he asks, "So, what was occupying your thoughts just now?"

I hesitate to tell him, which makes no sense since I hired him to investigate Samantha's disappearance. If I can't trust him, who can I trust? "Oh, I was just thinking about Mr. Hodges."

"Yeah, what about him?"

Good question. Although I hired Peter, I don't know him well. He's going to have to earn my trust. He's peering at me now; I've taken too long to answer, and I can't even remember what he asked. "Sorry," I breathe, "what did you ask?"

"I asked what exactly you were thinking about Mr. Hodges?"

"I confronted him in class today."

"You did? What did you do?"

"I called him out on his fake name right in front of the whole class." Peter frowns and I feel like a kid about to be scolded by the principal of my school. "He dismissed the class. He wanted to talk with me individually."

The yellow and white streetcar arrives and we climb aboard. We find a seat together and I place my backpack between us. I don't like it sitting so close to him and I pick it back up, placing it on my lap. Peter watches me do it, gives me a curious look and asks, "So he told you about being fired from the University in Florida?"

I nod. "He also told me about his wife. About how she was killed in an accident and how he spiraled into depression. He told me about going to a frat party at the University and waking up in jail."

"What did he say about teaching here under an assumed name?"

I'm hugging my backpack in front of me like a drowning man holds a buoy. "After he was fired, he checked himself into a rehab place. He said after he got out, he didn't have a job or anything to fall back on. His reputation had been shattered. Another professor, Carter, helped him get the job here. He took it as an opportunity to restart his life." Peter begins absently rubbing his beard as he listens.

The streetcar is completely full now and we stand to give up our seats to two elderly women. It's an unseasonably warm day, and with the crowding of the streetcar it feels like we're sitting in a sauna. A man is standing next to us with his arm up, holding the leather strap that hangs from the ceiling. The aroma from his armpit makes my stomach turn.

"So, do you believe him?" Peter asks me as we stand facing each other.

I'm holding my backpack in one arm, the handle of the streetcar in the other. "I think so...but if he didn't take Samantha, who did?"

We reach my stop and Peter says he'll get off with me. He wants to talk more and I'm guessing he can use the fresh air. We fight our way to the exit, bumping and pushing against people on the way out.

When we are finally off, I hesitate but he just starts walking toward my apartment. I shrug and begin walking along with him. He's looking down at the sidewalk when he asks the next question. "Why are you so sure she's been taken?"

I look at him and I'm not sure what to say. "What do you mean?"

"Just now, you asked who took Samantha. You didn't ask what happened to Samantha. Why would you say it that way?"

"Uh...I don't think I meant...that," I stammer. "I just don't think she's dead or anything. And I don't think she just left Budapest. That means someone must have taken her."

We've reached my apartment building now and Peter seems to want to say something else. But he doesn't. He just stands there looking up.

"Are we ever going to find out what happened to Samantha?" I ask.

He's looking at the building, seemingly paying no attention to me. Eventually he brings his gaze back down and looks me in the eyes. "Unfortunately, there isn't much to go on. We don't know her full name, where she lived, or even who her roommates were. It would help me to have at least a picture of her; you were going to get one for me?" As soon as he says it, I feel a pang of guilt and anxiety. "How's that coming? Do you have it?"

I look down as I shake my head. "No, not yet."

"Why? It should be ready by now."

Peter's watching me closely and I feel myself squirming under his gaze. "I forgot to go and get the film developed. It's still sitting in my camera." The look he gives me is like the look I would receive from my father if I brought home an F for a midterm in pre-calculus. "I'll go and get it developed right away."

Peter frowns. "Maybe you should give the film to me. I know a company that can get it developed in a couple days; much faster than the three or four days most places take."

"Great! That's even better. Do you want to come up and get it?"

We enter the building and I call for the elevator. My backpack is slung over my shoulder opposite Peter as we enter. The elevator stops at my floor, and I step out followed by Peter. As I fumble with my keys, Peter says, "What was the name of that professor who helped Hodges?" I open the door and walk through with Peter behind me.

"Professor Carter," I tell him.

Peter shakes his head. "I don't know what it is, but I can't seem to remember that name. Do you have something I can write it down on? Maybe a notepad? I just need a single sheet?"

I am in the front room, and he waits at the threshold to the door. "Yeah, let me look around. I'm sure I have one on my desk."

Peter pointed to my backpack. "How about in your bag there?"

I keep my eyes forward, looking at him. "No, I don't think so. I just have textbooks in there. I'll get you one from my desk. Wait here." I walk into my bedroom, place my bag on the bed, and rummage around my desk. A few seconds later I reappear with a single sheet of paper and the name Carter written on it. Peter takes the paper from me but continues to look around the room.

After a moment, he turns back to me, looking in my eyes. "So, are you going to get me that film from your camera?" Oh no, I forgot again. I nod and walk into my bedroom, find my camera, and come back out, placing the film in his hand. He's looking at a picture I have of my family on the shelf.

"Is this your family?" he asks.

"Yep, that's my sister Liz, my dad, and mom."

"Nice family."

"Thank you."

Peter puts the film in his pocket and heads for the door. Before reaching it, he turns back to me. "Stephen, why did you not take this film to get developed?"

"I forgot. I told you."

"You claim to like this girl enough to hire a private investigator. I asked you to get this film developed and you didn't. What was the real reason?"

I feel myself begin to fidget even as I try and control it. "I really did forget. But I'm embarrassed to admit, I didn't take it in because I didn't know how. I didn't know how to say it in Hungarian."

Peter stares at me, and it's the kind of stare I can't read. Is Peter beginning to think I had something to do with Samantha being missing? There it is again, he wants to say something, but he doesn't. Finally, he tells me he'll be in touch, and he leaves, closing the door behind him. After the door closes, I walk over and lock it. I make my way back to my room and grab my backpack. I sit down on the bed and open the notepad. I flip to the page I didn't want Peter to see.

Dear Samantha,

I'm sitting in my Entrepreneurship and Family Business class, listening to the professor drone on and on and can't stop thinking about you. It's my last class of the day. I used to watch the clock in this class with both excitement and nervousness. I knew I would be seeing you soon in the courtyard. The day would be over, and we would meet there. Do you remember the time after class when we got in that argument? You were asking me how I liked Mr. Fredrickson's Leading and Managing People class. I told you I didn't think leadership could be taught. I thought it was something you were just born with. I'll never forget what you said to me: "And here I thought you were smart."

I was a little shocked, then I got angry. I'm sorry about my temper. Sometimes I act too emotionally and don't really think it through. I just had a long talk with Mr. Hodges. It turns out Hodges isn't really his name. His name is Fredrickson. He left America to come teach here because he had been fired by his University in Florida. His wife was killed and he kind of lost it. He came here to get a new start. At least that's what he told me. I'm not sure how much I believe. I can't forget what you told me about him. About seeing him in the library and how you told me he seemed creepy.

That really brings me to what I wanted to say to you. I don't really feel like I can tell anyone about this so I thought I would write it to you. It's been eating me up inside and I have to express it. I'm sorry for what happened on our last date. I didn't mean for that to happen. Did it even happen? I know, I keep telling you that I'm sorry but I don't think you can hear me. Or maybe you just don't want to hear me. Why do you keep ignoring me? Stop it and come back to me. I love you.

Stephen

Chapter Twenty

Peter

As Peter leaves Stephen's apartment building, he notices his friend, Tom, sitting on the park bench smoking a cigarette. Peter walks over to him. "*Ez nem egészséges,*" (That's not healthy) pointing to the cigarette. Tom looks at him like he's just bitten into a lemon.

"*Mikor lettél az anyám?*" (When did you become my mother?) Peter can't hold his stern expression and begins to laugh.

"What's going on with you?"

"I'm just trying to get a little me time. My wife is driving me crazy." They're still speaking Hungarian as Tom prefers Hungarian. Having both lived in large English-speaking cities, they became fast friends when they met. Tom is about twenty-five years older but otherwise they have a lot in common.

Peter laughs and sits down beside him. "You're the one that decided to get married."

Tom smiles. "How are you, Peter? How are things?"

Peter looks at his friend and exhales slowly. "I don't know, Tom. I'm beginning to wonder if I've lost my touch."

Tom gives him a mischievous grin. "Wouldn't you need to have touch in order to lose it?"

Peter rolls his eyes. "I've got two cases I'm working right now. I just started on the one, a woman suspecting her husband of cheating, but it's the one you sent over to me, with your American friend, Stephen. I'm not sure if I can help him."

Tom looks at him with surprise. "What do you mean? What's going on with him?"

Peter shakes his head. "That's just it; something seems very off about the whole situation. He really knows almost nothing about the girl. He doesn't know her last name, her roommates, her phone number, not even where her apartment is. I can't decide if it's because he doesn't know or doesn't want to tell me." Tom takes a drag on his cigarette, nearly choking. He begins coughing and Peter considers patting him on the back.

Once Tom gets a handle on his breathing, he asks, "What do you mean? You think he knows more than he's telling you?"

"Something is going on. I just don't see how the kid could like the girl as much as he professes yet has almost no information about her. And why did she pursue him like she did?" Peter leans forward on the bench and extends his hand almost like he is offering Tom something. "When I first talked to him, I asked if he had a picture of her. He said he did, but it was on his camera and the film needed to be developed. I asked him to go get that done right away and he promised he would." Peter turns his hand over and shows Tom the film canister. "Today I learned he still hadn't developed the film. Now why would a guy, so in love like he claims, not develop the film with a picture of the girl? Especially when the PI he hired asked him to do so. It's not like I've asked him to do much. That's the only thing I've asked from him."

Peter closes his hand around the film canister and sticks it back in his jacket pocket.

Tom grimaces. "I see what you mean. That doesn't make a lot of sense." Tom leans back, putting his arm up on the back of the bench, and takes another drag on his cigarette. "So, what are you going to do?"

Peter purses his lips and considers the question. "I'm not sure yet. Will you tell me everything you know about him?"

Tom gives him a sideways glance. "Sure, I don't know him well, though. Can I ask you a question first?"

Peter shrugs. "Of course."

"Is Stephen a suspect?"

Peter smiles wryly. "I think you know the answer to that. I was hired to find out what happened to Samantha. That's what I intend to do."

"I thought so."

Tom then tells him how he first met Stephen, how he could tell he was American, and how timid and socially awkward he seemed. He told him about Stephen's disappointment following his first date with Samantha.

"Was there anything in his behavior that seemed odd to you?"

Tom laughs. "Didn't I mention he's socially awkward?"

"Yes, but did anything about the story or about his behavior strike you as odd?"

"No, not really. I can't think of anything. I was surprised a kid of his age was so clueless with women. That struck me as almost unbelievable."

Peter had the same thoughts. "Have you had any other interactions with him?"

"I've seen him out here several times. Mostly after he comes home from school or has gone running. And obviously, I talked with him after Samantha left."

Peter wants to hear about this. "Okay, and how did that conversation go?"

Tom leans back again and looks up at the sky. It's late afternoon in Budapest and the temperature is dropping. A slight breeze blows and the looser brown and orange leaves on the trees fall around them.

"He seemed broken-hearted. He reminded me of a kid that lost his puppy."

Peter looks down, lost in his thoughts. "Anything unusual in that conversation?"

"Yeah, he seemed convinced something happened to her. It's like he knew something happened and couldn't consider that maybe she just left. He also told me about the professor; that guy sounded shady. Have you checked him out?"

"Yes, I'm in the process. There is something going on there." Peter puts his elbow on the back of the park bench and leans a little closer to Tom. "Do you think it's possible that Stephen had anything to do with Samantha disappearing?"

"No, I don't think so. Plus, why would he hire someone to investigate a crime he might have committed?"

Peter has to agree with that. "Yeah, that would be strange, but the kid is odd." Peter stands and pats his friend on the shoulder. "Thanks for talking with me, Tom. I need to take this film to be developed. I've got a little surveillance work to do in Central Buda which would put me closer to Szép Ilona's restaurant."

Tom gives him a quizzical look. "Isn't that up in Central Buda, in the hills? That's a long way from your apartment."

Peter smiles and winks. "It is, but I like the bartender."

Chapter
Twenty-One

Director Toth

" **A** re you going to the Fradi–Újpest match Saturday?" I sit across the table from Nemeth Laszlo, mayor of the fourth district of Budapest. We've come to my favorite Chinese restaurant in Pest called Tan Mu Xiang. Laszlo, like many sports fans everywhere, believes the winner of the football match has more bearing on their happiness than crime levels in the city. Those other people, however, are not mayor of one of the busiest portions of Budapest.

"I don't think so. Last time wasn't exactly a good look for Újpest, the fans, or the police force." All too well I remember my disappointment meld into disgust, then to anger, as I watched Fradi dismantle Újpest on the pitch. My mood went from bad to worse as the fans transformed into a mob dismantling seats and throwing them onto the field. Eventually, they left the stadium smashing cars and breaking windows. Worse became embarrassing when my riot police turned cowards and ran away from the mob in fear.

"If you aren't there, don't you worry your force will be unprepared for a situation like last time?" Laszlo asks me.

I give the mayor and my childhood friend a steely look. "No." The word comes out more clipped than I intend. "I've put major emphasis into preparing and training them since that match. If a situation like that happens again, I would resign my post. There will be good behavior at the match. I guarantee it."

Laszlo knows my hard tone isn't directed at him. We grew up together in Újpest. We attended school and even played on football teams together. We've been friends as long as I can remember, and he knows how fierce I can be when something doesn't go my way.

"Well, maybe Újpest will actually win this time. It may be a non-issue," he says trying to lighten my mood.

I raise a single eyebrow at him as I shovel sweet and sour pork into his mouth. "Yeah, then it will be the Fradi fans who want to riot."

Out of the corner of my eye, I see our server approach. The young man slows his step as I turn and look at him. I've been told I can be intimidating. I'm so used to people being frightened when they talk to me, I barely notice it. As the young server approaches, he's as timid as Bilbo Baggins entering the dragon's lair.

"Director Toth?" he ventures.

"Yes."

"You have a phone call." The young man motions behind the bar to the telephone on the counter. I stand and the young man steps back.

I turn to the mayor. "Sorry, Laci. I'll be right back." As I turn back to the waiter, he cowers like a dog expecting to be kicked. I stride over to the bar as the bartender points to the phone. I pick up the receiver and place a finger in the opposite ear. This is a very popular restaurant, and the lunch specials always bring a crowd.

"Yes, this is Director Toth."

"Director? This is Tibor." I grip the phone harder and press my finger deeper into my ear. It's unusual that he would call me outside of the office. I don't want to miss a word.

"Yes, Tibor. What do you have for me?"

"He's got another shipment going to Croatia tomorrow. He asked me to drive the truck with Zsolt." My eyes narrow as I consider the implications. I nod as I think. "Director? Are you still there?"

"I am. That's good work, Tibor. You've gained more trust from him than any other agent we've had. Be careful but gather as much intelligence as you can. I know it will be hard, but now is not the time to interfere. It took a long time to get you in this position. Don't blow it. We need to know how far this runs." Tibor agrees to call me again when the opportunity arises and I hang up. As I turn to rejoin the mayor at the table, thoughts buzz in my head. How far will I allow Tibor to go before he's likely to be killed?

Chapter Twenty-Two

Peter

Peter walks into Szép Ilona's and immediately looks toward the bar. He feels a surge of relief—Zsuzsa is there talking with a customer. Not only is she nice to look at, but she likely has information he needs.

"Hi, welcome back." She's wearing a tight-fitting white tank top and jeans.

"Thank you. Glad to be back." He can't help the smile that comes looking at her.

"What can I get you? Another Dreher?"

He raises an eyebrow at her. "You remember what I had?"

She blushes. "I do. I don't always with new customers, but I do with you." She smiles and looks down and Peter can feel his pulse quicken.

"Well, I don't want to disappoint you. Yes, please, I would love a Dreher."

She winks at him. "Coming up."

Peter takes the opportunity to look around the bar and the restaurant. It's 5:00 p.m. and much busier than the last time. Most of the tables are occupied with diners and the bar has five other men besides himself. The other men are sending him withering looks. It would appear they aren't too keen on a new guy coming to see their girl.

Peter looks in the direction of the hallway behind the bar where he noticed the office. While he's looking, a man emerges. He's tall, has dark hair touched with gray at the sides, and muscular, although he doesn't appear to work out regularly. Instead, he has the look of someone who grew up an athlete and has now allowed middle age to set in. The man fits Kata's description of her husband to a T. He walks from his office to the entrance of the restaurant surveying the crowded tables as he goes. His gait is extremely confident, almost boarding on a strut. When he reaches the hostess at the front of the restaurant, he leans in close and says something in her ear. She looks up at him, smiles, and blushes. Andras smiles back then begins strolling through the restaurant, stopping at tables and talking with the guests.

Zsuzsa returns and places a frothing beer on the counter in front of Peter.

"*Egészségedre,*" she says smiling at him. "Are you wanting to eat as well?"

"Of course."

She hands him a menu. "Go ahead and look it over and I'll be back in a few minutes to take your order." She walks to the other end of the bar and talks with a customer.

Peter opens his menu and looks it over but continues to watch Andras. The man is smooth. He's like an actor who is in full control of his performance. As he stops at every table, he smiles, laughs, and genuinely acts interested in whatever nonsense the customer is saying to him.

As Andras moves on to another table, one woman says to her husband, "What a nice man. I just love coming to his restaurant."

Peter turns back to his menu and is startled to see Zsuzsa has returned and is watching him.

"Are you going to just look around the restaurant rather than eat?" she says in a disapproving tone.

"Oh, I know what I want," he reassures her.

"Okay, sir, let's have it. What will you be eating tonight?"

Peter points to the middle of the second page. "I'd like the chicken Kiev, please, with a cucumber salad."

Zsuzsa smiles and holds out her hand for the menu. "How do you know all my favorite dishes here? Are you psychic?"

He hands her the menu and shrugs. "I knew you were going to ask me that."

She laughs. "I'll be back in a bit." And again, she's gone. He grabs his beer and takes a swig. Immediately, he embraces the bold, rich flavor. He takes two big gulps then sets it down.

"How is the Dreher tonight?" a male voice says right beside him.

Peter turns to find Dobo Andras standing to the left of him. He's smiling and Peter can see why he could land such a striking wife. He's clean-shaven but would have a thick beard if he chose to grow one. His jaw is chiseled like granite and he has a sharp pointed nose, bright blue eyes, and a mouthful of straight, white teeth. The man is movie star handsome.

"Excellent," Peter responds.

Andras lowers his eyebrows. "Good to hear. I don't think I've seen you in here before?"

Peter shrugs. "I've been here once. I came in a couple days ago and quite liked it."

Andras's smile grows in warmth. "I love to hear that. How did you find us?"

Peter has to think quickly. "I have a friend who recommended it. He said the food is delicious and, based on my first experience, I would say he's correct."

Andras pats him on the shoulder. "You are too kind. What's your friend's name? I will have to thank him for the referral."

"Lantos Tamas," Peter lies.

Andras furrows his brow. "Hmm, doesn't sound familiar. I'm not sure I know him."

"Well, he highly recommended it and I'm glad he did. The food is excellent, and your help isn't bad to look at either."

Andras chuckles and bows. "Is there anything men like more than good food and attractive women?"

They both laugh loudly, maybe a little too loudly.

Andras drops his voice as he leans in closer to Peter. "Well, enjoy your beer and dinner and thank you for coming to Szép Ilona's. I hope to see you again soon."

Peter thanks him and he moves on to the next person at the bar. Peter watches as Andras continues to greet the customers at the bar. It appears Andras has the charisma to charm the men as much as the women. He takes another swig of his beer. Before long, Zsuzsa returns with his food and places the warm platter in front of him.

"Looks pretty good, huh?" He has to agree. His mouth waters at the sight of the breaded chicken. "Would you like me to refill your beer?" Peter bobs his head, and she takes his mug.

For the next fifteen minutes, Peter eats his meal and watches Zsuzsa interact with her customers. He knew she was good at her job, but this is quite impressive. She has a knack of making each man feel like she appreciates having him there. Andras finishes greeting the customers then goes into the kitchen. After another fifteen minutes, he slips back into his office.

Peter sits and debates his next move. Typically, infidelity cases are easy to solve. You just follow the philandering spouse and eventually they meet their lover. But this situation is more complicated because Andras owns another restaurant. And not just another restaurant in town, but one in another country. Peter fears he's going to have to follow Andras to Croatia to catch him cheating. What would that mean for the case of Samantha? Could he afford to travel to another country chasing an adulterer when a woman is missing? Does it change the urgency if Samantha is no longer alive as he suspects? As he sits debating these points, Zsuzsa returns.

"How was the chicken Kiev?"

"Very good," he replies.

"Better than the stroganoff?"

"No, that was excellent; this was just very good."

She laughs. "Now my challenge will be finding something you like even more than the stroganoff." He knows she's flirting with him again, but he can't determine if it's simply because he's a customer and she wants a good tip. He decides fortune favors the bold.

"I don't know if there is anything I could eat here that would compare with how much I like the bartender."

Zsuzsa wasn't expecting the compliment and ducks her head blushing. "Well, you've tried the chicken Kiev and the stroganoff, but you haven't tried the bartender. Maybe you should?" Peter had never considered himself to be a savant when interpreting signals from women, but you'd have to be a neanderthal not to pick up this one.

"When can I?" he asks.

Zsuzsa looks into his eyes. "I don't work too late tonight. If you want to meet me around eight, we can get a drink together."

"I'll be here." Peter tells her.

Chapter Twenty-Three

Peter

The street is loud, especially when a bus passes. Peter sits on a park bench across from Szép Ilona's Bisztro waiting. For what? He isn't sure. Andras probably. His hope is that Andras will leave, meet his lover, and Peter can snap a few pictures. Maybe the rendezvous takes place at a hotel and Peter can convince a bellboy or front desk attendant to dish on the couple. Just like that, the case is over and Peter can focus on Samantha.

The sun is setting and Peter pulls his jacket tight. He's always loved the month of October. The leaves are turning color, but typically, it isn't too cold and doesn't rain much. Something about today reminds him of his youth. Peter grew up with a reputation as an intelligent but rambunctious boy. Although he excelled in school, he got in more fights than other kids. He'd rather be punched in the face than lose in a game. He wasn't one to follow the rules either and his father lacked the patience to deal with him. As he grew, his willingness to rebel did also. After school, Peter was expected to come home and complete his chores. He had to chop wood, gather the eggs from the chicken coops, and do his homework. He would procrastinate arriving home and would dawdle with his friends. He was quick to agree when his friends would suggest a store detour. It was always a source of contention in the house. Imre and Miklòs, his two best friends, were given money by their fathers. Peter never had any money. His friends would buy snacks and he would steal. He had gotten away with it so many times that he began to be complacent.

On the day that would turn out to be his last in Hungarian school, he stole some bread and Kolbász (Hungarian sausage). As he and his friends exited the store, the shopkeeper called Peter back. He asked him to open his jacket.

The shopkeeper summoned the police, and he was taken to jail. His father made him wait for a few hours before coming to get him. He repaid the shopkeeper and promised to keep a better eye on Peter. When Peter saw his father, he recognized the furry boiling underneath. He had never been his father's favorite child. In fact, his father admitted he wished Zoltan, his older brother, had not been killed in the war and that Peter had instead. As they had walked home, Peter apologized to his father, fearing the punishment headed his way. His father never looked at him, choosing to stare straight ahead instead. Reaching the front gate to the house, his father commanded him to wait there.

A few minutes later, his father emerged from the house carrying some of Peter's things. "It's time you go make your own way in the world," he told Peter, handing him his clothes in a bag along with 5,000 forint. "You are no longer welcome in my home." Peter stared at him. He was expecting a beating, or at the very least, no supper. But he never expected to be kicked out at sixteen. His mother had come to stand on the porch but was unable to look at him. This was his father's decision, like any other major decision in the house.

At that moment, something snapped in Peter. He defiantly looked in his father's eyes and said, "*Jól van, Uram.*" (Very good, my Lord) He took his things, squared his shoulders, and walked away with nowhere in the world to go. After having wandered the streets of Pecs for a couple hours, he realized his home city held nothing for him. He'd seen pictures of the beautiful bridges in Budapest and the castle overlooking the city.

When night fell, he snuck his way onto a train headed north having no idea where it would lead. He had been lucky; the train went to Budapest. As they entered the city, he was astonished by the size of it. They traveled for miles and still didn't reach the station. As the station came into view, he jumped from the moving railcar. He hit the ground hard, knocking his head on a rock and scraping his knees. His eyes became blurry, and he could feel a pounding in his head. He lay on the side of the tracks and, for the first time since leaving home, cried. It wasn't the physical pain; it was the look he saw in his father's eye. He saw relief. He was ridding himself of some awful burden. At that moment, Peter realized his father had never loved him.

A Volkswagen Passat slams on its breaks right in front of Peter, pulling him from his thoughts. Once the traffic clears, he focuses on the restaurant across the street. The front door opens and a young woman comes out and begins walking down the street. Peter recognizes her immediately. It's the same young woman who ushered him to the bar tonight. The same woman Andras was flirting with. The girl wears a short skirt with black tights, and a tight knit top that reveals her pierced belly button. None of that strikes Peter as odd, but the speed with which she moves is. She meanders down the walkway as if she has nowhere to go. At this pace, she might make it to wherever she is going next year.

Again, the restaurant door opens. He immediately recognizes the figure exiting the restaurant. The man is tall and has a confident stride with graying hair. He turns in the direction of the wandering girl and quickly gains ground on her. When she notices him, she flashes a big bright smile. He smiles back and puts an arm around her. They appear to be headed toward the bus stop.

Peter stands and calls for a taxi, making sure to keep out of their line of sight. As they stand waiting for the bus, Peter notices they seem very comfortable with each other. Several times she laughs and Andras seems very attentive to her. The taxi pulls up and Peter gets in.

"Just stay here for now. Once the bus comes, I want you to follow it. I'm trailing those two at the stop." Peter points out Andras and the young woman.

After about three minutes the bus arrives. The taxi driver allows the bus to move away before he pulls out. At each stop they pull to the side of the road keeping distance from the stop. After five stops Andras and the girl get off. They're holding hands now laughing and talking as they walk. Peter tells the taxi driver to follow but to keep his distance.

After walking several blocks, they turn and climb the steps to the Hotel Tiliana a small hotel in Central Buda. Peter shoots several pictures of them as they walk, but he wants one in the actual hotel. He pays the taxicab driver and walks in. The lobby is empty short of the check-in desk with a single employee working. Peter considers walking to the desk to interrogate the desk clerk. But he decides against it. This isn't far from Andras's restaurant and it's likely Andras is a repeat customer.

The hotel features a small café. Peter figures he might be waiting a while and walks over to order a tea. He positions himself at a table that allows him sight to the stairs and the hotel rooms. He'd like a picture of them leaving together. After only five minutes, Andras comes down the stairs alone. He waves, saying something to the desk clerk, and walks out. Peter sits debating on what to do. Should he follow Andras or wait for the girl? He decides to wait. A picture of the girl in the hotel would still be powerful.

After another twenty minutes Peter has lost his patience. He decides to make a bold move. He exits the hotel café and reenters via the main doors. He calculates that the clerk never looked at him when he walked in the first time. This time he walks straight to the desk and introduces himself.

"Hello, my boss Andras was just here. He left something behind in the room and told me to come get it," Peter tells him.

The front desk clerk looks skeptical. "Andras told you to come?"

Peter frowns. "He wasn't happy." The clerk looks like he wants to quiz Peter further but Peter cuts him off. "Look, don't get me in trouble. Just give me the key to the room. I'll be back in five minutes."

"What did he leave?"

"I can't tell you that."

That convinces him. He reaches up and grabs the key and hands it to Peter. Peter walks up the stairs before examining the key. The key is to room ten. Peter walks to number ten and knocks. Nothing happens. He knocks again and still nothing. Finally, Peter uses the key and opens the door. It's empty. The bed looks like it has been laid on but not inside the blankets. Peter checks the bathroom but nothing is left behind. The girl seems to have disappeared.

Chapter Twenty-Four

Stephen

"Hello?" I ask as I pick up the phone.

"Oh no, did I wake you?"

I immediately recognize my sister's voice on the other end. "Liz?" I ask.

"What time is it over there?"

"Umm..." I walk back toward the bedroom to see the alarm clock. "It's seven p.m."

"Oh, okay good. I was worried I woke you."

"No, I was studying." I sit down at the kitchen table; the long swirling phone cord stretches from the hallway to my ear. I'm wearing the jeans and T-shirt I had worn to school. I'm barefoot and the wood floor feels cold against the bottom of my feet.

"What are you studying?" Liz asks.

"Oh, nothing really. So, how are you?"

One question was all she needed. She's off, telling me about school, and how she's enjoying her classes at Ohio University. She complains about her friends, but they are also her support system and she loves them. She's always been the outgoing type; popular in school with a welcoming personality. Everyone seems to like her.

"It's good to hear your voice. I worry about you," she tells me.

I lean back and chuckle in the chair. "You worry about everything."

"I do not," Liz responds hotly, "and I resent the implication."

I can hear the smile. "How are you? How's Dad?"

"I'm doing pretty well," she responds. "Dad is fine. He still seems to love Maggie; heaven only knows why."

I've never been particularly fond of Dad's new wife, but Liz seems to downright despise her. It's not a big surprise. Both women are strong personalities that seem to think they know what is best for Dad and the family.

"Are you judging me because I don't like Maggie?" she asks. "I didn't have Chuck to get me through Mom's death and Dad's funk like you did."

This makes me laugh out loud. Leave it to Liz to lighten the mood. "You could have. You just don't have as creative an imagination as me." I can't believe she remembers Chuck. Chuck was my imaginary friend I created after my mother died.

"How are things there in Hungary?"

"It's taken some getting used to, but I'm pretty happy here now."

"I heard you're dating someone?"

I hesitate. *Should I tell her? How much should I tell her?* "I am. Well...we've been out a few times. I really like her." I tell her about Samantha; about meeting her and the dates we've been on. I can't help the excitement in my voice as I talk about her.

"Oh, Stephen, I'm so happy to hear that. I was worried about you, you know?"

"I know. You told me. Remember?"

"Come on! Going to a foreign country with a foreign language and you really don't know anybody? That's a lot for anyone. Especially someone like you." Liz probably knows me better than anyone else in the world. Being only siblings, we are naturally close, but after our mother became sick, we grew even closer. After her death, it felt like we only had each other.

"So, when are you seeing Samantha next?"

"Well, that's the thing, I'm not sure."

"Why? Haven't you asked her out again?"

"Yeah, I would except I don't have her number. And I haven't seen her in school lately."

"What do you mean you don't have her number?" Liz is incredulous. "And what do you mean she hasn't been in school?" There's little point in holding back now. I open up and tell her almost everything. Liz stays quiet on the other end of the phone until I'm done.

"I hired a private investigator."

"You did? Why haven't you talked to the police? Has the investigator been helpful? I assume it's a man?" She is talking fast now.

"He's been somewhat helpful." I tell her about Hodges and how that isn't his real name. About how his real name is Mr. Fredrickson and he was fired from Central Florida University. How Fred Carter helped him land the teaching job here in Budapest. "Actually, I'm glad you called; I could use your help. I need to find out if this Mr. Carter is real. How would you feel about finding his number and calling him?"

Liz can't hide her excitement on the other end of the phone. Her volume is high even through the crackling connection. "Do you think Mr. Fredrickson or Hodges, whatever his name is, had something to do with Samantha disappearing?"

"Yes. That's why I need to know if Mr. Carter is real. I need to know if Fredrickson's story is true."

"I'll work on it. Let me see what I can find out and I'll call you back."

Something about hearing her voice stirs emotion in me. I miss her. "Liz, thank you. I love you."

"I love you too, Stephen. I'll call you when I find out."

I hang up the phone and head back to my desk but I don't pick up the textbook. Instead, I sit and stare out the window. The sun is setting over Budapest now and I begin to feel guilt. Why couldn't I be honest with Liz? Why couldn't I tell her everything?

Chapter Twenty-Five

Peter

P eter stands outside Szép Ilona's waiting for Zsuzsa. They had agreed they would meet when she got off work at 8:00 p.m. He had arrived only a couple minutes ago when she appeared.

"Hi," Zsuzsa says as she sees him. He approaches and they exchange a hug. "Do you have a place in mind?"

"No, I was thinking I would rely on your expertise."

Zsuzsa turns and begins tapping her finger to her lips. "How about a place called Eper? It's only about a five-minute walk from here."

"That sounds great!"

After walking to the bar and ordering their drinks, they find a booth at the back. The bar is sparsely populated with only a few patrons, outside of them. Nobody seems to be paying any attention to them.

Once they are settled on opposite sides of the booth, Zsuzsa asks, "Do I get to know anything about you besides your name being Peter?" She's teasing him with her eyes. The booth and table are large. It could easily fit three people on each side. The leather's worn and tearing on the seats but neither seem to mind.

Try as he might to fight it, Peter finds himself intoxicated by her. It reminds him of the first time he met his wife. His wife had been out of his league also. He smiles at her. "You can ask me one question."

She frowns back at him. "Only one?"

"Let's start with one and then we'll see."

"Hmm," she muses taping her lips with her index finger. "What should a girl ask in this situation?" Her eyes brighten. "I've got it!" She leans back. "Have you ever been in love before?"

"Yes," he says simply, taking a sip of his drink. Zsuzsa rolls her hands in a circular motion as if to tell him to keep going. "Hey," he responds, "that's your question and I answered it."

She frowns and exhales. "That's not fair."

He can't help but chuckle. "Should have asked a better question Have you ever been in love?" he asks her.

"I'm not answering that," she tells him.

"Why not?"

A guy at the bar is angry because he's been cut off by the bartender. They both turn to watch before losing interest as the man leaves the bar. Zsuzsa looks back at him and shakes her head. "Because you tricked me."

"What?" Peter asks.

"Because you tricked me," Zsuzsa repeats with a slight pout.

Peter chuckles again. "Tricked you? How did I trick you?" Peter knows she's flirting with him, and he can't help but be drawn in.

"Because you knew what I meant, and you still haven't answered my question."

"Okay, how about this, you answer my question, and I'll let you ask another."

Zsuzsa smiles and her eyes sparkle. "Deal!" She sits back in the booth thinking. Almost immediately, her eyes get wide and she responds back. "Yes." She's clearly pleased with herself and Peter chuckles again. "My turn," she says. "Tell me about the woman you loved."

Now it's Peter's chance to sit back in his seat. How does one describe the woman who still represents his whole life? "She was ravishing. She was medium height, had a lovely figure, dark hair, and dark brown eyes like chocolate. She was kind and engaging. She had a way of challenging me and making me want to be better."

Zsuzsa's eyes are studying him. "What happened to her?"

Peter smiles and holds up his index finger. "Only one question."

She laughs. "Okay, okay, hurry up and ask your question so I can hear more."

Peter decides to take it easy on her. "Where were you born?"

"Százhalombatta," she responds then quickly asks, "How did you meet her?"

"I was in New York City. I left Hungary when I was only sixteen and lived in NYC for most of my life. I was working as a detective in the NYC police department and got a call to investigate a break-in at an apartment near Midtown. I rang the bell and when she answered the door, her eyes made me stop dead. She had obviously been crying but I couldn't get over how rich her eyes were. They reminded me of when I had been to a chocolate factory in Belgium and watched them make dark chocolate. She had such fine soft features." Peter's heart aches at the memory of her. To that point he had never believed in love at first sight. "Her apartment had been burglarized and I made a note of all missing items. What upset her the most was a missing pendant necklace given to her by her grandmother. I made it my mission to get it back."

Zsuzsa is so engrossed in the story she can't help but ask, "So did you find it for her?"

Peter wants to remind her she has already asked her question but decides to just answer.

"I did," he tells her. "I found that the burglar had hit several other buildings in the area. When we picked him up, I questioned him, and he remembered the pendant. He told me he had sold it to a jeweler in Brooklyn. The store owner there had already sold the necklace but had the information for the person who had purchased it. I went to them and reclaimed it as stolen property."

Zsuzsa gets a concerned look on her face. "You mean you just took it from them? After they had paid money for it?"

Peter nods. "I did, but they were able to return to the jewelry store to get their money back; I had already worked this out with the shop owner." Peter leans back. "I think I've given you way more information than your question required."

She smiles. "I'll owe you one, and I always pay my debts, but you can't stop there. I want to hear the rest."

Peter laughs. "Then I think you are going to be in even greater debt to me."

She smiles. "Fine. Ask a simple question."

"Will you tell me the story of how you met the man you loved?"

"No," she says simply. "What happened when you returned the pendant?"

Peter laughs again. She really is so cute. "I brought it to her, and she cried again. She thanked me over and over and kept asking what she could do for me. I asked her if she knew how to cook and, next thing you know, she started cooking for me." Peter shrugs. "We fell in love." He stops and taps his finger on the table with a far-off look in his eye. "No, I shouldn't say we fell in love. I should say I loved her from the moment I first saw her. I finally convinced her to love me back."

"Where is she now? Why did you come back to Hungary?"

"That's a little harder to talk about. The simple answer is, she died."

Zsuzsa's face fell. "Oh, I'm sorry," she tells him, "I don't mean to be insensitive, and you don't have to answer, but what happened?"

Peter turns and looks at the bar. This trip down memory lane has affected him more than he would like to admit. He doesn't want Zsuzsa to see the pain he's feeling. He still finds it difficult to believe how much it hurts to think back on that time. His speech is slow and his voice low as he explains, "She was a nurse and would often work late. One night, she never came home. Her remains were found in an alley several days later. We never found who did it and, to this day, the case has never been solved. I stayed in NYC for another year looking for answers but never found any. I quit my job. I just couldn't handle the prospect of investigating anything that might remind me of her. I was full of feelings of hate and rage. I wanted revenge." Peter shrugs. "I still do." He rubs his beard. "I hate the prospect of her killer still being out there. I couldn't deal with the idea I might cross him on the street. That's when I decided to come back to Hungary. There were too many memories of her in NYC. Of us together. I needed a fresh start. I didn't want to forget her, but I needed to be in a new environment. I started to feel a homesickness for my homeland."

Without a word, Zsuzsa slides out of her seat and comes to the other side of the table, she slides in next to Peter, and hugs him. "I'm so sorry. You've been through so much." It's been a long time since Peter has been this close to a woman and he can feel how much he's missed it. He loves the smell of her perfume, and the feel of her body against his. Perhaps he hasn't known how lonely he has become. Zsuzsa finally lets him go but doesn't move back to the other side of the booth. She stays next to him with her hand on his.

"You know what the worst part is?" Peter looks down as he says it, feeling the regret. "I'm responsible for her death."

Zsuzsa stares at him. "What? Why? How?"

Peter shakes his head. "I'm almost one hundred percent sure whoever killed her did it to get back at me. It must have been someone I put in jail. Or someone who loved the person I put in jail."

Zsuzsa puts her hand on his cheek and turns his face to look in her eyes. "Peter, that's not your fault. You can't carry that kind of burden." They fall silent, looking in each other's eyes. Peter had been told the same thing by others, but he didn't believe them just like he doesn't believe her.

"Peter," she asks, "what do you do for work now?" She is looking at him intently and he debates his answer. Normally he'd lie and make something up, but something inside him says he can trust her.

"I'm a private investigator," he tells her.

She leans away from him, her face falling. "Did you come into my restaurant for work?"

Peter decides lying to her would be pointless. "Yes," he says simply.

"Are you investigating Andras?"

He's slow to answer and she sees it. "Yes," he finally replies.

She looks down and starts rubbing the glass with her index finger. "Did you come and sit at the bar because you were hoping to get information about him from me?"

Peter winces at the question. He exhales slowly and answers, "Yes."

Without warning, Zsuzsa slides out of her seat and rushes toward the door. Peter drops some cash on the table and rushes after her. As he exits the bar, he blinks. It's completely dark outside and his eyes take a moment to adjust. He looks around wildly, trying to find where she's gone. After a moment, he sees her hurrying along the sidewalk. He runs to her, feeling the stiffness of his legs.

As he approaches, she hears him and calls over her shoulder, "Leave me alone, Peter. I don't want to talk to you."

Peter reaches her and grabs her by the shoulders, turning her to him. When he does, he can see tears streaming down her cheeks. "Zsuzsa, what's wrong?"

She looks up into his eyes. "He scares me," she admits.

Peter inhales. "Are you having an affair with him?"

Zsuzsa frowns. "Of course not. You thought I was having an affair with him?"

Peter shakes his head. "No, I just didn't know what you meant."

She furrows her brow and looks intensely into his eyes. Her voice dropped to a whisper. "I'm talking about the girls. The girls that keep disappearing."

Now it is Peter's turn to be confused. "What girls keep disappearing?"

"You don't know about them? That isn't why you're investigating him?"

Peter shakes his head but he feels a lurch in his gut. "No, I'm investigating him because his wife thinks he's having an affair."

Zsuzsa scoffs softly. "Oh...well, there's way more going on than that." Now she grips his arm and her whisper becomes fierce. Her long nails dig into his flesh. She looks around then steps closer to him. "But you didn't hear any of this from me. He's dangerous and powerful. I don't want to vanish also."

Peter stares in her eyes seeing the fear. "I promise, Zsuzsa, he won't know you helped me."

She cracks a half smile through the tears. "You know that's not the only reason I'm crying." Now Peter worries what she might say next, and she sees it in his face. "I thought you liked me. Not just wanted me for a spy." Peter smiles. He places his hand under her chin and raises her face to his. He leans over and kisses her, feeling her soft lips against his. When she opens her eyes, she turns and grabs his hand. "Come on, we have more to discuss, and my apartment is just down the street."

Chapter Twenty-Six

Peter

P eter looks around the apartment as Zsuzsa gets out a kettle and fills it. The apartment is small but clean, and he likes the way it's decorated. His own apartment is boring and sparsely furnished. He has almost nothing that would tell a guest anything about him. Zsuzsa's, by contrast, is expertly appointed. The walls are painted different pastel colors. She has numerous pictures and art pieces on the walls. Her small table includes a lovely centerpiece of flowers and candles.

"*Tejet akarsz?*" she asks. He shakes his head. He had never understood why people put milk in tea. "*Citrom?*" she asks.

"*Igen,*" Peter bobs his head. He never passes on lemon.

"Go ahead and sit down," she commands and points to the small table. Peter obliges but he worries he might pick a bad spot given the size of the centerpiece on the table. Zsuzsa senses his uncertainty and comes over to the table. "Let me just get rid of some of this stuff." In a flash, she has picked up the flowers and candles and places his tea down in front of him.

As she sits down, Peter is anxious to get some answers from her. "Tell me about Andras?"

Zsuzsa takes a deep breath. "Peter, just forget what I said. I really think it's better if I don't talk about him."

This is going to be harder than he thought. She knows things about Andras, but she's scared and has clammed up. She's white knuckling her teacup and she has a difficult time meeting his gaze. He knows he needs to be careful here. If he pushes too hard, he isn't going to get any information from her. He needs her to feel she can trust him.

"Zsuzsa, can I tell you a story?" She looks at him warily but agrees. "When I was in NYC, I dealt with some difficult and scary situations. As you can imagine, people don't contact the police because everything is going great. The same is true of a private investigator. Sometimes, I've become desensitized from hearing and witnessing so many difficult things. Anyway, one day as a detective, a woman came into my office. She told me that her daughter had been killed but the police were calling it a suicide. I could see the pain in the woman's eyes, but, I'll admit, I was skeptical. You see, nobody wants to believe their child would commit suicide. They want to believe there must have been some other reason." Peter takes a sip of his tea. He looks in Zsuzsa's eyes and knows he's getting through to her; she's completely engrossed in his story.

"Anyway, I told the woman that I would investigate the suicide and get back to her. To be honest, I really told her that to get her out of my office. I had rarely come across instances where I had found the police were wrong. Well, I talked with some of my contacts at the NYC police department and they shared some of the case evidence with me." Peter looks away and shakes his head. "The evidence was compelling that it had been a suicide. I went back to the mother and told her that I investigated and found she had in fact committed suicide. The mother wept but thanked me for my time." The memory is painful, and he has a difficult time hiding it. He barely blinks as he speaks. "A few weeks later, I learned that the mother also committed suicide. Apparently, she felt responsible for her daughter's death. Three months later, I was investigating a serial killer in NYC. After several weeks, we caught him. He kept pictures of his victims and one of the pictures was the girl of the mother who had hired me. The mother was right, her daughter hadn't committed suicide. She had been murdered."

Now he leans forward and places his hand on hers, "Zsuzsa, I understand you are scared. And if you don't want to tell me about Andras, I won't force you. But just know, that experience changed me. I made a promise to myself that I would never lie to a client or to anyone when it came to a case. I promised myself that I would never betray anyone's trust. And I would investigate to the fullest. If you tell me what you know about Andras, I will not reveal where I got the information. I will do everything in my power to protect you."

The apartment is silent aside from the subtle sound of their breathing as they look in each other's eyes. "Andras is a very bad man," she says. "Girls keep disappearing and nobody seems to notice."

"What girls?" Peter asks.

She takes a deep breath and puts her hands on the table. She lowers her voice even though they are alone. "As you can imagine, we hire a lot of young girls in the restaurant business. It seems like we constantly hire new hostesses, servers, and bartenders. That's not unusual. Any place I've worked did the same. The jobs just aren't typically career positions. They have large turnover." Zsuzsa begins to move her hands as she talks. "But lately, I've noticed so many of these new girls just disappear. Most of them are from places outside Budapest, many from Hungarian portions of Romania. They work in the restaurant for a couple weeks then we never see them again." She stops and points her index finger at Peter. "But the really weird part is that they vanish. It's like they never existed."

Zsuzsa stops and looks down at her hands in her lap. Her cat is rubbing against his leg, "So, I asked Andras about it one day. He passed it off like it was normal, but I kept pressing until he snapped. He grabbed my arm, looked in my eyes, and told me that if I didn't stop asking, I would disappear also."

Peter raises an eyebrow. "He said you would disappear?"

Her lower lip trembles. "I've never seen him look like that. He is always so friendly and outgoing, but now I saw a different side to him. I immediately recognized his charming, friendly demeanor was only an act."

Peter takes a sip of his tea and considers what she has told him. "Zsuzsa, what do you think is happening to these girls?"

She tilts her head as she considers. "That's something I've thought a lot about. Whenever we hire a new girl, I want to warn her to run, but I'm so frightened of him I keep quiet. I'm stuck. I don't think I could quit, because if I did, I think he would kill me."

"So, is that what you think? You think he's killing these girls?"

Zsuzsa shrugs. "What else could it be?"

Peter purses his lips. "Yes, I see what you mean. But to what end? What's the purpose? He has another restaurant in Croatia, right?"

She furrows her eyebrows. "You think it's happening there also?"

Peter shrugs. "It could be. Has anyone else confirmed there actually is another restaurant?"

Zsuzsa's eyes go wide. "You don't think he has another restaurant?"

"What if it's just a front for something else?"

"A front? For what?"

Peter leans back. "To help him make these girls disappear. Maybe they're being sold into sex trafficking." He can see her head is spinning. "I'm not saying that's what is happening," Peter reassures her. "I'm just saying, it's possible. And it's just as possible that he has a restaurant there." Peter begins tapping his finger on the table. "I really need to follow him into Croatia. See what is really going on."

Zsuzsa jumps in her chair. "He's going to Croatia tomorrow."

Peter raises an eyebrow. "He is?"

She nods her head. "Yes. Someone said he is headed down to Zagreb."

Peter stands up from the table, his tea forgotten. "I'm sorry, Zsuzsa, but I need to go. I need to try and find out how he is traveling and when."

"That's okay. I understand," she tells him as she stands. Peter heads for the door but stops as he feels Zsuzsa grab his arm. When he turns around, she's looking up at him. "Peter, please don't let him know I told you anything."

He instinctively reaches out and hugs her. "Zsuzsa, I promise you. He will never know." He turns back around and reaches for the door. As he turns the knob, he thinks of one more question. "Zsuzsa, in the last few weeks, was there ever a redhead from England in your restaurant?"

Zsuzsa considers the question. "You mean working in the restaurant? No, I don't think so. I would remember her."

Peter strokes his beard. "What about just eating or drinking in the restaurant?"

Zsuzsa furrows her brow trying to remember, then a memory dawns in her eyes. "Yes! I remember one a few weeks back. She was there at the bar with a few other girls. They were all foreign. I don't know if she was from England, but I remember a pretty redhead and she was speaking English."

Chapter
Twenty-Seven

Peter

It takes Peter almost an hour to get home. At 10:00 p.m., the public transportation options become limited in Budapest. He had to wait twenty minutes for the streetcar, and another fifteen for the subway. The long commute gave him a much-needed chance to think. He had gathered so much information over the last couple days from his conversations with Gretchen, Stephen, Tom, and Zsuzsa that they seemed scattered and unorganized in his head. After talking with Gretchen, he had begun to think Mr. Hodges had done something to Samantha. Otherwise, why would she be deleted from the school database? But then, after talking with Stephen and Tom, he thought Stephen might have done it. There were so many odd aspects of Stephen's story and behavior. Hiring Peter could mean Stephen was a psychopath. If Peter was able to uncover the truth, Stephen could simply kill him before he was able to alert the police. Peter knows he needs to be careful with Stephen moving forward. He must be aware that his client is also a suspect. What makes it even worse is that

Tom had told him where Peter lives. If Stephen truly is a psychopath, could he be waiting for him in the apartment? But finally, after talking with Zsuzsa, and learning about Andras and the pretty redhead in the restaurant, he thinks Samantha could be a victim of Andras.

As he walks into his apartment and down the hall to his office, he notices the light on his answering machine is blinking. He walks over and pushes the button.

"Message one 3:14 p.m."

"Hey Peter, it's me, Kovacs Lajos. I investigated this Dobo Andras fellow you were asking about. Uh...you better call me. I'd rather not say anything over the answering machine. I'll be around the office late today. I'm working on another case. Call me."

"Message two 8:42 p.m."

"Peter, this is Dobo Kata, I was wondering if you have any new information for me about my husband. You can call tonight until about eleven p.m. or anytime this weekend; he will be gone to Zagreb. Anyway, please call me. I'd like to hear if you know anything."

Peter sits down at the desk next to his phone and begins to dial the number. He looks at his watch, it's 10:45 p.m. There's still time. After several rings, she picks up.

"Hello?"

His finger is next to the hook in case it's another voice he hears. "Hi, Kata, it's Peter."

"Oh, yes, Peter. Thank you for calling me back."

Peter taps his pen on the desk. "Unfortunately, I don't have much news for you. I've been in Szép Ilona's a couple times now and I met Andras. I'm starting to think it might be important for me to follow him to Zagreb. Do you know when he is going again?"

He can hear her excitement build from the speed and cadence of her voice. "Yes, he's actually going tomorrow morning."

"Okay, great. How's he traveling? Is he driving?"

"No, he always takes the train. It usually leaves around nine thirty a.m. from Keleti."

Peter smiles. This is exactly the information he needs. "Great! I think I'll be on the same train. Also, do you have the address for his restaurant in Zagreb?"

There's a pause on the other end of the phone. "No, but I think I can find it. Hold on."

Peter sits looking up at the ceiling as he reclines back in his chair. After several seconds he hears muffled voices. *Has Andras come home?* He hears footsteps grow louder then a man says, "Why is the phone off the hook?" Peter strains to hear, but he thinks he hears Kata ask, "Is the phone off the hook?" She's further away and her voice doesn't carry as well.

A few seconds later, he heard Andras, "Hello? Is there anyone there?"

Peter sits quietly, holding his breath. He doesn't want to hang up, because he doesn't want Andras to hear the line go dead. The only thing he can do is sit and quietly wait for Andras to give up and hang up himself.

His plan backfires when someone outside his building begins blaring their car horn. Peter moves his hand over the mouth of the receiver, but the damage is done.

"Hello? Who is this?"

Peter has no choice and slides his finger over the phone hook, hanging it up. He slowly sets the receiver down, already thinking about the implications. Now Andras knows Kata has been talking with someone and lied to him about it. Peter sits contemplating what to do next. He's jerked from his thoughts by the sound of his ringing phone. The sound is blaring in his small apartment. *Could this be Andras calling back?* It could be someone else, but if it is Andras, what would he do? Would Andras recognize his voice? Peter acts quickly, reaching over and unplugging the answering machine, allowing the phone to ring and ring. Eventually, whoever is on the other end of the line, grows weary and hangs up.

Peter doesn't move, he just sits by his phone considering the implications of what has just transpired. After a few minutes, he plugs the phone back in and dials Detective Kovacs.

"Yes," he hears Kovacs say.

"Kovacs? Andrassy Peter here."

Peter hears Kovacs sigh. "Well, I looked into the restaurant owner, Dobo Andras."

"What did you find out? Anything on his record?"

Kovacs responds quickly. "No, clean as a whistle." Now Kovacs drops his voice to barely a whisper. "But something strange happened. After I did the search for him in our database, and it came up clean, my director called me and asked why I had looked into Dobo Andras."

"Is that unusual?"

"Very," Kovacs replies. "I do those types of searches all the time and have never had him call me."

Peter considers that for a moment. "So, what do you think it means?"

Kovacs is silent on the other end of the phone for a few seconds. "I'm not sure, but for some reason, my director is keeping close tabs on the guy."

It seems Peter may not be the only guy looking into him.

"Hmm... What about the other guy? The professor at the school?"

"I don't have anything on that one yet. I've got a call in to the states. I'll let you know when I hear something."

Peter hangs up the phone but doesn't stand from his desk. His thoughts are on Kata. Andras is a very dangerous man and he knows she's lying to him.

Chapter Twenty-Eight

Stephen

I walk out of my apartment building early this morning. The sun hasn't come up yet, but it will soon. The sky will become increasingly brighter and the stars will fade. I walk into the park next to the building and begin some light stretching. As I stretch my calves and hamstrings, I consider where I should go. I like the idea of something punishing. Something that will leave me exhausted.

After stretching, I start running at a moderate pace. Reaching the end of Bogdánfy utca, I turn right. I run for a few blocks and reach the river and Petofi bridge. As I turn and head upriver, I survey the three bridges on the horizon. I consider turning and running across the nearest one, Liberty, but decide against it. The Pest side of the river is almost completely flat and I want elevation. In front of me, stands Gellert Hill. Gellert will provide the type of challenge I'm looking for. Leaving the river, I cross the street at the traffic light. I wait at the traffic light, jogging in place. Once it changes, and it's my turn to go, I'm nearly hit by a car coming through the intersection. The driver honks his horn and flips me off. Cautiously, I continue across the street. Since I've been here, I've noticed Hungarians seem to believe cars have the right of way not pedestrians. This isn't the first time I've almost been hit. As I grow closer to Gellert, still running along the sidewalk, I'm still dogging cars. These are parked up on the sidewalk. I'm looking down, careful of where I step. Hungarians love their big dogs and don't always clean up after them.

Finally, I reach the base of the hill. I've come here before and know exactly where to go. The trail head begins on the southeast corner and runs from the base all the way up to the Citadel and massive statue at the top. I hesitate only a second, thinking back to the last time I had been here. *Is this really somewhere I want to be?* I shake it off and start on the trail. It's a grueling twenty-minute climb and when I reach the top my hamstrings are burning. I taste iron as I cough, I'm breathing so hard. My lungs tingle and I feel sweat trickle down my forehead. Walking into the Citadel, I wipe at my head with the palm of my hand. I traverse the steps and walk out onto the wall of the Citadel. The very spot I had planned on. Sitting down, I take a swig of my water and look out over the city. To the east, I notice the sun is just beginning to rise over the buildings. This is my first time watching a sunrise in Budapest and the vantage point of being at the top of Gellert Hill on the Citadel wall doesn't disappoint.

The scene in front of me does exactly what I was hoping. I begin to recall my final date with Samantha with perfect clarity. She was upset by my actions from the last date and wasn't going to see me again. I begged her to agree to have dinner with me and after a few days of making me wait, she finally relented. We had agreed to meet at Moszkva tér, our normal meeting spot.

"How do you always beat me?" she asked.

"Well, I ride the streetcar and it only runs so often. If I hadn't been on that one, I would have been fifteen minutes late," I tell her. I stood there awkwardly unsure what to do. After a couple seconds, I stepped toward her and gave her an awkward side hug.

She patted my back saying, "Oh."

I stepped back blushing. "Sorry. I'm not really a hugger." She smiled at me and took both my hands in hers and moved so she was standing directly in front of me. Slowly, she placed her hands on my waist.

"Okay, now put your arms around my shoulders and give me a little squeeze," she said. I did and she did as well. As I held her, I could feel her body pressed to mine and the smell of her hair; it left me feeling a little dizzy. She let go and, as she did, I forced myself to release her.

Samantha looked up at me, holding both of my hands. "So, Mister, are we going to dinner?" As we walked to the streetcar, we held hands. "You know, I haven't really been south of the castle area yet," she admitted.

I turned to her and smiled. "Really? Well, I can be your tour guide again."

We got on the streetcar and headed south. I pointed out some of the other bridges she had only seen in the distance, Elizabeth and Liberty. The Elizabeth Bridge was named after Queen Elizabeth, a Hapsburg princess in Vienna who was one of the queens of the Austro-Hungarian Empire. I also pointed out Gellert Hill and Hotel. I enjoyed how interested Samantha seemed with everything I told her. She genuinely loved touring the city and learning, albeit modestly, what history I knew. The streetcar finally reached my stop and I guided her off the car.

As we leisurely strolled to my building, she broke the comfortable silence we had fallen into. "Oh, this looks pretty nice; nicer than my building."

I was surprised. "Really? What's yours like?"

"Well...my building is just more central in the city. We don't have the nice little park and tennis courts." We went in and rode the elevator up to my floor. I made sure to position myself so that she couldn't see the graphic sexual pictures on one of the elevator walls.

When we reached my door, I stopped and looked at her. "You aren't going to judge me too harshly, are you?"

She laughed. "What do you mean?"

"It's not a fancy apartment."

She smacked my shoulder. "I'm sure it will be great." I moved forward in the dark hallway and opened the door. After guiding her in, I heard her exclaim, "Wow! It's so beautiful!"

That was the reaction I had hoped for. I set the table with the best plates, silverware, and cups I had. I even included a vase with fresh flowers I had purchased that afternoon.

"Feel free to look around the apartment," I told her. "I've got a couple small things to finish before we eat." I walked into the kitchen and got the cucumber salad from the fridge. I prepared all the food earlier in the day and left the Paprikas Csirke on the stove at a low temperature to keep warm. As I began to start dishing up food, I heard music coming from the bedroom. *I guess she found my CD player,* I thought. I have a collection of about thirty different CDs ranging from rock, metal, rap, country, R&B, even some movie soundtracks. I was surprised to hear the choice she had made.

Samantha came walking into the dining area of the kitchen. "Is this music okay?" she asked.

"I'm pretty sure this is from my CD collection, and I rarely hold on to CDs I don't like. I just didn't know British girls liked Garth Brooks."

"You clearly don't know how fast his concerts sold out in England."

I pulled out a chair for her. "This is your seat, my lady." She curtsied, sat down, and I slid her chair closer to the table. I walked to the other side and sat down.

"This looks very fancy," she smiled. "But I'm not familiar with this. What is it?"

"Have you been to any Hungarian restaurants yet?"

She ducked her head. "No," she admitted, "I was too afraid. I've pretty much stuck to the places I'm familiar with: McDonald's, Pizza Hut." She laughed as I gave her a disapproving look.

"What a shame, you're in a place with amazing food and you're too afraid to try it?"

She laughed. "So is this Hungarian food then?"

I leaned back. "Well...we are in Hungary, and this is food, so I would say so."

She rolled her eyes at me. "I mean," she started, "is this food Hungarian cuisine?"

I chuckled. "Oh, I sure hope so. It's not my grandma Erzsi's food but it's her recipe and I hope you like it." Samantha picked up her fork and speared some of the chicken. I watched her do it with anticipation. I was nervous.

"Mmm, that's really good."

"Yeah? You aren't just saying that are you?"

"No, it's really good."

I tasted it and she was right, it was delicious.

"So, you weren't lying to me when you said you could cook, were you?" Samantha was watching me closely.

She caught me by surprise, and I eventually flashed her a crooked smile. "Okay, maybe I don't cook that often, but I've seen my grandma make this a bunch of times. I knew I could do it with practice."

"Practice? How often did you make this?"

"Before this week? Never. This week? This is my fourth time." I ducked my head and smiled. Suddenly, Samantha got up from her chair and came around the table to me. Before I knew what was happening, she leaned down and kissed my cheek.

"Thank you," she whispered in my ear. Her perfume lingered in my nostrils as I watched her move back to her chair and sit down.

The rest of the meal was relaxing for me. We talked a little more about our childhoods. I told Samantha about the time I was hit by a pitch in the championship game of my little league baseball game. About how I tried so hard not to cry that I lost track of the pitch count for the next batter and was easily tagged out. After telling her the story, she admitted to me she knew nothing about baseball and understood none of the story. She told me about her first childhood crush and about how he had kissed her on the schoolyard then kissed her friend the next day. It was her first heartbreak. When we finished, I stood and went to take her plate. She looked up at me, sliding her plate away.

"What do you think you're doing?" she asked.

"I was going to take your plate to the sink."

"Go sit back down," she ordered. "You did all this cooking all week, the least I can do is tidy up."

I smiled at her. "That's sweet, Sam, but I needed to make you dinner to make up for being such an awkward fool." I reached for her plate again but, again, she moved it away from me. "Give me that plate," I commanded with mock gruffness to my voice. She stood to face me and as she did, unleashed a breathtaking smile. *Wow, she's so beautiful.*

"Okay, I will give you this plate on one condition." She was standing close to me and I could smell her fragrance as she held her plate behind her back.

"Okay, what's the condition?"

She looked up at me with eyes that looked like large emerald pools. A mischievous smile began to play at the corner of her lips. "I want a kiss from you."

I had dreamed about kissing her since the day I had met her outside the school building. Standing here in his intimate kitchen I knew the timing was right. I stepped a little closer while looking in her eyes. I was surprised to see her step back away from me.

She placed her hand on my chest. "But I don't want just any kiss. I want a kiss like you mean it." Her brow furrowed as she said it and I knew she was no longer teasing me. The force of her words hit me, and I felt my breath become shallow. I didn't feel confident about my kissing prowess. I hadn't kissed many women and those I did, I liked more as friends. I knew I needed to channel my inner Humphrey Bogart in *Casablanca. Humphrey Bogart, what am I—eighty?!* Samantha was closing her eyes as I stepped closer but now opened them, probably wondering what was taking so long. I reached out and put my hands around her waist. *Kiss her like you mean it,* I thought to myself. I leaned down and put my lips on hers. I told myself not to be too firm but make sure she felt it. I could feel her tense body as I initially held her but then I sensed her relax in my arms. I felt the softness of her lips as I pressed mine to hers. After a few seconds, I pulled back and looked at her.

She opened her eyes and smiled. "You can have my plate now, but I get to help."

I took her plate and walked around the cabinets into the kitchen. My head was spinning a little; I had never experienced a kiss like that—nothing that meant so much. Since I had no garbage disposal in the sink, I scraped the plates clean into the trash. Samantha came in and handed me some of the dishes. She smiled at me as she did and I got the sense she had liked the kiss. I began to wash the dishes in the sink with my back to her. I sensed Samantha come up behind me. She wrapped her arms around me and laid her head on my back right between my shoulder blades.

"Stephen?"

"Yes."

"How are you liking the school?"

"I like it pretty well. How about you?"

Samantha continued to burrow into my back. "I like it too. For the most part." I turned around and looked down into her eyes.

"What do you mean? For the most part?" I asked.

She leaned into me and put her head on my chest. She wasn't looking at me now and I could smell her hair.

"I don't know," she began. "I like the school, it's just a little odd being in a school with people from all different countries, isn't it? And some of the professors are a bit different." I could agree that the teaching styles and techniques were certainly very different from the schools in the US.

"Which professors do you have the most trouble with?"

"What do you think of Mr. Hodges?" Originally, when reviewing my schedule, I had felt that class would be a waste of time. I didn't believe good management could be learned. But Mr. Hodges was changing my perspective and I was finding myself enjoying the class.

"I like him. He has an interesting way of teaching. I think he makes the curriculum interesting. Why? What do you think of him?"

She moved her head off my chest and looked up at me, "Creepy."

She said it so matter-of-factly I couldn't hide my surprise. "Why do you say that?"

"I don't like the way he looks at me," she responded. She was now looking at me and I could see genuine fear in her expression. "One day I was in the library, and I caught him watching me." She leaned in closer, and I could feel her body shudder against mine. "Maybe I'm reading too much into it, but I just don't feel safe around him."

I began replaying all the interactions I had with Mr. Hodges. I couldn't think of anything that would qualify as creepy or unsafe. "I think it's probably more in your head than reality. The school wouldn't hire him if he had done anything in his past." But even as I said it, I wasn't sure that was exactly true. Maybe that was the reason Mr. Hodges had left the US. "Hey, I have something I want to show you. We can finish the rest of the dishes later." With that, I grabbed her hand and led her out of the kitchen.

As we left my apartment and headed down in the elevator, Samantha couldn't help herself. "So, where are we going?"

"You'll just have to trust me."

She laughed. "Can you at least give me a hint?" The elevator reached the main floor and we exited.

"Okay, hmmm, we're going to need to get on the streetcar again."

She smiled. "Oh, are you finally taking me shopping? You know you still owe me from last week; you said we would go shopping but we never did." She raised one eyebrow at me. I knew she was teasing me, but I suddenly felt bad. I hadn't intended to go shopping today; if I was honest with myself, I never wanted to go shopping unless absolutely necessary. But I had mentioned it to her and now I thought maybe I should take her. *No, my other idea will be better.* We had reached the streetcar stop now and she was staring at me. "Did I guess it? Is that why you won't answer?"

"Oh, sorry, what did you ask me?"

She rolled her eyes. "I guessed you were going to take me shopping."

"No, we aren't going shopping. But maybe sometime this week we can go." We got on the streetcar.

"Then, where are we going?"

"You really don't like surprises, do you?"

"I like surprises as long as I know what they are." She laughed at her own joke which made me laugh right out loud. We only rode the streetcar up two stations and got off at the Gellert Hotel. I was still holding her hand as we exited. "Stephen, you are taking me to a hotel? What kind of girl do you think I am?"

I hadn't even thought of how this might look and began to blush furiously. "No, we aren't going to the hotel."

"Oh, that's too bad." She laughed again as she saw the shocked look on my face. I had guessed correctly, there were some taxicabs parked out in front of the hotel. Where we were going, Samantha would never be able to walk in those heels. Now would be the tough part. *How was I going to say what I needed to the taxicab driver in Hungarian?* I stopped before going up to one. I just stood there staring at them. Samantha looked up at me and gave me a little nudge.

"Sorry, I'm just not sure how to say it," I told her.

"Say what?"

I decided I knew enough to struggle through it and walked up to the car, ignoring her question. Seeing us angle directly for him, the driver got out of the car and began opening the back door.

"*Jó estét kívánok,*" I said to the driver, "*Kérem, a Gellért-hegyre.*"

"*Persza,*" the man responded, and we got in the back seat.

"What did you just say to him?" Samantha asked.

"I asked him to take us somewhere."

She rolled her eyes again. "I know that. Where did you ask him to take us?"

"A little place I like to call 'you'll see.'"

As we drove, I noticed the cab driver kept looking at us. He probably wasn't used to people speaking English. It didn't take long for us to make it to the top of Gellert Hill; probably only about five minutes. When we reached the top, I paid the man and he drove away.

"What is this place?" she asked me.

"It's the top of Gellert Hill. At the base of the hill is that hotel where we got the cab." It was easy to understand why Samantha was disoriented. In the dark, it wasn't obvious where we had driven. The cab drove up on the backside of the hill. At the top of the hill sat the Citadel with a huge statue of a woman holding something overhead. The statue had lights all around. We walked so that we could stand in front of it and see it better.

"What does the statue represent?" she asked me. My memory went back to several years before. I had stood on this very ground gazing up at the statue asking my Grandma Erzsi the same question as she held my hand. I'll never forget the disgust I saw on the face of my grandmother as she glared at it.

"It was given to the Hungarians by the Soviets because they," I held up my fingers on both sides like I was creating quotation marks, "freed the Hungarians from Nazi occupation. But of course, the Soviets then did the same thing and never left. Well, not until 1991." As we stood looking at the statue, I felt as big as an ant. I imagined this must be how people feel looking up at the Statue of Liberty in New York.

I turned to look at Samantha. "Come on, I want to show you my favorite part of the hill." I led her back the way we had come until we reached the side of the Citadel and began walking inside. Samantha stopped, "Are you sure we can go inside there?"

"No," I replied.

She laughed. "Okay but slow down a little; I'm wearing heels on cobblestone."

I guided her inside the Citadel. I had read it was built during the Austro-Hungarian empire as a military post. We walked up steps then

I showed her that we could walk along the wall out to the corner of the building. Samantha removed her shoes. We were up at least thirty feet from the ground and a fall from that height could kill a person. I guided her slowly out to the corner of the wall. From this point, if you looked to the north, you could see the Chain Bridge, the castle, and Parliament. The lights sparkled against the black sky. What an incredible view it was. Not only was it beautiful, but it was secluded. When we had been on Fisherman's Bastion during a prior date, the view had been amazing but we were surrounded by people. Although there were a few people down on the street outside the Citadel, we felt alone up on the wall.

The breeze was lightly blowing from the south making it feel cooler than it was.

"Are you cold?" I asked her as we sat on the wall staring down at the city.

"A little bit." I put my arm around her and hugged her to me. "I loved the view from Fisherman's Bastion, but this is even better. How did you know about this?" she asked me.

"I came running up here a few days ago," I answered. We fell into silence as we gazed out over the city.

"Can I ask you something?" She didn't look at me; just kept staring at the city lights.

"Sure."

Now she turned her head to look at me. "Have you dated very much?"

"Was I that bad of a kisser?" I asked.

"No, that's not why I'm asking. I loved the kiss. In fact, I think you should kiss me again." I leaned down and kissed her. This time, longer and more passionately. When I pulled away, she opened her eyes and smiled, "Mmm," she said.

"So why do you ask if I have dated very much?"

She looked back to the city. "I don't know. You just seem shy, and as I think about the guys I've dated, most of them pursued me."

"No, I haven't dated very much. I mean, I dated a little in college but rarely."

"Why do you think you are so shy and timid around women?"

I looked out over the city considering the question. I had asked myself this very question many times. I knew if my mom had been around as I got older, things would have been different. I was sure my mother would have encouraged me to date.

"Probably fear of rejection, mostly. But I'm sure a psychiatrist somewhere could have a field day with me." After a few moments of silence, we made eye contact again. "Why did you pursue me like you did?" I asked her.

"Good question." She laughed as she said it. "First, I thought you were cute. And you got my attention when you hit your head in class. I had noticed you before and thought you were handsome but when you hit your head... I don't know, it was just so cute and I felt bad for you. From that point on, I wanted to get to know you."

"So that worked for you, huh? Me making a fool of myself?"

"I didn't think you were a fool. I'm just glad you weren't hurt. You hit it quite hard."

Again, we fell into a comfortable silence as I held her. I had never experienced that kind of comfort with a woman. We had only known each other a few weeks but it felt like an eternity to me. I leaned over and smelled her hair right by her neck. I loved her fragrance. I leaned in closer and kissed her neck. She seemed to hold her breath and I could tell she liked it.

Chapter
Twenty-Nine

Peter

P eter scans through the arrival and departure names which include both Hungarian and international cities like Vienna, Zurich, Kiev, and Bucharest. Finally, he sees Zagreb. He examines the board closer; the train would be leaving at 9:37 a.m. from platform number seven. He needs a ticket. He rarely, if ever, travels from this station, so he isn't familiar with the platform locations or the ticket window. He looks up at the large clock on the wall, it reads 8:52 a.m. He exhales with relief. He has plenty of time, a luxury he isn't accustomed to. After looking around for far longer than he should have, Peter laughs at himself; below the Departure and Arrivals board sits the ticket windows. The fact that he hadn't noticed them shows his level of anxiety.

He strides over to the windows but quickly finds each has a line. Without hesitation, he turns and walks to the back of the shortest. After a ten-minute wait, he finally reaches one of the windows. A woman sits behind the desk. She has dirty blonde hair and wears a uniform that looks like she should be working on the train, not selling tickets. The uniform is wrinkled with multiple stains and Peter wonders how long it has been since it has seen an inside of a washing machine.

"Yes, how can I help you?" The woman couldn't have said it with less expression and enthusiasm had she been trying. She doesn't even look at Peter, keeping her eyes down at the metal platform under the glass window.

"I'd like a ticket on the nine thirty-seven train to Zagreb please."

The woman still doesn't look up. "What class?"

Peter should have thought of this. He doesn't want to be in a train car with Andras, but he also needs to be close enough to keep eyes on him. Peter assumes Andras would be riding first class, and there must be many compartments. How likely is it that they would be in the same one?

"First class, please."

The woman refers to her rate sheet. "17,431 forint," she says, again, in her robotic tone. Peter winces. That represents half of the deposit Kata had paid him to take the case. If Andras isn't on the train, it would cripple him.

"Can you tell me what your refund policy is?"

The woman finally looks up. She is older than he originally thought, maybe late thirties or early forties. Her fingers have a yellow stain, and when she speaks, her teeth are also stained yellow and crooked. "There is no refund policy. If you buy a ticket, you have a ticket. If you don't make the train, you are out of luck." Peter stands looking at her, considering this. After a few moments, the woman grows impatient. "Are you going to buy a ticket or not?"

Peter gets a pained expression. "I'm waiting for a friend to join me and if he doesn't come, I don't want to pay the fare for a trip I won't be taking."

The woman gives him a curt nod. "Then get out of my line. Come back when you decide." She looks past him and says to the next man in line, "Yes, can I help you?"

Peter steps to the side and lets the man come to the window. *Sweet lady.* What to do now? He can't afford to buy a ticket until he knows Andras is taking the same train. His only option is to wait, see Andras at the station, then go buy a ticket. He just hopes Andras arrives soon. If he comes late, Peter runs the risk of missing the train.

Peter looks around. He can't do anything to rush Andras but he can prepare for his arrival. He needs to find platform number seven, but after walking back and forth, he can't see anything indicating which platform is which. Near the ticket windows, off to the side, he notices a man begging. The man has no legs, only stumps below his waist. He is standing on the stumps and carries wooden blocks in his hands. The man walks by placing the wooden blocks on the ground then swinging his body forward landing on his two stumps.

Peter walks over to the man. "Good morning! Can you tell me where the number seven platform is?"

The man looks up at Peter with a sour expression. "Yeah, of course I know." He then points to the hat he has lying in front of him containing small change and a few bills. "But you won't know unless you help me out." He's salty but who can blame him? Living a life with no legs would try anyone's patience. Peter leans forward and puts 500 forint in the hat.

The man looks satisfied. "It's right behind you, man." Peter turns and looks at the platform. A very small sign has the number 7 on it with no other indication.

Peter takes a few minutes to survey the station and the platform. He finally decides the best vantage point for seeing all passengers on and off the train is from a park bench sitting near the ticket windows. He sits on the bench and looks at his watch, 9:20 a.m. People are already starting to board the train but still no sign of Andras. It would make sense for Andras to be late if he is coming. Whenever someone does something regularly, they know just how much time they need. Peter looks to his left as the guy with no legs comes swinging by.

The man sees Peter. "How stupid are you? You still can't find number seven?"

Before Peter can respond, the man is gone, swinging his body, and moving the wood blocks before him. Peter pities the man. He wonders if the man gets away with treating people like this because of his handicap, or the handicap has made him bitter and angry.

Peter continues to sit people-watching, feeling his anxiety grow as the minutes count down. He looks at his watch, it's now five minutes from the train departure and still no sign of Andras. What does this mean? His thoughts drift to Kata. Did returning her call last night cause this? Maybe Andras had done something with Kata and that's why he isn't here for the train. Or maybe Andras took another train. Peter stands and walks forward to read the Arrivals and Departures board again. He notices that two other trains will depart for Zagreb today, the next one being at 2:00 p.m. He feels the pang of disappointment, realizing he's likely to spend the entire day in the train station. He turns away from the board having lost all hope and sees a tall figure walking briskly past him toward the number seven platform. He recognizes the confident stride, dark but graying hair, and athletic but slightly overweight build.

Peter reacts by turning and running for the ticket window. Like before, the window has several people stacked in line. He looks down at his watch, 9:35 a.m. The train is scheduled to leave in two minutes. The line decimates his chance at making the train. He walks past the line and right up to the window. The apathetic woman with the blonde hair doesn't notice and seemingly doesn't notice the traveler she is currently supposed to help. Peter steps in front of the woman standing at the front of the line and lays twenty thousand forint on the counter. "I really need that ticket to Zagreb," he says to the ticket attendant. She looks up but is already shaking her head. Peter cuts her off before she can speak, "I know you don't want to sell it to me, but the train departs in two minutes and my friend just arrived. If I stand in line, I'll miss it." Peter pleads to her with his eyes.

The woman stares at him, her expression unchanged. "You should have purchased earlier." What could he say? She was right. There they were staring at each other through the window when the woman nonchalantly reaches out and grabs the money. With her other hand she slides the ticket across the counter. Peter smiles and thanks her, but just as he is about to turn away, he realizes he never got his change. "What about my change?"

She glares back at him. "If I get your change, you will miss the train."

Rather than argue with her, he turns and runs for the train. As he does, the train begins to pull out. He groans and begins to sprint. He's no longer a young man nor is he in great shape and he knows he's running at a pace he can't sustain for long. His knees agree, feeling like they might break, and he can already feel his chest tighten. The train has only traveled a couple hundred feet, moving slowly almost as if it were waiting for him. He catches it and pulls himself up the stairs. Once on the train, he leans over and sucks in huge breaths of air sounding just like the engine that propels them forward. His lungs are on fire and he feels light-headed. After a couple minutes, he finally has the presence of mind to look at his ticket, first class car four, compartment five.

As he stares at his ticket, a train conductor comes to him. "Can I help you find your seat?" He nods, still not trusting himself to speak.

The run wasn't long, maybe three hundred meters, but for a man of his age and cardiovascular shape carrying a bag, it feels like he had run a four-minute mile in the Olympics. He holds out the ticket to the conductor.

"Oh, yes, I'll show you. Follow me."

Peter takes the ticket back but still doesn't speak. He walks behind the conductor through several train cars. Finally, the conductor stops and points to the door in front of them. "This is it. Enjoy your trip." With that, the man heads back the way they came. Peter opens the sliding door, excited to be sitting down soon. The cabin has two bench seats, a window, and an open space in the middle. As Peter looks in, he notices the cabin is occupied by only one passenger—Andras.

Chapter Thirty

Stephen

I walk into the Strategic International Management building and head to my first class. I'm ten minutes early and the second student to arrive in the class. As I sit down, I look at the clock on the wall: nine minutes until class will start. I gaze out the window; it's a charming autumn day in Budapest. The leaves on the maple trees outside are beginning to turn orange and yellow. I've now been in Budapest over a month, and although I'm more comfortable than when I first arrived, today I'm anxious.

My leg is bouncing up and down as I wait. More and more students fill the room. A tall guy with dark hair and a wiry build comes and sits down. He and I have been sitting next to each other for a month now, and I can't remember ever hearing him speak. Not only that, but we've also never even acknowledged each other. That's going to change today.

"Hey, do you know that redheaded girl that usually sits over there?" I point to where Samantha typically sat.

The guy looks up, now recognizing I'm talking to him. "What?"

"There's a redheaded girl that usually sits in that seat over there. Do you know her?"

The guy looks to where I'm pointing, "What girl?"

"She's not there right now. She usually sits there. Do you know her?" I fight to keep the irritation out of my voice.

The guy shakes his head. "I don't know who you're talking about."

I point again, "The girl that sits right there. The pretty redhead. Do you know her?"

"Sorry, man. I don't know who you're talking about."

I look back out the window as the guy goes back to reading his notebook.

I glance at the clock on the wall: two minutes until class is to start. The room is now full of students; only a few missing. Three more minutes pass, and Mr. Hodges comes through the door. "All right everyone, let's get started." Mr. Hodges wears a green button-down shirt, a sweater vest, khaki-colored pants, brown belt, and brown Doc Marten shoes.

"Is anyone familiar with the antitrust laws in the United States?" Mr. Hodges surveys the room and begins to walk. He's looking down but appears to be keeping an eye out for anyone raising their hand. Nobody raises their hand and all eyes look blankly back at him.

"Okay, how about this. Does anyone know anything about what antitrust means? I'll give you a hint: Parker Brothers owns one of the most popular, if not the most popular, board games about this concept."

I think about some of the board games I've played before—Risk, Axis & Allies, Chutes and Ladders, Life—but none of those options make sense. Mr. Hodges seems disappointed. "I forget I'm teaching in an international school. Maybe some of you never had the game in your countries, or maybe it wasn't popular." Mr. Hodges looks down and rubs his chin. "Hmm," he says, "one more hint: this game includes houses and hotels. You try to acquire property."

"Oh, Monopoly!" someone shouts from the middle of the class.

Mr. Hodges feigns exhaustion. "Yes! Finally!" He looks up and smiles. "Antitrust refers to a monopoly. Meaning one company owns too much of the market in a particular industry." Mr. Hodges walks to the other side of the room. "The United States, along with several other countries, have enacted laws to prevent monopolies. Why?" He looks around the room waiting for someone to respond.

Sandra, the self-proclaimed teacher's pet, raises her hand. "If one company owns the market, they can control the price. If there's nobody to compete with them, then quality and value can suffer."

Mr. Hodges nods his head. "Yes, exactly." He turns and walks the other direction. "Have any of you ever heard of a man named John D. Rockefeller?" This time, nobody responds. Rockefeller was from my hometown of Cleveland and I had written a report about him back in middle school; I've even seen his house. Mr. Hodges looks at me almost like he's reading my thoughts. "Stephen, where are you from again?"

I feel my anxiety rise as several people turn to look at me. "I'm from Cleveland, Ohio."

"You must have heard of Rockefeller? That's where he lived."

"Yep, I'm familiar with him."

Mr. Hodges smiles. "Okay, great! Enlighten the class. What can you tell us about him?"

I duck my head; this is not what I want. He knows I don't like speaking in front of everyone. "I think Rockefeller was born in New York. His family moved to Cleveland when he was young. He began working as a bookkeeper when he was sixteen, and by the time he was twenty, he began partnering in an oil refinery business. He started a company called Standard Oil and profited on the growth of kerosene and gasoline."

Mr. Hodges starts moving his hands like he's turning a wheel. "Keep going, Stephen, you're on a roll."

I sigh but continue. "At that time in the United States, light was produced by kerosene lamps, not electricity. Automobiles were also starting to become more popular and there was an increased need for gasoline. Rockefeller was a ruthless negotiator and began crushing his competitors in the oil industry. He also negotiated with the railroads and used them to transport his oil around the country."

Mr. Hodges takes off from there, speaking more quickly as he paces. "At one point, the railroads tried to play a hard negotiating line with Rockefeller. They realized his only way to move his product was through the railroads. They joined together and increased the price to a point that upset Rockefeller. Rockefeller countered by building the region's first oil pipeline. It's estimated that at its peak, Rockefeller and Standard Oil controlled ninety percent of the country's oil." Mr. Hodges always walks around the room and waves his hands while talking. I often think of him as a stage performer acting in a Broadway play. "In 1911, the United States Federal Court ruled that Standard Oil must be dismantled because the company held too much market share and was too powerful. The company was then broken up into several smaller companies that still exist today, including ExxonMobil and Chevron Corporation."

I look around the room, I've got to hand it to Mr. Hodges, the man knows how to command a room. Everyone in the class seems completely engaged in the story.

"Rockefeller was criticized for how he built his empire. Many claimed his ruthless business tactics hurt other people and companies. Rockefeller himself was quoted as saying, 'if a company isn't growing, it's dying.'" Mr. Hodges stops pacing and looks at the class, "So, what do you think? Was Rockefeller a good leader? Does a good business leader have to be ruthless? Does he/she have to crush the competition?"

A movement just outside the door catches my attention. A woman with long hair has been looking in the class but ducks out of view when she sees me notice her. *Was that Samantha? How could it be?* I feel my heartbeat quicken.

Before I know it, I get up from my chair and hurry out of the room. I ignore the fact that the class discussion stops, and everyone stares at me. I blink a few times—the hallway is much darker than the classroom. The woman is walking on the other side of the hall, moving quickly. I begin running, and as I draw closer to her, I begin shouting her name, "Samantha." Finally, the woman turns around but as she does, my hopes are dashed. She cowers before me, like she's afraid I'm going to hurt her. Fear is in her eyes. I begin backing away. "Oh, I'm sorry. I thought you were someone else."

I turn around and as I head back to class, I notice everyone in the hallway is looking at me. As I reenter the class and sit down at my desk, I look back out the window. The classroom discussion has moved on, but I'm lost. But it's not because of the discussion, it's because of me. I was so sure that was Samantha. Could it be that I wanted her to be Samantha so much that I imagined her to be?

Chapter Thirty-One

Peter

Peter nods his head and says, "Good day," to Andras.

Without waiting for a reply, he sits down on the other side of the train cabin, opposite Andras. As they look at each other, Peter notices Andras's eyes narrow in recognition. The cabin features a large window and two rows of seating facing each other with only a few feet of space between them. Above the seating sit large luggage shelves.

"Good day," Andras replies. Andras points his finger at Peter. "You were in my restaurant last night?"

Peter nods. "I was. What a coincidence that we would see each other again so soon."

"Yes, isn't it? I almost think one of us is following the other." Andras says it without a hint of suspicion.

Peter leans back and laughs, maybe a little too loudly. Don't overdo it, he tells himself. "Well, if you are following me," Peter responds, "I feel bad for you. You won't get much excitement from a lonely man like me."

"Same here. Well, I'm not lonely, but a restaurant owner doesn't have the most exciting life."

"So, what takes you to Zagreb?" Peter is trying to act as nonchalant as possible. He figures some personal questions would be natural from a relative stranger. "Oh, sorry. I don't mean to interrupt your reading." Peter motions to the magazine Andras holds in his hands.

Andras seems to be perfectly comfortable with the question and brushes aside the notion of being bothered. "I go to Zagreb quite often. I opened a second restaurant there several months ago. It's just like the one in Budapest that you've been to. Having a second restaurant requires me to split my time."

Peter nods and rubs the beard on his chin. "I would imagine that could be a daunting task. How is the new restaurant going so far? I sure liked the one in Budapest."

Andras leans back, putting his left arm over the top of the bench. "It's going well. It was a little slow to get off the ground, and I've had to put quite a bit of money into marketing, but things are beginning to pick up now. I was able to find a good chef."

"Can I ask, why Zagreb? Wouldn't it have been easier to open another restaurant in Hungary?"

Andras cocks his head to one side and purses his lips. "Oh, believe me, I thought about that. But after the civil war that just took place in Yugoslavia and with Zagreb being the capital city of Croatia, I loved the opportunity I saw there. There are a lot of Hungarians in Zagreb, and it doesn't take too long to get there. Just a simple train ride." Andras smiles at the last part and raises his right arm in front of him with his palm pointed up as if he's Vanna White demonstrating the Grand Prize on *Wheel of Fortune*. "And I'm sorry, I don't remember your name. I'm Andras." Andras stands and leans forward, extending his hand to Peter.

"I'm Peter." Peter takes his hand and is impressed by the firmness. "I'm on my way to visit my daughter. She and my son-in-law moved to Zagreb recently." Peter knows with any lie the less information you give the better.

"What part of the city do they live in?"

Peter doesn't like this. The more digging Andras does, the more he has to lie and the more likely Andras can catch him.

"Right downtown. Where is your restaurant?"

Andras leans back with both arms up on the top of the bench seat. His demeanor shows he has very little interest in Peter's responses, but his eyes never waver. Peter has the feeling he is seeing right through him. The calmness is an act. He's reading Peter. Peter has seen enough interrogations to recognize one.

"My restaurant is right near the Cathedral of Zagreb. Are you familiar with that area?"

Every time Peter tries to turn the conversation back to Andras, Andras answers but never expounds and asks another question. "No, I'm not familiar. I've never been to Zagreb before. This will be the first time."

"Oh, you're going to love it. It's a nice city. Not as pleasing as some of the other parts of Croatia like Split or Dubrovnik, but still very nice. Have you been to either of those cities?"

Peter feels himself relax a little. This isn't safe ground necessarily, but it's certainly safer than drilling him on his knowledge of the city and his fake daughter.

"No, I've never been to any part of Croatia. This will be my first time."

"Croatia is irresistible. People in the west often travel to Italy, and Italy is lovely, but Croatia is just as nice. It shares the same coastline in the Adriatic Sea. Almost the entire country is coastline. It has over a thousand islands off its coast. And the Plitvice Lakes are amazing!

You've never seen water that has such a vibrant color. You really should travel the country. How long will you be there?"

Peter shakes his head and shrugs. "Oh, not long. I'm only going for the weekend."

Andras frowns. "I'm sorry to hear that. Next time you go, make sure you visit the rest of the country. It's worth it." Andras smiles and looks out the window and Peter has the feeling the conversation is over. Andras turns back to his magazine and begins to read. Peter reaches over to his bag and begins searching for his book when he hears Andras's voice. "Hey, where does your daughter live? What's her address? With you not being familiar with the city, you're going to need help finding it."

Peter has no answer for this. Luckily, he has turned away from Andras which gives him time to fix his expression. He turns back to him once he has his book in his hands. "I don't remember the address. My daughter is supposed to come meet me at the train station. I don't really need it."

Andras purses his lips and shrugs but something in his eyes betrays his nonchalant demeanor.

For the next couple hours, Andras reads his magazine and Peter his book, John Grisham's *The Firm*. Several times, Peter looks up to gaze out the window. Peter hasn't traveled this route before, and he finds it fascinating. After leaving Budapest, the train heads west passing Lake Balaton. The lake is a favorite vacation spot for not only Hungarians but Austrians, Germans, Czechs, and Poles. Peter has never vacationed on the lake, but he's heard it's magnificent. As he looks out from the train window, he can see the description is accurate. It's Fall and he loves the charming autumn colors on the trees with the water in the background. Having lived so long in New York City, it still surprises him when he gets out in the "vidék," or country, and sees thatched roofs on the houses. Funny, he thinks, he grew up in a house like that. But that seems like centuries ago. He has seen so much in his life since then.

Once, Andras left to use the toilet. Peter was sorely tempted to snoop through his luggage but knew he couldn't run the risk of Andras catching him. They are in Croatia now and, although the landscape hasn't changed drastically, Peter does perceive a more Mediterranean look in the scenery and culture. Peter finds himself reading for ten minutes then looking out the window for five. He repeats this over and over again.

"You speak English, I guess."

It's more of a statement than a question. Andras is speaking to him and motions toward the book in his hand. Peter looks down and realizes it's in English. Being fluent in both English and Hungarian he rarely thinks about what language he's speaking or reading.

"I do," Peter responds.

"How did you learn English?" Andras has put his magazine aside now and seems to want to restart their conversation. Peter isn't sure how much information he wants to divulge.

"I lived in New York City."

Andras raises an eyebrow. "Wow, New York. How did you get there? You speak Hungarian like a Hungarian."

Peter shrugs. "I was kicked out of my house when I was sixteen and had to make it on my own. I decided to make it an adventure and leave Hungary for greener pastures."

"That had to be hard. Did you speak any English when you went there?"

Peter shakes his head "no."

"I've been studying English. It's not going that well." Andras smiles a very toothy smile and Peter is reminded how white his teeth are. Not only are they white, but they are very straight, which is rare among Europeans; dental work has never been a priority, especially behind the Iron Curtain.

"I was forced to learn it," Peter tells him. "I was thrown into NYC, and nobody spoke Hungarian. I didn't have a choice but to learn English, and fast."

"What brought you back to Hungary?"

Peter is uneasy but he doesn't see any problem in answering the question. "I missed my homeland. When I had left here, I was a boy. Although I had lived in New York longer than I had lived in Hungary, I still saw myself as Hungarian."

Andras smiles again. "What do you do for work?"

"I'm a schoolteacher," Peter lies.

"A schoolteacher? Really? What do you teach?"

Peter has always used schoolteacher as his profession when he doesn't want people to know what he really does. "I teach history in middle school."

"Sounds awful. I remember the kid I was in middle school, and I'd rather have my fingernails pulled out than do what you do." Peter can't help but notice the change in Andras. His smile seems forced, and Peter senses anger behind those eyes.

"Have you ever been married?"

Peter considers the question and wonders if this is his way of digging or if he is simply making conversation. "I have."

"Is your wife Hungarian or American?" Andras is watching him closely now.

"She was American," Peter responds.

Andras begins to pull at his lip as if he's considering something. "And your daughter lives in Croatia?"

Peter can see where this is going now. "Yes, she does."

Andras looks confused. "How did your daughter end up in Croatia if she grew up American?"

Peter has anticipated this. "Her husband is from Croatia."

Andras nods.

"Are you married?"

"I was," Andras's voice is suddenly cold, "but the whore is gone now. It's about time I lost that forint sucker." Andras gets a look on his face like he knows he has said too much. He turns back to Peter and the charm returns. He chuckles. "You know what I'm saying. Every man is better off without a woman. Sure, some of them are fun to look at and play with, but who wants to have them control your life? Better off keeping them as playthings."

What has this guy done with Kata? Peter feels the brakes engage on the train and realizes they have stopped in Zagreb at the Glavni Kolod station. Andras stands and gathers his luggage. "Enjoy seeing your daughter, Peter."

Peter bows his head and thanks him. He turns and picks up his own bag as Andras effortlessly slides open the door to their cabin and walks out, striding down the hallway.

Peter rushes to the door as he follows Andras. He doesn't want to lose sight of him. Now everyone in first class is coming out of their railcars. An old, heavy-set woman moves in front of Peter. In order to move her girth, she shuffles side to side as much as she moves forward. He can still see Andras, but he has already descended the stairs and is walking through the station. Peter remains behind the old woman, losing patience as Andras slips away from him.

Chapter 32

Peter

Peter leaves the train station from its main doors at the front of the building. As he exits, the sun is on his left about to sink behind the tall buildings of downtown. Shadows extend to the right, but the weather is warm, and Peter embraces the opportunity to stretch his legs. Outside, a street runs in front with taxicabs lined up on either side. Across the large crosswalk, Peter can see a streetcar station and, beyond that, some type of public square with a large historic building.

"*Oprostite gospodine.*"

Peter turns in the direction of the voice. A young man stands looking up at him. He's speaking Croatian, but Peter has no idea what he's saying. Hungarian and Croatian have nothing in common. Hungarian is like Finnish and Estonian while Croatian is a Slavic language like Russian.

The young man recognizes Peter's bewilderment by the language and tries again in English. "Do you speak English?" The boy's English is heavily accented.

Peter nods. "Yes, I do."

"I think so," the young man responds. He looks to be about seventeen or eighteen years old. He's wearing a hat turned backward, a T-shirt with a black leather jacket, and jeans with tennis shoes. He's average height and thin with a little facial hair growing at his chin and mustache but nothing close to a full beard. "I'm Luka. First time to Zagreb?" Luka's smiling broadly, and Peter raises an eyebrow while he analyzes him. What is this kid up to, he wonders, but decides to play along.

"Yes, I've never been here before."

Luka smiles. "I drive taxi and could be happy to be your city guide. Much better price than those." Luka points in the direction of the other taxicabs lined up on both sides of the street. Luka waves with his hand as if Peter should follow him. Not waiting for a reply, he begins walking as he talks. Peter, too curious not to see this through, hurries after him. "My car is around side. What brings you to Zagreb? Here for business?" Luka holds up his right hand and rubs his thumb to his fingers in the universal sign for money.

Peter can't help the smile that creeps across his face. There are plenty of self-confident people in the world. Some are obnoxious, but he finds this kid endearing. "I'm here to visit my daughter," Peter tells him.

"Oh, that's great!" He's walking fast, and Peter has to hustle to keep up.

Luka stops suddenly and looks at Peter. "Why did she no come for you at train station?"

Excellent question, Peter thinks. "Turns out, she must work. She's a nurse in the hospital." Luka nods, seemingly satisfied, and begins walking again.

After a few short paces, he stops in front of an old 1985 lime green Trabant. The Trabant was discontinued in 1990 but even now, ten years later, you can still find them all over Eastern Europe. To say the car is an improvement to the horse and buggy wouldn't be fair to the horses. Trabants first made their appearance in East Germany in 1957. Peter didn't know if it was true or not, but he had heard that cardboard could be found on the inside of the doors. He once overheard someone call the car "a spark plug with a roof". Without turning to look at Peter, Luka opens the driver side door and says, "Hop in. I will take you anywhere you need to go."

Peter hesitates. "You aren't really a taxi driver, are you?" He stands in front of the car on the curb, looking at Luka.

Luka looks up at him. "Yes, I am."

"Then why are you parked over here rather than out front like the other taxis? Why are you driving a Trabant when all of those other cars are Volkswagen and Opel?"

The boy was looking at Peter, but now averts his glance. He speaks so quietly it's hard for Peter to hear. "No, I no work for those taxi companies. They don't hire me because I am too young. This my car." Now Luka shut his driver's door and comes around to the front of the car closer to Peter. "But I need money." He's pleading with Peter now. "I give you half price from those taxis and I answer anything you want to know about Zagreb. Everything I know about Zagreb." Peter can't help how much he likes the kid. How could it hurt to have someone drive him around and act as his guide? Peter walks over to the passenger door and opens it.

"Let's go."

Luka's smile looks like it might split his face if it grows any bigger. "Okay! You won't regret."

Chapter Thirty-Two

Peter

When Luka starts the car, the engine reminds Peter of a chain saw. He realizes that's because it probably has the same horsepower. It chugs and spurts like an old woman choking on her coffee. Peter looks around the car and can't help but be impressed. He can see Luka takes pride in the car; it's old and the interior is worn but it's clean. As Luka shifts into reverse and begins to back out, Peter has the distinct impression he's riding in a car two clowns couldn't fit in. He has to keep his hands in front of him and his arms close to his body otherwise he'd be brushing against Luka. His knees are in his chest, and his bag takes up the entire back seat.

"Where do you like me to take you?" Luka asks as they rattle their way down the road in what feels like an enclosed go kart.

"I need to find a place to stay overnight."

Luka has a little trouble shifting gears as they slow to a stop at the light. "What part of city do you want?"

Peter knows almost nothing about the city and where he wants to stay. His only reason in coming is to find and follow Andras.

"Do you know a restaurant called Szép Ilona?"

Luka furrows his brow as he considers the question. "Oh, yes, I know. It's new. In city center."

Peter smiles. "Okay, well, I'd like to stay somewhere close to the city center."

Luka taps his finger to his chin. "What kind of place you want? Nice?" He lifts his right hand and rubs his thumb against his fingers again. *He likes money.*

Peter chuckles. "Not too expensive. Something that demonstrates Zagreb. Maybe something older but not run down and not too much money."

Luka grimaces as he thinks. Finally, he snaps his fingers. "I know. Hotel Jägerhorn. It is nice but not too much money. It is the oldest hotel in Zagreb. It is right in city center on Ilica Street. I think you like."

"That sounds great, Luka. Let's go see if I can get a room there."

Luka smiles and nods knowingly. "You will get room. My girlfriend, Mia, works there." He winks at Peter as he says it and Peter can't suppress the laugh that busts from his lips. As they drive in the cardboard box with wheels, Peter looks around at the city. Zagreb has similar architecture to Budapest but with subtle differences, one being almost all the buildings feature red tile roofs.

"Luka, tell me about Zagreb. What do you know about the city?"

Peter can see Luka smile and puff his chest out. "Zagreb is the capital city of Croatia. Population of the city and surrounding is 1.1 million. Zagreb started as Roman city, but not called Zagreb until about AD 1200." Peter smiles and wonders if Luka has memorized this speech. "Zagreb is located near the Sava River." He points out to his left. Peter can't see a river but assumes that must be where it's located. "Zagreb is also in the foothills of the Medvednica mountain."

Peter isn't sure how much more Luka has in this memorized script, but he decides to cut it off. "Luka, what is the best part of Zagreb?"

"In Zagreb? Or Croatia?"

Peter shrugs. "How about both? What's the best part of Zagreb and the best part of Croatia?" Luka thinks for a minute, losing concentration on the road. A couple times he's made Peter nervous because he tends to slam on the brakes and, more than once, he's yelled at other cars.

"Best part of Zagreb is Old Town. Best part of Croatia is Plitvice Lakes. The lakes are bewitching. The water is blue-green color, and the waterfalls are big." Luka raises his arms high and Peter wishes he would just keep his hands on the wheel.

Luka slams to a stop. "Hotel Jägerhorn," he announces and points to the right. The hotel is a cozy little place with several open-air courtyards and white arches leading to the front doors. It seems to be right on a pedestrian street and Peter wonders if Luka is going to be in trouble for driving on it. As he looks around, he sees no other cars on this section of the road and the streetcar track runs right down the middle. It seems not to bother Luka as he climbs out of the car talking. "Hurry, come; we will talk to Mia."

Peter wonders about the wisdom of leaving a car here but decides it isn't his ticket and gets out. As they enter the small hotel, Peter's impressed. It's very well maintained, clean, and right in the center of the city. He begins to worry about the cost. Luka motions for Peter to follow him and walks right up to a blonde woman at the front desk. Luka smiles broadly and greets her in Croatian. As warm as Luka's greeting is, the girl's is cold. She doesn't seem happy to see him. Luka doesn't bother to translate for Peter, he just starts yammering to the girl in Croatian. She's an attractive girl but by no means a heart-stopper. She has long blonde hair that she wears straight to her shoulders. Her face is void of makeup and she's wearing a conservative cream-colored blouse, black skirt, and heels.

Luka must have mentioned him because she looks up and smiles at Peter then goes back to scowling at Luka. The longer the conversation goes on, Peter gets the impression Luka is either in trouble with Mia or has exaggerated the idea that she's his "girlfriend." Mia politely responds to Luka, but the iceberg that hit the *Titanic* was warmer and softer. Peter couldn't understand her words but he could see the emphatic shake of her head.

Finally, Luka turns to Peter as Mia walks away. "No rooms but Mia is going to check and see what she can do." Mia crosses the room and enters an office only twenty paces away. She's presumably gone to talk with her boss. After a couple minutes, she returns. Again, she shakes her head at Luka, saying something as she waves her hand. Luka now speaks even more excitedly and begins to wave his arms around. Finally, the girl holds her hands up and says something about kuna. Peter recognizes the word for Croatian money but doesn't understand any of the other words being said. Luka's arguing with her about something. Finally, he gives up and turns back to Peter.

"She says you can stay but six hundred and twenty kuna."

Peter does a quick calculation in his head. That would be about 30,000 forint or almost 100 American dollars.

Peter glares at Luka. "I thought I told you I didn't want an expensive place?"

Luka shrugs. "I thought my girlfriend would help," he says lamely.

"Girlfriend? I'm not your girlfriend." Mia is shaking her head having just spoken perfect English.

Luka immediately goes red and begins to backtrack. "You are girl and you are friend. That's girlfriend."

Mia rolls her eyes at him. "That's not what you said. You probably told this poor man I would give him a good deal because I am your 'girlfriend.'"

Luka looks sheepish and Peter knows he's been played.

Mia turns to Peter. "Sir, because this guy treated you this way, I will help you out. We have a special rate we can offer periodically. Will three hundred kuna work for you?"

Peter can't believe his ears. That's less than half the original price. "Yes, that would be great. Thank you." Mia smiles and helps him get checked in, eventually handing him the key and explaining how to reach his room. She's smiling a pleasant smile and never looks toward Luka again.

Peter turns to Luka. "How much do I owe you?"

Luka has moved over in the lobby away from Mia. "One hundred kuna." As Peter hands Luka the hundred, he takes it and snaps his fingers. "But you still need dinner. I will drive you to Szép Ilona."

It's true, Peter does need a ride and Luka would be as good an option as any. The cost of the ride here was cheap. "Okay," Peter replies. "But I need to go up to my hotel room for a minute. Will you wait for me down here?"

Luka smiles. "Yes, I wait. You go. I go check on my car." *Good idea. It could be towed by now.*

Peter goes upstairs to his room. After using the bathroom and changing clothes, he comes back down, relieved to see Luka sitting in a chair waiting for him.

"You are ready?"

"I am."

"Okay, my car is in garage. We will need to walk for five minutes."

Perfect, Peter thinks. "Luka, why don't you go get the car? My knee is hurting me and I don't want to walk."

Luka frowns as he looks down at Peter's legs. "Okay, I go. You rest here." Luka points to the chair he was sitting in then rushes out the door. Once he's gone, Peter walks over to Mia without any pain or limp.

"Mia? That's your name, right?"

"Yes, it is. How can I help you, Peter?"

Peter smiles. "Can I ask you how you know Luka?"

Immediately Mia's eyebrows arch downward. "I'm not his girlfriend if that is what you want to know."

Peter shakes his head holding up his hands. "No, I knew that. It was very clear. I want to know how long you have known him. Does he do this taxi driver thing full time?"

Mia doesn't answer, choosing instead to look at him warily.

"I just want to know if I can trust him."

Mia senses the truth of the statement and her guard drops. "Oh, yeah, you can trust him. I mean he might say stupid things and bend the truth sometimes, but he's just trying to help you out. He means well."

"How long have you known him?"

"Almost my whole life," Mia replies. "We went to school together."

"Does he do this driving gig all the time?"

Mia shakes her head. "No, he is studying in school to be a doctor. He does this to earn money. And I think he likes it; it fits his personality. He also works sometimes in a new restaurant just a little way away."

So, Luka has been lying to me.

Peter looks out and sees Luka has come back and is waiting in his cardboard box on wheels. Peter thanks her and heads out.

Chapter Thirty-Three

Stephen

I walk out into the hallway following my last class of the day, and as usual, my mind wanders to Samantha. It's an everyday occurrence. She and I used to meet outside the school on the park bench once classes had ended. Each day, since she left, I hope to see her again but my hopes are dashed as I exit the school and see our park bench empty. Why does it seem that I am the only person missing her? Doesn't anyone else wonder where she's gone? What about her Italian roommate? Is she looking for her? I exit the building, and just like every other day, I see a solitary park bench. I move down the steps and across the courtyard toward the administration building. A couple girls move in front of me, maybe five paces ahead. I'm not eavesdropping on them, but I can't help hearing their conversation.

"Where is she from?" one of the girls asks the other.

"Somewhere in England. I can't really remember spot. They all sound the same to me." This girl says her w's like v's and i's like ee's.

What accent is that? Russian maybe? I'm not trying to listen but I am intrigued and slow my step to keep pace behind them.

"When was the last time you saw her?"

"Saturday night. She was going on date with guy she met here at school. He was making her dinner, or they were going to dinner. Something like this."

I feel the blood pumping in my veins. One of the girls looks back and notices me walking behind them. I nonchalantly look to the ground hoping she hasn't noticed I'm listening. They've reached the administration building now, opening the door and entering. I'm far enough back that they don't hold the door for me but I catch it before it closes.

"And you haven't seen her since then? I guess she has a boyfriend now, huh?" The girl who says it bumps her hip into the other girl and laughs knowingly. "Lucky you. Sounds like you have the apartment to yourself now. Maybe she's staying with him now."

"I guess so. I think she came home to get some clothes or something. The door to her room was open it was closed before. I hope she keeps paying her part of the rent. I don't care where she sleeps."

The other girl grabs the roommate by the arm and pulls her to the side. "Hey, I need to go to the bathroom before we leave."

They veer off and I continue straight, not looking at them. As I exit the front doors to the school, my eyes take a second to adjust to the brightness. The sun's shining bright, and I feel the warmth of its rays. As I walk across the street toward the streetcar stop, I'm thinking about the girls. No wonder I feel like I'm the only one looking for her. I probably am. Her roommate sounds like she doesn't even know she's missing or cares. I wonder how long it will be until the roommate realizes she's not with a boy. It's nearing the end of the month now and rent is going to be due soon. Maybe only another week before the roommate starts looking for her. What then? Will they come looking for me? I climb onto the streetcar, find a seat, and look out the window.

Chapter Thirty-Four

Peter

Peter gets in the car and Luka revs the engine. It sounds like a lawnmower being pushed up a hill and moves almost as fast.

Peter keeps his eyes on the road but says to Luka, "She isn't really your girlfriend, is she?"

Luka doesn't keep his eyes on the road, turning to check the demeanor of Peter. When he sees he's not angry he smiles and ducks his head. "No, she's not. But it is a pretty good trick."

"Trick? What do you mean trick?"

Luka smiles even bigger now. "I know she be mad if I say she is my girlfriend. She feel sorry for you and give you a good room."

Peter chuckles in spite of himself. "Thank you. You are a handy guy to have around, Luka."

After that, Peter and Luka fall silent as they make their way to the restaurant. Luka tries to strike up a conversation, asking Peter about his daughter, but he quickly deflects it. Peter needs to pay close attention to where Luka is taking him. If he has to come back on his own, he needs to remember the way. Finally, after only five minutes, Luka pulls up to a building with a sign that reads "Szép Ilona." It's not the first sign he's seen in Hungarian in the city, and it doesn't surprise him given that some of present-day Croatia was part of the Austro-Hungarian Empire.

"Here you are, Mr. Peter, Szép Ilona restaurant," Luka declares.

Peter turns as if he's going to reach for the door but instead reaches in his jacket pocket, pulling out his pistol. He holds it up to Luka as he screams and puts his hands in the air.

"What are you doing?" Luka asks.

Peter sits calmly, keeping the gun low. The street's dark, but Peter doesn't want to take any chances of someone seeing them. "Put your hands on the steering wheel and don't move them," Peter commands. Luka looks scared enough to pee himself. "Why did you lie to me, Luka?"

Luka shakes his head, turning to look at Peter but keeping his hands on the steering wheel. "I no lie. What do I lie?"

Peter sighs. "Now you're lying to me again. You know what you said. Don't treat me like I'm stupid. Who told you to pick me up?"

"Nobody. I see you come out of train station and..."

Peter smacks the dashboard of the little Trabant hard, maybe too hard. He wants to make Luka believe he's losing his patience.

"Okay, my boss told me to get you."

"And who is your boss?"

Luka looks at Peter. "His name Andras." Now Luka switches to flawless Hungarian. "Are you from Hungary?" Luka asks him. Peter nods but says nothing. "I thought you might be. My family is from Hercegszöllős, which used to be part of Hungary but is now part of Croatia. In Croatian, it's called Kneževi Vinogradi. We moved to Zagreb when I was twelve but always spoke Hungarian in our home. Andras knew my uncle and offered to give me a job in the restaurant. I went to the train station today because it's my job to pick up Andras when he comes to town. This time though, when he came out of the front doors, he told me he wanted me to pick you up."

"Why did he want you to pick me up?"

Luka shakes his head. "I don't know. I just know he told me that he wanted me to pick you up. He said to make you an offer that you wouldn't be able to refuse but tell you nothing about him or the restaurant."

Peter keeps his gun on Luka but waits before he comments. "Has Andras ever done this before?"

"Never."

Peter scowls. "Luka, my name is Peter, as I told you before. I came to Croatia to follow Andras. His wife hired me because she believes he is cheating on her with a woman here in Zagreb. I've come to see if that's true. Is it?"

Luka shakes his head. "I don't know. It might be. But there is more than that." Peter hoped Luka would say this, but now Luka seems to think better of talking and holds his tongue.

"Luka, this is going to be a lot easier if you just tell me what Andras is doing."

"I'm not sure what he is doing, but I know he came to Croatia to do more than open a restaurant."

"Why do you say that?"

"Because…" Luka hesitates, "look, I don't want to get further involved."

"I don't want you to look right now, but there is a silver Mercedes about a block behind us. It's been following us since we left the train station. Andras is having me followed. My guess is those guys aren't as innocent as you. You can either help me or leave me here to fight it out with them and whoever else Andras has."

Luka surreptitiously looks in his rear-view mirror and sees the two men in the Mercedes. This prompts him to spill his guts. "One day at the restaurant, a shipment came in from Hungary. Usually, the manager goes and takes care of it, but he was dealing with an angry customer so I went back to see if I could help and heard muffled screaming coming from the truck. It was several women trapped in the truck. When I went around the back of the truck to let them out, the driver came up and pointed a gun at my face. He told me in Hungarian that I was putting my nose somewhere it didn't belong. Just then, my manager came out and stopped him, telling him I worked in the restaurant and was helping out. He turned to me and commanded me to go back inside. I ran in as quick as I could. A few minutes later, the manager came and pulled me to the side. He told me that if I wanted to live, I would keep my mouth shut about what I saw. I've never told anyone but you." Luka now looks like he might cry. "I felt so bad for those women, but I was scared. I don't know exactly what they are doing with them, but whatever it is, it's not good. I wanted to help them, but I didn't want to die either."

Peter sits considering what Luka has said and what his next move might be. Finally, he puts his gun away. He prides himself on being an excellent judge of character and he trusts the kid. "Luka, I'm going to go investigate the back of this building. After I get out of the car, I want you to drive around the block then go in the restaurant, find Andras, and tell him I'm looking around the back of the restaurant. Tell him I told you I was here to investigate him. Don't tell him anything you just told me." Luka shakes his head, but Peter goes on before Luka can say anything. "Then go and call the police. Tell them you heard gunshots behind the restaurant."

"But Andras will come right back there for you."

Peter nods. "I'm counting on it."

Chapter Thirty-Five

Peter

It's full dark as Peter exits the car. He hadn't noticed the threatening rain clouds that had rolled in while he was in Luka's car. He intentionally looks straight ahead, pretending not to notice the guys in the Mercedes who have been following him since the train station. Now he just hopes they will both follow him a little longer.

As Peter walks around the back of the restaurant, he scans the area. There are two tall buildings on either side along with a tall apartment complex behind it. The small parking lot is nearly vacant with only a couple vehicles and two large garbage dumpsters. Both vehicles are trucks, one being for produce, the other for refrigerated materials. Peter, knowing he won't be alone for long, steps behind the refrigerated truck and waits. Sure enough, seconds later, both guys come around the corner looking around frantically. One of them takes the lead by silently motioning for the other to go in the restaurant back door. As the second one turns toward the building, the first one begins looking for Peter playing right into his hands. All along his intention was to split them up, and it would appear he's accomplished that.

The big man circles the truck in search of Peter, having no idea Peter is now behind him closing fast. As the thug bends over to look under the produce truck, Peter rushes forward and hits him squarely in the back of the head with the butt of his pistol. Immediately the big man slumps to the ground. As Peter leans forward placing his fingers to his neck and checking for his pulse, he hears the back door to the restaurant open.

Without a sound, Peter moves away from the restaurant toward the apartment building in the back. Silently, he opens the door to the building and goes up to the first floor where he can see the entire parking lot from the window. Sitting low, and out of sight, he watches as Andras and the second thug begin searching for him. Quickly, they find thug number one lying flat on his face under the produce truck. Andras is scowling at the second man, waving his arms and yelling something Peter can't hear. The second man stands guard looking around for Peter as Andras checks on the first guy. Andras smacks him in the face and the guy wakes up. Now Andras stands, never moving, looking from building to building. Finally, he walks over to the back of the produce truck and begins fiddling with something Peter can't see.

After a few seconds, Andras opens the back of the truck. The door swings wide and completely blocks Peter's view. He can't see anything other than the two big men Andras has working for him. Grunt number two is looking back toward Andras as grunt number one sits on the gravel trying to figure out where he is. After several seconds, Andras emerges from the back of the truck. He has a woman with him. She's tall, thin, and well proportioned. Her arms are tied behind her back and her mouth is gagged. Andras pulls her to the front of the truck, forcing her to her knees. He steps back a couple steps and points a gun squarely at her head. Peter knows exactly who she is. She's Andras's wife, Kata. Peter closes his eyes knowing Andras has him. There's no way out of this without risking Kata. Peter hides his gun in a ventilator shaft, stands, and walks down the stairs. A few moments later, Peter emerges from the apartment building with his hands up. As soon as he hears the door, Andras turns in his direction.

"Peter! So nice that you could join us." He then motions to Kata as she looks up toward Peter. "You remember Kata, don't you?"

Chapter Thirty-Six

Peter

Andras's henchman steps up and gruffly turns Peter around then ties his hands behind his back. Andras pulls Kata up from the gravel and they both lead their captives toward the restaurant. Andras opens the door leading Kata inside followed by Peter and the big man. The room is a kitchen, decent in size, maybe thirty feet by twenty feet. It's full of restaurant equipment which makes it feel more cramped. They lead Kata and Peter to the lone empty wall and force them to sit on the ground. Kata looks at Peter and he has a chance to examine her. Her eyes are puffy and red. She's obviously been crying, but one eye is badly swollen. She's been hit and probably not just once. Her blouse has a tear in it and her knees are cut and bleeding. Andras beat her following the phone call last night. As Peter looks in her eyes, what he sees troubles him most. When he met her in the café, she had been so put together. She exuded confidence. Now fear permeates her eyes.

After a couple minutes, Andras comes back in the room. He had left Peter and Kata with his brutes. Andras walks over, hunches down, and speaks to Kata.

"Do you want me to take this gag out of your mouth?" She nods. "No more screaming. Are we agreed?"

She nods her head again. Andras pulls out a knife and quickly cuts the bandanna that has been tied around her mouth. With her lips now exposed, Peter can see dried blood and swelling. She moves her mouth back and forth and Peter wonders how long she's been wearing the bandanna. Andras stands and starts pacing back and forth, tapping the knife against his off hand. He looks like a man who can't make up his mind between several choices. To his right, Peter hears a low voice like a whisper. Although he's sitting right next to Kata, he can't make out the words. Andras stops pacing and turns to look at her.

"Do you have something to say, Kata?" She continues looking at the floor but this time her words are clear.

"Andras, how could you do this to your wife?" At this, Andras comes unglued, striding over to her, gripping her by the chin, and raising her face to look at him while he screams.

"How could I do this to you? How could you do this to me? You were supposed to be my wife and you hire this man to follow me?" Andras lets her go and Kata slams back against the wall. Andras fights to get control of his temper as he stands up and begins tapping the knife in his hands again.

"Kata, I'm going to ask you some questions. And I don't want lies, not like last night. I want the truth. Do you understand me?" He turns back to look at her and Peter. She continues to stare at the floor. "When did you hire Peter?" Kata doesn't look up. Andras turns to one of his brutes. "Get me another bandanna."

At this, Kata looks up. "I hired him this week. Only a few days ago."

Andras scowls and starts pacing again. "Why did you hire him?"

Now Kata looks at Peter. She seems uncertain about how much she should say. "I hired him because I thought you were having an affair."

Andras purses his lips. "And am I?"

"I don't know," Kata says.

Now Andras looks at Peter, smiling. "Looks like you weren't worth the money, Peter. You can't even answer her question." He walks back to her, hunching down so he can look in her eyes. Kata recoils from him. He reaches out and puts his hand under her chin, raising her face. "I never cheated on you, Kata. Oh, sure, I had plenty of opportunities." He looks deeper into her eyes. "I loved you."

When Kata speaks, it comes out in a whisper. "Then why are you doing this to me?"

Andras frowns and shakes his head. "Oh, Kata, I don't want to do this to you. If you had been a good wife and supported me, I would have never done this to you. But instead, you hired someone to follow me. You had to ruin what we had."

At this, Peter can't hold back and scoffs at him. Without a word, Andras spins and slaps him hard in the face. Peter feels the burn of Andras's hand on his cheek.

Andras scowls at him. "Peter, you will not speak unless spoken to. If there are any other outbursts from you, I will be forced to silence you for good." Andras stands and stares down at him. "But, Peter, since you seem so keen on speaking, let's hear your side of things. What have you learned about the incredibly evil Dobo Andras?" As he says this, he emphasizes the "incredibly evil" part and bows. Peter looks at him and they lock eyes glaring back and forth. "Don't be shy, Peter. Tell me about myself. What have you learned?"

Peter doesn't respond, uninterested in playing this game. "Fair enough, Peter. If you don't want to answer my questions, I'm sure I can make you talk." Andras walks over to Kata and holds his knife under her chin. She grimaces in pain.

"You are incredibly charismatic," Peter blurts out.

The blade freezes. Andras wasn't expecting the compliment, and it makes him turn and smile. "Well, thank you, Peter. I think Kata would agree. What else?"

"You are a talented businessman. That's clear from owning two different restaurants. You are obviously a great cook. I loved the food especially the beef stroganoff I had in Budapest."

Andras smiles even more now. "That's one of my favorites also. Kata likes it as well, don't you?" She's turned away looking at the wall and doesn't acknowledge the question. Andras is looking at her and his jaw hardens. Peter, trying to deflect the attention from her, rushes on.

"You have the talent to do amazing things in this world." Andras turns back to Peter, forgetting Kata for a moment. "But you lack the wisdom."

Peter sees Andras smirk. "Go on, Peter. Tell me how unwise I am."

"You allowed greed to take you in a different direction. Kata tells me things were great up until about two years ago. My guess is that's when you decided a successful restaurant and charming wife weren't enough. You allowed your need for more to cloud your judgment. You became a monster."

Andras laughs right out loud at this, and Peter sees it's a defense mechanism. Peter has struck him closer to home than he wants to admit.

Peter sees an opportunity, so he continues. "It's not too late, though, Andras. You can still get back to what you had and that begins by letting us go."

Andras starts pacing again, before stopping and smiling at Peter. "Let you go? Oh, I'm way beyond that, Peter, but I will do something for you. Tell me who else knows about me and I'll let you die quickly without pain. Who have you talked to in your investigation? What do they know?" Peter's mind flashes on Zsuzsa. He made a promise to protect her. He also thinks about Luka. *Where is Luka now? Has he returned to the restaurant?*

"I'm waiting." Andras insists.

"I didn't talk with anyone," Peter lies. Andras makes a face and begins walking toward him but then stops, as if he has a better idea. He veers slightly to his left toward Kata.

"Nobody, huh?" he demands of Peter. Peter shakes his head. Andras bends in front of Kata and puts his knife to her neck again. This time, Kata rears back as the blade begins to pierce her skin and blood trickles down.

"Okay," Peter cries, "there was someone!" Andras stops and turns back to Peter, never taking the blade from Kata's neck.

One of the henchmen steps forward. "Boss?"

Andras waves him off. Peter thinks he hears a shuffling sound outside.

"Who?" Andras asks.

Peter's racking his brain. What can he say to this? If he lies and Andras knows it, Kata's going to be dead. But how can he give up Zsuzsa or Luka? Instantly, an idea pops into his head.

"Detective Kovacs with the Budapest Police." The surprise is evident on Andras's face. Peter goes on. "When I first started investigating you, I contacted him to do a background search. I wanted to check your criminal history. I typically do that for people I'm investigating."

Now Andras lowers the knife and turns to him. "And?"

"Well, as you probably know, you don't have a criminal record. It came back empty." Andras seems annoyed and turns back to Kata. She recoils from him, and Peter knows he's running out of time.

"But then," he goes on and Andras stops but doesn't turn around, "Kovacs received a call from his Director only a few minutes later." That does the trick and Andras turns back to Peter, alarm obvious on his face. Peter is talking slowly, thinking about his options. "His Director wanted to know why he had done a search for Dobo Andras in the system." Andras sits hunched over, waiting for Peter to finish. He's still in front of Kata but clearly paying attention to Peter's story. "Kovacs told him the truth. That he was doing the search for me."

"But why did the Director care about me?" Andras asks.

Peter hesitates, then hears the sound of a pistol being cocked.

Andras whirls around and sees one of his henchmen holding a gun pointed straight at him. The other stooge reaches inside his coat, going for his gun.

The huge man holding the gun turns on his companion. "Don't even think about it, Zsolt!"

He keeps his gun trained on Andras but points to his partner. Zsolt doesn't listen, instead pulling out his gun and raising it toward his partner. The big man with the gun turns and fires at Zsolt and Peter thinks his head will explode from the noise that reverberates in the small kitchen. Zsolt's eyes widen as he feels the impact of the gunshot to his chest. As he slams back against the nearest wall, the outside door smashes open and armed police officers fill the room. They hold a gun to the gunman who has just shot his partner. Both sides are yelling until he puts the gun down. Another police officer rushes over to the shot man. In the madness, Peter instinctively leans his body over Kata to shield her. Nobody seemed to be watching Andras in the chaos and Peter finds he's gone.

Chapter Thirty-Seven

Peter

Peter sits next to Kata in the dining area of the restaurant. The henchman that shot the one named Zsolt is an undercover officer from Budapest named Nemeth Tibor. He obviously isn't working with the Croatian agency, because when they rushed in, they disarmed and handcuffed him. It took several minutes before they were able to retrieve his identification and call Budapest to verify. Zsolt was taken out on a stretcher. After disarming the undercover police officer and tending to Zsolt, a female Croatian officer comes to Peter and Kata.

"Do you speak English?" she asks with a heavy accent.

"Indeed, I do," Peter replies.

Kata only shakes her head. Like most people in Europe, she understands at least a minimal amount.

The woman looks at Peter. "Are you hurt?"

"No, but she is," he tells her, motioning to Kata. "Please help her. I can wait."

The woman turns to Kata, finds a knife, and cuts her hands loose. She turns back to Peter. "Would you translate?" He nods and the woman turns back to Kata. "Do you have pain?" Kata looks at her while Peter translates.

"Not too bad. My face hurts, and I think my right hand might be broken. But other than that, some cuts, and bruises."

Peter turns to the female officer and translates. The officer asks Kata for her hand and she offers it. The woman begins tenderly checking each bone and Kata gasps and winces a couple times. The officer turns back to Peter. "I think she has broken a couple bones in her hand. We'll need to transport her to the hospital, but it will be a few minutes." Peter translates this to Kata, and she nods and thanks the officer. The officer turns back to him. "What your name and the woman?"

"My name is Andrassy Peter, and this is Dobo Kata."

The officer has a notepad and writes down their names. "How you know?" pointing to Kata.

"I'm a private investigator," Peter tells her. "Kata hired me to follow her husband, Andras, the owner of this restaurant. She thought he might be having an affair." Peter isn't sure if the officer understands the "affair" part.

The woman looks back to Kata but speaks to Peter. "She is Andras's wife?" Peter bobs his head. The woman has been crouching in front of them. Now she stands and tells Peter, "I be back. I go talk with my boss."

"Before you go, will you untie me?" Peter asks.

The woman turns back to him. "I will untie you soon. I be right back." She turns and walks out.

Peter looks across the kitchen and notices they are still talking with the undercover cop. Peter turns to Kata. "Are you okay?"

She looks at him and he can see that she's trying to process all that has transpired since last night. Her eyes well with tears, but she fights them back. "Yes, I'm going to be okay."

Peter hesitates to ask but his curiosity is too great. "How did you get here?"

Kata takes a deep breath and shakes her head in disbelief. "Well, when he picked up the phone yesterday or whatever day it was, I knew I was in trouble. I had never seen a look in his eye like that. After he hung up, then called you back, I sat trying to come up with some type of story but couldn't think of anything. He went to the bathroom as I sat in the bedroom on the bed wondering what I should do and what he would do next. I couldn't tell if he knew anything. After a few minutes, he came walking into the room and sat on the bed next to me. He seemed really calm, like nothing had happened. He looked at me and asked me if I had been talking on the phone. I told him I had been talking with a friend and thought I had hung up the phone. I told him I was sorry and that it was just a mistake." Now she shakes her head. "Without saying anything, he slapped me hard on the cheek. It knocked me back on the bed." Peter can see tears well up again and her voice grows in intensity. "He had never hit me before. In all the time we were dating and married, he never hit me. I was in shock. I tried to get away from him, kicking my feet and trying to roll off the bed, but he just climbed on top of me and held me by the wrists." Kata hugs her body as she speaks. "When he spoke again, it was with a menacing tone. He said he knew I was lying and that he had no use for a lying wife. I started to scream and, this time, he punched me in the face. I saw the clenched fist coming but I couldn't get out of the way. I could only turn my head. The next thing I knew, I was in the back of a truck, in the dark, driving on the road. My arms were tied behind my back and my mouth was bound. I was lying on my stomach and had things packed all around me, but it was so dark, I couldn't make anything out."

Kata loses control of her emotions and begins to cry. Big tears roll down her cheeks. "How could he do this to me, Peter? How could I be married to an animal like that and not even know it?"

Peter sighs. "Kata, how could you know? He was an actor and never showed you who he really was."

Tears continue to stream down her face and she wipes her nose with her left hand still favoring her right. She looks at Peter and asks earnestly, "But, Peter, who is he then? Who is Andras? Is he the man I married? Or is he the man he has been the last two years?"

Peter shrugs. "He's both. I don't think he's always been the monster you see now. I think he's become that man."

"When I was in that truck, I thought I was dead. I had no idea where I was going." Realizing what she has just said, she looks around. "Speaking of, where am I? How did you get here? What language was that policewoman speaking?" When she asks these questions, Peter realizes she has no idea she's in Croatia. Kata surveys the room. "I'm scared, Peter. They didn't catch him, did they?"

"The police are looking for him. They'll find him soon."

Kata looks into Peter's eyes, and again he's taken by her beauty. Her eyes are bloodshot, her lips bleeding, her face bruised, and her dark hair snarled. Not many women can make that look work for them.

The policewoman who had talked with them before comes back now. She speaks to Peter. "I need to take Mrs. Dobo now. The Hungarian police want to talk to you." She motions toward the undercover officer who is finally sitting alone.

"She's been through a lot in the last couple days, please don't leave her alone. Her husband is a dangerous man," Peter says.

The officer nods. "I will stay with her."

Peter turns back to Kata. "They want to take you to the hospital now."

Peter sees the look of concern in her face. "Are you coming with me?"

Peter shakes his head. "They want to talk with me." Kata begins to protest. "Don't worry. This officer will stay with you and once I'm done, I'll come to the hospital."

Instinctively, Kata reaches out and hugs Peter. He can feel her trembling. He wants to hug her back and reassure her but is still restrained. He turns to the officer. "Will you please release me now?"

She apologizes and comes over to cut Peter loose. As he moves his arms forward, he has to hold his breath. His limbs aren't accustomed to being bound and the blood flow returning to his extremities hurts.

Chapter Thirty-Eight

Peter

Peter walks over to the big undercover Hungarian police officer who had posed as one of Andras's brutes. This is Peter's first experience being this close to him and he feels overwhelmed by the mass of the man. He's tall, but not outrageously so. His girth is what impresses Peter. He's late thirties, early forties with dark, almost black hair and a seemingly constant frown to his face. He's the kind of man you think of when picturing Goliath.

"I understand you would like to talk with me?"

The man bobs his head and extends his hand. As Peter takes it, he thinks it might completely swallow his. "Nemeth Tibor *vagyok*."

"Andrassy Peter."

"I'm sorry if I roughed you up a little earlier. It couldn't be helped." The man's voice matches his look, low and gravelly. Peter wonders if it's even possible for him to smile; if he tries, it might split his lips. "Is Kata going to be okay?" the big man asks. She had just left with the Croatian female officer.

"I think she will be. It's a big shock for her," Peter says.

Tibor grunts and nods his head. "How long have you been on to Andras?"

"Kata hired me just a few days ago. She believed he might be having an affair. Obviously, this was way more than I had anticipated."

Tibor nods his head. He takes out a cigarette and presses it to his lips then pulls out a lighter and lights it. He takes a long drag then eyes Peter. "Well, I've been with Andras for much longer than that; I've been working for him the last six months. Or I should say, pretended to work for him."

"I bet you've seen a lot."

Tibor shrugs. "I've seen things I'll never be able to erase from my mind. I've seen things that make you want to stay in your house, lock the doors, and never emerge." Peter wonders what those things are, but he also doesn't want to know. Kind of like driving by a head-on collision and seeing a body lying in the street. Tibor goes on, "Had I been better at my job, maybe we could have stopped him earlier. But Andras answers to someone else, and we were trying to find out who that person is. That's the crux of it. Find that person, and you blow the whole thing open. Until then, you're plugging holes in a boat with only your fingers."

This revelation surprises Peter since he assumed Andras was the mastermind. Tibor sees his surprise and decides to explain himself. "Andras has been working for the Ukrainian mafia. They have a strong hold in Budapest, almost like the KGB back in Soviet times. Anyway, Andras would receive a quota of women he needed to abduct in Budapest each month and in exchange, he was paid handsomely." Peter had pieced at least some of that together without the mafia affiliation. "Andras would ship the women from Budapest to Croatia in his restaurant trucks, then deliver them to the mafia who would, presumably, sell the women."

"How many each month?" Peter asks.

"Usually, five or six. Pretty sad situation."

"Couldn't you stop it?" Peter can't believe they would allow this to go on and on.

"The problem is, Andras is a middleman. The mafia could easily find someone else to take his place. We needed to find who is calling the shots. When the women would be delivered, we would follow them and, in some cases, buy them or, in other cases, bust the sale. But we had to be careful not to spook them until we found who was orchestrating it at the top." Tibor shakes his head. "Unfortunately, we're going to have to start all over again. Andras was careful to never allow me to know who he dealt with and today, I've blown my cover." Tibor shrugs and shakes his head again and all Peter can do is nod.

"Why did you blow your cover?" Peter asks him. "I mean, I'm grateful. Very grateful. But why didn't you let Andras kill us?"

"Maybe it was, in part, Kata. I really felt bad for her. I had met her a couple times at the restaurant in Budapest and she was very kind to everyone." Tibor kicks his foot against the tile floor. "I also heard the Croatian police outside. Someone had called them, and I wasn't interested in getting in a shootout. I made the decision to save you and Kata rather than keep my cover. But that's not why I wanted to talk to you. Andras is still out there. He's smart and charismatic and very angry. He's a vengeful man and you can bet you're at the top of his list. I'm on there also. But he's going to blame you for this. Watch your back, Peter."

Peter had been in some nasty situations during his time as a detective in New York and his work as a PI, but this is one of the only times he can remember being frightened.

Tibor leans forward and puts one of his big paws on Peter's shoulder. "I mean it. He'll be coming for you if we don't find him."

He starts to walk away but Peter stops him. "Tibor? Kata would be high on that list also."

Tibor raises a hand. "I'm way ahead of you there, Peter. I'm headed to the hospital right now. I won't let her out of my sight. I didn't blow my cover for her to die now."

Peter smiles and, for the first time in two days, he feels Kata is safe. "Can I ask you one more thing?" Peter can see Tibor is anxious to leave but he needs to ask. "Did you see any of the girls that have been taken recently?"

Tibor shrugs. "I saw a few but not many. I wasn't involved in that aspect much."

"Do you remember any with red hair? British?"

Tibor thinks for a minute. "No, I don't remember any like that. But like I said, I didn't see many." Peter's disappointment must show on his face.

"Why do you ask?" Tibor inquires.

"I'm working another case and I'm wondering if that girl was a victim of Andras."

Tibor grimaces. "Well, we're going to review all the records we can. It will take a few days, but we might find something."

Chapter Thirty-Nine

Stephen

"Why are you keeping me here?" Samantha asks the hooded man.

The man has her locked in a room that looks like a cellar and only opens the door to give her food and water three times a day. At least he's provided a toilet and a bed, but aside from that, there are absolutely no furnishings.

She's been asking this same question of the man since she arrived and he's never even so much as looked in her direction. She has no idea how long she's been here or even why she's here. The room is absent natural light and having no clock, she's lost track of days and time. She doesn't even know if it's day or night.

Her leg is bound to the base of the bed with a metal shackle. When she first arrived, she pulled and tinkered with the shackle hoping to remove it. After rubbing the skin raw, she eventually gave up. The length of the chain only allows her to reach the toilet and the bed. She's been unable to explore the rest of the room. Samantha climbs off the bed and kneels on the cold cement floor. She looks as if she is going to pray to or beg the man for her release. Instead, she begins to cry. This is certainly not the first time she's cried since being abducted, but it's the first time in the presence of the man. "Please," she begs, "please tell me why I'm here. Please tell me where I am!"

He's tall but always wears a hood and his face is engulfed in shadow. The darkness is only interrupted by a single light bulb hanging above the bed. The man never approaches her, treating her as if she might infect him with a deadly disease. He places the food on the floor, as far from her as possible but within reach of the chain. He turns to leave but stops and turns around. He's watching her, analyzing her. He says nothing as he stares at her from the shadows.

"Who are you?" Samantha pleads. "Why are you doing this?"

Something's changed in him. He begins to slowly move. He reaches up to the hood surrounding his head and pulls it back. Samantha wipes at her eyes and leans forward, struggling to see. Recognition dawns and she gasps, all the air leaving her lungs. She feels as if she might vomit as she looks at the face. There, standing in front of her with a sneering face, is Stephen.

I sit straight up in bed gasping for breath. My body is clammy and sweaty. I feel as if I've been drowning and I'm sucking in large quantities of air. The room's dark, but there's a ringing sound coming from the hallway. I swing my legs off the bed and begin walking in the direction of the sound, the wood floor cold on my feet. I extend my hands in front of me, feeling for the bedroom door. After a few cautious steps, I reach the door and turn the knob. I'm in the hallway now and the ringing fills the apartment. I pick up the phone.

"Hello?"

"Stephen? Oh, I'm sorry. Did I wake you?"

I recognize the voice immediately, "Yes, Liz. But it's okay, I'm glad you did."

She hesitates on the other end of the phone. "I'm sorry, but you told me to call as soon as I spoke with Professor Carter."

My mind's clearing now from the nightmare. "Right. What did you find out? Did you talk with him?"

Liz's voice is steady on the other end of the phone. "I did. He confirmed everything your Professor Fredrickson said. He told me about Fredrickson's wife, about him being fired, and about how he helped him land the job in Budapest." I feel an odd mixture of relief and disappointment. If Fredrickson was telling the truth, it makes it more likely he had nothing to do with Samantha's disappearance. It means the person I was sure was responsible, isn't.

"Are you sure it was Mr. Carter you spoke with? It couldn't have been someone posing as Mr. Carter?"

Liz sighs on the other end of the phone. "What do you mean posing as Mr. Carter?" she exaggerates the "posing as Mr. Carter" part.

"I mean you confirmed it was him?"

"Well, I didn't see him; it was over the phone. But I called the phone number listed for the business department in the school and they transferred me to him. He didn't answer, so I left a message and about thirty minutes later, he called me back."

"Okay, so what did he say when he called you back? Did he say he heard your message?"

Liz is silent on the other end of the phone and I'm afraid we've lost connection. Then she speaks, and when she does, her annoyance has ratcheted up. "Stephen," she says my name with deliberate slowness, "it was him. Nobody knew I would be calling. There's no way Fredrickson could have intercepted the call. It was him. Mr. Fredrickson was telling the truth."

She's right, and I know it. I slump down on the chair next to the phone. "You're right, Liz. I'm sorry. I was just so hopeful I'd finally have some kind of lead. Something that would make me feel like we were making progress."

Liz is silent on the other end of the phone again. When she speaks, her tone has grown kind, patient. "Stephen, are you okay? I mean are you really okay? You seem more upset now than when I spoke to you a few hours ago."

I tell her about the nightmare. About me being the one who abducted Samantha. "Liz, I just don't know what it means. Why would I have a dream like that?"

"Hey, it's just a dream. Do you think all your dreams are telling you something? I'm sure you've been thinking about her all the time. All your thoughts are occupied by her. I'm sure you worry that she's a prisoner somewhere and the longer it takes you to find her, the longer she will suffer." Now Liz becomes stern, channeling our late mother. "But listen to me, for all you know, she went back home to England. She could be perfectly fine. In fact, if I were to bet, I would say that's exactly where she is. I know you don't want to accept that because it hurts you, but more than likely, she pulled out of school and left to go home. Maybe she had a family emergency and didn't have time to get word to you. You need to stop beating yourself up over this. Have you even been going to school?"

I tell her I had, but that I was having a hard time concentrating. "She's all I can think of."

"Stephen, you hired a private investigator. You need to let him do his job and you need to stay focused in school. You went all the way over there and paid a bunch of money. You're going to regret this if you don't do your best." She's right. I know she's right, but I also know that she doesn't fully understand my predicament. She's too far removed. But rather than try to explain it to her again, I agree and tell her I'll follow her advice.

After I hang up, I walk back and climb into bed. I look at the alarm clock: 2:12 a.m. My body is exhausted, but my mind is racing. That dream was so real. As I lay staring up at the ceiling, I know it was more than just a dream. It was my subconscious mind acknowledging that I'm responsible for what happened to Samantha.

Chapter Forty

Peter

After spending another twenty minutes with a Croatian detective, Peter walks out the front doors of Szép Ilona. He promised Kata he would come to the hospital, but after learning Tibor was headed there, he felt she would be safe. He's exhausted, and he needs sleep. He decides to head back to his hotel. But before he does, he knows there is one more thing he needs to do. At the corner of the building, he turns and heads to the back. He crosses the parking lot and reaches the apartment building. As he tries the door, he's relieved to feel it give and come open. He walks to the first landing and retrieves his gun from the ventilation shaft. Now the test is whether he can remember his way back to the hotel. He tried to pay attention as he drove with Luka, but he wasn't sure how well he had done. The streets are almost completely deserted now, and it's even darker. Thankfully the rain has stopped, but large puddles abound. His shoes are wet, and he can hear the echo of the squish of water leaving his shoes as he walks along the silent street.

As he walks, he keeps his hand in his pocket, clutching the revolver. Tibor's warning remains firmly in his mind. Andras is a vengeful man and he's still at large. Peter knows he'll be coming for him.

To his right, Peter sees a movement. Like an old gunslinger, his revolver is out and trained at the person in front of him. "Who's there?" he says in English. A small man emerges from behind the phone booth. He's wearing a backward hat and looks young.

"Peter? It's Luka." He's speaking Hungarian.

Peter exhales with relief. "What are you doing out here? I almost shot you."

Luka comes into view now. "I wanted to make sure you are okay."

Peter smiles in spite of himself. "Yes, Luka I'm okay. Thank you for calling the police."

Luka looks relieved. "I had to convince them I had heard a gunshot in order for them to come."

Peter claps him on the shoulder. "Good job! Thank you!"

Luka smiles. "Where are you going? Want a ride to the hotel?"

"You don't even know how much I would appreciate that."

Luka points to his left. "My car is just right here."

When Luka starts the car, Peter half expects someone to lean out of their window and curse at them. The Trabant splutters and spurts as it starts then melts into a high-pitched whine as Luka pulls out. Peter closes his eyes as they drive, and Luka, sensing Peter's exhaustion, keeps his conversation to a minimum. By the time they reach the hotel, Peter had dozed off and Luka has to elbow him awake.

"Are you going back to Hungary tomorrow?"

Peter hadn't thought about it but considering he is done with Kata's case, he figures that makes sense. "Yeah, I guess I am. I'd love to stay and travel around a little bit in Croatia, but I need to get back. I have another case I need to solve."

"Would you like a ride to the station? I know there's a train to Budapest that leaves at one p.m."

"I would love one, Luka. You've been a wonderful city guide. I'm grateful Andras sent you to me."

Luka has a look on his face like someone has just awarded him a first-place trophy. "I'll be here at noon to pick you up and meet you in the lobby. Might give me a chance to chat with Mia. She misses me."

Peter laughs out loud as he gets out of the car. Before he walks away and into the hotel, he leans down to the car, looking through the window. "I'll see you tomorrow."

Luka puts the car in gear and drives away. As he reaches the end of the road, he comes to a red stop light. He considers driving right through since nobody is on the road at 3:00 a.m., but he decides it would be just his luck that a police officer would be parked in the shadows, and he can't afford another ticket. He has three already and only got his license a year ago. As he sits waiting for the light to switch to green, he doesn't notice the figure emerging from the dark walking toward his car. As the driver side door opens, Luka turns his head in surprise. Through the glow of the streetlights, he sees the glint of a metal knife slicing toward him. Before he can react, the knife slices across his neck. He tries to take a breath, but nothing happens. He reaches his hands to his throat as blood rushes from the wound. He looks over in shock at the figure now receding from him. He can't mistake the broad confident stride of his boss, Andras, as he walks away.

Chapter Forty-One

Peter

"Hi, Mia, do you remember me?" Mia looks up from the desk as Peter stands looking down at her.

She smiles. "Of course, I do. You are Peter."

"That's right. I need to check out of my room, but before I do, I wondered if you would be able to help me?" Peter had slept in this morning and didn't have a lot of time before Luka would be here again to pick him up.

"Sure, I can. What do you need?"

"I have a friend who is in the hospital, and I'd like to call her, but I don't have the first clue how to do that. Do you think you could help me?"

"Of course. What hospital is she in?"

Peter fishes out the note he made on the back of the card Tibor gave him. "University Hospital of Zagreb"

"Okay, great. What's her name? Do you know her room number?"

Peter shakes his head. "No, I don't know her room number, but her name is Kata Dobo. She was admitted last night."

"Give me just a couple minutes and I'll see if I can get her on the line."

As Peter stands listening to Mia rattle on in Croatian, he takes the opportunity to look around the hotel. Luka said this was one of the oldest hotels in Croatia, or at least in Zagreb, but it didn't look it. They had done a great job of updating it, inside and out. It had a delightful courtyard where one could sit and drink tea or coffee alongside a nice café. The setup was different than he had ever seen before. Coming from the street, travelers enter the hotel via an arched gateway leading to the courtyard, then up a few sets of steps and through the doors on the left and arrive at the reception desk. From there, guests could climb the stairs to their rooms.

Before long, Mia is speaking to him again. "Peter? I have Kata on the line for you." She reaches across the desk and hands him the phone.

"Kata? How are you doing?"

"Hi, Peter. I don't like being here, but I got some sleep and I'm feeling better already."

"I'm glad to hear that. I'm sorry I didn't come to the hospital last night, but Tibor told me he was going to be with you."

"Yes, he came last night and has stayed with me. The Croatian officer was nice, but she and I couldn't communicate with each other. It's nice to have someone here that speaks Hungarian."

That makes sense to Peter. "Do you know how long you'll be there?"

"I'm not sure. I think I'm going to head back to Hungary tomorrow. Tibor says he will be with me until they find Andras."

"Yes, he told me the same thing last night. Well, if it's okay with you, I'm going to head back to Budapest today. I have another case I need to work on."

"Yes, that's fine. I understand. I also need to pay you for solving the case."

Peter hesitates. "Did I really solve it? I'm not sure if Andras cheated on you."

"Oh, come on, Peter. This case turned into way more than either of us thought it would. You saved my life last night. I'll forever be in your debt. When I get back to Budapest, I'll get you paid."

Peter looks at his watch. "Thank you, Kata. I'm supposed to be on a train soon. I have Luka, a kid who called the police for us last night, coming to pick me up. He's been my guide in the city."

"Tell him thank you from me," Kata says.

"I will. Please call me when you get home to Budapest."

"Oh, and Peter, please be careful. Andras is still out there, and he might be coming for you."

Peter agrees. "I will, Kata. Thank you. I'll talk with you soon." Peter hands the phone back to Mia. She takes it, seemingly troubled by something. She asks him to wait for just a minute while she helps the man behind him.

Peter thinks the request is strange but agrees. He steps to the side and waits while she helps the short, squat man standing behind him. After Mia finishes with the man, she comes around the desk and asks Peter if he will step outside into the courtyard. He follows behind her, even more curious now.

When they arrive in the courtyard, she turns to Peter. "I'm sorry to tell you this, Peter, but Luka won't be coming to pick you up." He can't help the look of surprise and Mia seems hesitant to explain. After pausing to look in his eyes, she tells him, "Luka was found dead in his car last night. Someone cut his throat."

Peter stares back in her eyes, not comprehending. "How? How do you know this?" he asks.

"When I was coming to work this morning, I saw his car. His body had been taken away, but I spoke with one of the officers."

Peter can see that her cheeks are flushed, and she's wringing her hands. "I'm sorry to be the one to tell you that."

Peter's head is spinning. He knows Andras is a very dangerous man and has revenge foremost in his thoughts, but he assumed Kata and himself would be the targets. Maybe even Tibor, but he had no idea it extended to Luka. Peter can feel the news has unnerved him and Mia suggests they sit at one of the tables.

As Peter sits, Mia watches him. "I overheard your conversation. I don't speak Hungarian, but I heard you say Luka's name. Was he supposed to come meet you here?"

"Yes, he was going to give me a ride to the train today. I'm headed back to Budapest."

"Can I call a car for you? I can have one here in five minutes." Peter thanks her and she rushes off. He sits at the table in the courtyard, his head spinning but he wills himself to think. First, he considers changing plans and going to Kata but decides the last thing he wants is to have himself, Kata, and Tibor all together in the same room. Then his mind shifts to Luka. Why him, Peter wonders? But he quickly comes up with a reason. Luka was easy to get to. When Andras had interrogated Peter, he wanted to know who helped him. Luka had been one of the names that came to mind, but he never expressed it to Andras. How did Andras know then?

Peter strikes his own forehead with the palm of his hand. *I should never have let Luka give me a ride home last night.* If Andras had been following him, he would have seen Luka and known he helped. What about Zsuzsa, Peter wonders. *Does Andras know about her?* Suddenly, Peter feels he needs to get to Budapest right away.

Chapter Forty-Two

Peter

Peter sits looking at the print in his book. He can't get his mind to concentrate on the words on the page. He's now on the four-hour train ride north to Budapest. Unlike when he had come to Zagreb, this time he purchased a second-class ticket. There isn't a huge difference in the experience but there certainly is in the fare since the second-class ticket is half the cost. The second-class cabin is a big car with groupings of four seats per grouping and maybe ten or twelve in the whole car. There are no closed cars and no hallways. This particular train is pretty full, and Peter has two other people in his grouping of four seats. Next to him sits a man around forty with a shaved head, muscular build, average height, and dark beard with the first touches of gray. He half smiled at Peter when he first sat down but hasn't acknowledged him since. Peter guesses he's an American because he's reading a copy of *Sports Illustrated* with a white-haired man yelling on the cover and the title, "Fired: The Downfall of Bobby Knight." He has no idea who Bobby Knight is or what sport he plays.

Across from Peter sits a dark-haired, Hispanic woman. She looks to be about the same age as the man next to him. She doesn't acknowledge him as he sits down, which is usually fine for Peter. He doesn't particularly like making small talk with strangers on public transportation but today is different. He needs something to distract him from all the thoughts swirling in his head. She also holds a book in her hands, but she's much more attentive than Peter is to his. The cover of the book is dark with grey and red letters. Below the author's name and title is a picture of a storm drain. Peter can see she's about two-thirds of the way through.

"Have Beverly and Bill rekindled their love yet?" Peter says it with no warning and the woman and man look up and stare at Peter. Peter is looking at the woman expectantly waiting for an answer. After a moment, she realizes he's speaking to her.

"What?" she asks.

Peter points to her book. "Have Beverly and Bill rekindled their love yet?"

She turns the book over so she can look at the cover then back to Peter. "What do you mean?"

"Oh, nothing. I was just asking something about the book. Is this your first-time reading *IT*?"

She smiles and bobs her head. "My first time reading any Stephen King novel. I don't know why I picked this one. It's really long."

"It is but it might be his best. It's very good."

"Yeah, I brought it with me from home thinking it would be something good to read traveling around Europe. It's a lot of time on planes or on trains."

"Where are you from?"

"I'm from Southern California. A place called Oxnard."

"That's pretty close to LA, isn't it?"

Her eyes sparkle with enthusiasm. "It is. Really close. Do you know it?"

Peter shakes his head. "No, but one time I had strawberries when I was in New York and the packaging said they came from Oxnard, California."

"My father worked in those fields. Maybe he picked the ones you ate."

Peter shrugs. "Could be."

They fall silent and Peter has the impression he might lose her to her book again. "So, what brings you to Europe?" The man sitting to Peter's right now seems interested in their conversation, although he does his best not to show it. He keeps his *Sports Illustrated* up but his eyes dart back and forth between Peter and the woman.

"I work for Danone, the yogurt company. I'm inspecting some of our manufacturing plants here in Europe. You know Europeans," she laughs, "they really like their yogurt, so we have a lot of them here. It's been a great chance for me to see the continent, though."

Peter must acknowledge he is one of those Europeans and begins asking her questions about her job. Sometime during the conversation, they completely lose *Sports Illustrated* guy.

"I'm sorry, I pulled you away from your book," he tells her during a break in the conversation.

She waves her hand. "Oh, don't worry about that. I've been reading it for thirty hours and I'm not even close to being done. I needed the break. So, tell me about you. What do you do? Why do you speak English so well but claim to be European? You sound like an American."

Peter smiles. "I'd love to answer your question but I'm an old man and I've been riding on a train for over an hour. Let me find the toilet and then I'll be back."

She smiles as Peter stands and walks down the walkway toward the back of the train. After crossing through a couple train cars, he finally finds the restroom and goes in. There isn't much to it, a small sink and toilet.

The room is so small, he can easily reach his arms out and touch both walls. After he finishes, he washes his hands and reaches for the door. The door seems to be stuck as he pulls on it. Peter tugs again, feeling it start to give, then stop. Peter tries again and the door comes open easily. Hmm, he thinks. As he steps out and starts walking, he suddenly feels someone push him up against the wall and immediately something sharp presses against his neck.

"Don't speak!"

Peter feels his heart drop. Andras has found him.

"Come with me, Peter," Andras whispers in his ear. "And if you try to yell, I'll slit your throat so fast, your words will stick." Andras reaches his hand around Peter's waist and grabs his gun.

Peter knows not to yell. He remembers what happened to Luka. Andras has one of Peter's arms wrapped behind his own back and is guiding him down the hall past the restroom. As Andras forces Peter down the hallway, he can't help but wonder why he hasn't just killed him. Behind the bathroom, there's a small hallway then stairs leading to the train car exit. Andras forces Peter to the bottom of the stairs right by the exit door. If Andras were to push the door button, he could easily push Peter out of the moving train. In that case, Peter would be killed and nobody would be the wiser that Andras was his killer. Now Andras steps away from him. He's at the top of the stairs with his knife still pointed at Peter. Peter turns so he's no longer looking out the exit door but back up at Andras, his back against the exit door.

"I'm going to give you another chance, Peter. Tell me who helped you learn more about me and I'll ease your pain when you die."

Peter's heart is pounding. Andras certainly has the advantage here; his knife is pointing right at him, and he has the skill to use it. He also has the advantage of size, strength, and the higher ground. He has the upper hand in every way and has planned this perfectly. The only thing that would give Peter a chance would be his gun, but Andras has that now.

"What makes you think someone helped me?"

"Because you aren't smart enough to learn what you did about me on your own". Peter wonders if he should take offense.

"Was it Zsuzsa?" The name comes so quickly and so out of left field that Peter momentarily betrays himself. He flinches and Andras sees it. A smile steals at the corners of Andras's lips. "No need to deny it, Peter, your face gave you away. Make sure you don't play poker anytime soon—your tell would cost you a lot of money."

Peter knows there's little point in denying it. Andras has won.

Andras stands before Peter looking at his knife. The knife reminds Peter of the blade wielded by the Australian in the movie *Crocodile Dundee*. It's very large, and obviously a prized possession of Andras's. He stands sliding his thumb against the edge, admiring it. Without looking at Peter, he begins to talk.

"We've got a little time before your ride arrives," Andras says. Peter wonders what he's talking about. "Do you know why the knife is the perfect weapon?" Andras asks still not looking at him. Peter glares back at him. "It requires you to be very close to your victim. You can see the look in their eyes, and you can also feel the blade as it penetrates the skin. It's so much more intimate than a gun."

Andras looks at Peter but then goes back to admiring the knife. "When I was first learning to become a chef, I enjoyed the knife sharpening classes, but I especially liked cutting meat with a particularly sharp blade." Andras looks coldly at him and smiles. "I felt the knife slide easily across Luka's throat. Blood immediately oozed from the slice. I can't wait to cut Zsuzsa, but first, it's your turn."

Peter hears the blast of a train far away as Andras begins to move forward.

"Wait!" Peter pleads. "Before you kill me, can I ask you one question?"

Andras shrugs. "You told me what I wanted to know, even if it was by accident, and I'm feeling generous. Ask away but be quick."

Peter takes a breath. "A few weeks ago, did you take a redheaded British woman by the name of Samantha?" The surprise that crosses Andras's face confuses Peter.

Suddenly, Andras begins to laugh. "Why would you care? Oh, I get it. You're looking for this girl, right? You want to solve the case before you die?" Andras is teasing him. "You're pathetic Peter. You know, a few years ago, I was like you. I thought the idea of taking these women and selling them off was horrible. When I was first approached, I flatly refused. But my restaurant was struggling, and I needed money. I decided to just do a couple. They were girls that had come to Budapest from the country and didn't have anyone who would miss them. It was easy. I couldn't believe how easy it was and how much they paid me." Now he shakes his head. "I had worked so hard. I had put everything I had into my restaurant, and it was still struggling to survive. With the girls, in one day, I could make what the restaurant would make in a month or two. Before long, we were taking four or five girls a month. I was pumping that money back into the restaurant and business soared."

Andras shrugs. "And those girls, most of them, are happier than they were before. They don't need to worry about money. They don't need to worry about a place to live or what to eat. Everything is handled for them." Peter hears the blast of a train steam engine. Another train is about to pass them going in the other direction. Andras hears it too. "I'd like to say it's been nice knowing you, Peter. But why be insincere? It will be a pleasure to kill you."

Andras pushes the button and opens the exit doors. Peter feels the sudden whoosh of cool air as it rushes in, blowing him forward. Andras lunges with his knife, but Peter sees it coming and ducks as he falls forward. Andras trips on one of the steps and falls face forward, flailing his arms out, trying to catch the side of the door. Peter flips around on the steps watching as Andras splats across the front of the train like a bug on a windshield.

Chapter Forty-Three

Stephen

I walk out of my apartment and summon the elevator. As the doors open, I'm surprised to see a young woman inside. Typically, the elevator is vacant when I get on, which is fine with me. I'm always afraid someone is going to talk to me and I'll only be able to respond in broken Hungarian. The woman is young and very attractive. She has magnificent blue eyes and long curly dark hair. It's her outfit that leaves me befuddled. She's wearing a white see-through blouse and short skirt.

"*Szia,*" she says with a lovely lift to her voice.

"*Szia,*" I mumble, barely able to get the word out. I drop my head as I enter the elevator, not wanting to stare at her, but also longing to.

In Hungarian, the greetings and goodbyes can be used interchangeably. As we descend in the iron box, I worry she might try and talk to me. I'd be surprised if I could respond back with a single word in English, let alone Hungarian.

As we reach the bottom floor, I let her exit first. She walks in front of me, and I can't help but admire her as she reaches the exterior doors. She pushes one open, walks through, then holds it for me.

As I reach the door, she looks in my eyes and says, "Ciao."

I'm not sure how to respond. Isn't *ciao* Italian? She continues to look in my eyes as I realize she's waiting for a response.

"Ciao," I blurt out.

She giggles then walks away. I slowly follow her as I exit the apartment complex. After walking a couple blocks, I reach the streetcar stop. Two minutes later, the yellow and white streetcar arrives. As I climb onboard, I find an empty seat and sit down. The streetcar bustles with conversation and noise. All around me I hear conversations in a language I can't understand but none of that pulls me from my thoughts. Before long the streetcar passes in front of the Gellert Hotel. I let my gaze extend beyond the hotel to the top of the hill with the huge statue and citadel. Every time since running up there, when I pass by, I avert my eyes. I know I'm hiding from the memory. If I don't think about it, maybe it never happened. No, I need to face it. I force myself to look at the hill and experience the night again.

As I looked at her, I was struck by how lucky I was. I couldn't believe I was sitting here with her. "No, I haven't dated very much. I mean...I dated a little in college, but rarely."

"Why do you think you are so shy and timid around women?"

I looked out over the city. I had asked myself this very question many times. I knew the major part was a fear of rejection, but beyond that, I wasn't sure. I knew if my mom had been around as I got older, things would have been different. I was sure my mother would have encouraged me to date. "Probably fear of rejection mostly," I responded, "but I'm sure a psychiatrist somewhere could have a field day with me." After a few moments of silence, I looked at her. "Why did you show interest in me like you did?"

"Good question." She lightly punched me in the arm. "First, I thought you were cute. And I have to admit, you got my attention when you hit your head in class. I had noticed you before and thought you were handsome but when you hit your head... I don't know, it was just so cute, and I felt bad for you. From that point on, I wanted to get to know you."

"So that worked for you, huh? Me making a fool of myself?"

"I didn't think you were a fool. I'm just glad you weren't hurt. You hit it quite hard." Again, we fell into a comfortable silence as I held her. I was amazed how comfortable I felt with her. We had only known each other a few weeks but it felt like an eternity. I couldn't imagine my life without her now. I leaned over and smelled her hair right by her neck. I loved her fragrance. I leaned in closer and kissed her neck. She seemed to hold her breath and I could tell she liked it.

For the next thirty minutes, we sat on the stone wall kissing and looking out at the twinkling lights below us.

Finally, Samantha turned to me, "Come on, let's go. I'm cold and nobody else is around."

I had been so captivated by her; I hadn't noticed that people were no longer milling around the statue. It was silent other than the distant hum of the city below us. I knew she was right; it was very late, and we should be getting back. I helped her stand, and as I did, I took notice of how far we were from the ground. I knew it had to be at least thirty feet and the wall was quite narrow.

"I'll go on ahead so I can help you down. Be careful. Falling from here wouldn't be pleasant."

"Now that's an understatement," she said as she looked at the cobblestone road below us. In less than a minute I reached the end of the wall and climbed down to the walkway. As I turned back to look at her, I noticed she hadn't moved yet. She just stood there, smiling at me.

"What?" I asked her.

"What's your plan to get back?"

"What?"

"Did you have a plan to get back down from the hill?" Seeing the look on my face was answer enough for her. She began to laugh but as she did, she lost her balance. I watched in horror as Samantha fell from the wall to the street far below.

Chapter Forty-Four

Peter

Peter sits in a train station office in Siófok. Two men stand staring at him. It's been a half hour since anyone talked and his frustration is growing. He asked a couple times what they were waiting for and got only partial answers. After Andras had fallen from the train, Peter lay on the steps; he didn't dare move with the doors open and the suck of air pulling him toward the exit. Within a minute, one of the train conductors came running over, closed the doors, and helped him up. Peter was ushered to the front of the train while the man began asking him what had happened. He explained who he was and who Andras had been. The conductor's eyes grew as large as saucers when Peter told him about what happened in Zagreb and then on the train. He told Peter not to leave and sent someone back to get his luggage and coat. A couple minutes later, they arrived in Siófok where Peter was escorted off the train and into the office where he sat now, waiting.

Peter hears sirens outside. "Finally," he says.

After a couple minutes, two armed police officers enter the room. One of them, a wiry little fella, points at Peter but looks at the train conductor. "Is this him?" Peter's annoyed already. It doesn't help that he's beyond hungry, and his life has been threatened twice in two days.

No, Sherlock. I'm a random passenger who lost his bag and I'm just waiting for it to be found. Peter thinks all this but doesn't say it. He just sits impatiently bouncing his knee up and down on the chair. The officer, after receiving confirmation, sits down across from Peter. He's a small man with wire-rim glasses and a receding hairline he's unsuccessfully trying to hide by combing his hair forward. He reminds Peter of a peacock. Like the feathers of a peacock, his boisterous demeanor is used to distract his audience.

"Are you Andrassy Peter?" the peacock asks. Peter has been through so much over the last several days and his patience has long since flown. He knows the guy is doing his job but he just can't help himself.

"Nope, I'm just a random passenger sitting here waiting for the police to ask me some stupid questions."

The peacock's jawline goes rigid. "I'm going to assume that's a yes. Do you want to tell me what happened on that train?"

Peter sighs loudly. "Not really."

The peacock begins turning red and Peter wonders if he will soon be seeing his beautiful crop of feathers. "Look, I don't like your attitude, Mr. Andrassy. If you don't comply with us, it's possible we could charge you for murder."

Peter glares back at him. "Is that a threat?"

The peacock turns and looks at his partner who is younger and clearly timid. Peter also guesses he's put on twenty to thirty pounds in the last year. His belt is cinched in the last hole and a few of the buttons on his shirt seem stressed enough to pop off at any moment. The partner just shrugs, and the peacock turns back to Peter.

"I'm going to ask you one more time what happened on that train. If you don't answer to my satisfaction, we'll be moving this to our police station."

Peter is past the point of caring. "Why don't you go and ask the train conductor? I've already told him the whole story. Actually...why don't you call Kovacs Lajos of the National Police? He should be here anyway."

The peacock goes a dark shade of red and abruptly stands. He approaches Peter and commands him to stand. Peter complies, and the partner hurriedly shuffles over, clearly not sure what is going on but knowing he should help.

"Turn around," the peacock commands.

Peter sighs loudly and turns around. He knows better than to resist at this point. The peacock pulls out his handcuffs and slaps them on. This is the third time in two days Peter has his arms held behind his back and he's past tired of it.

The peacock motions to his partner. "József, take him to the car."

József tries to be rough but it's a little like the Pillsbury Doughboy trying to play Darth Vader—nobody's going to believe it. As József leads him out of the train station in handcuffs toward the police car, another set of police vehicles pull up. These aren't local; they're Hungarian National Police. They stop abruptly in front of Peter, József, and the peacock.

Kovacs Lajos jumps out of the lead car.

"Hey! What do you think you're doing?" he demands.

The peacock steps in front of József, puffing out his chest. "We're taking this man in for questioning."

Lajos is shaking his head, holding out his credentials. "No, you aren't. This is a national case and he's going with us to Budapest."

Five minutes later, Peter is sitting in the back of a police car with Lajos, his handcuffs removed. Peter tells Lajos about Andras, Zagreb, and the train. Lajos sits listening quietly and when Peter finishes, he lets out a low whistle.

"That's quite a story, Peter. You're lucky to be alive. I bet you're looking forward to some rest."

Peter shakes his head. "I still have one more case I need to close."

"Oh yeah? The one with the missing girl from England?"

"Right."

"Do you think she was a victim of Andras?" Kovacs asks.

Peter shakes his head. "I don't."

Kovacs raises his eyebrows. "Really? Seems pretty likely to me."

Peter looks out the window but then thinks of something. "Hey did you ever hear anything back on the professor? The American."

Kovacs nods. "I did. His story checks out. His wife had been killed and he lost his job in Florida. I'm not sure why he's teaching under a different name but he is Fredrickson. He doesn't have a criminal record other than a couple minor traffic tickets."

Peter looks back out the window. Something isn't making sense. "Maybe she was abducted by Andras then. Something just doesn't feel right to me."

"Do you have a picture of this girl?" Lajos asks him.

Peter starts to shake his head then stops. "I do, actually. Well, not yet, but I'll have one once I get back to Budapest. What day is today?"

Lajos thinks for a couple seconds. "Sunday."

"I turned in some film before I left. I bet I can pick it up tomorrow. It will have pictures of her."

"Get them to me. Tibor found files that include pictures of all the girls Andras took."

Chapter Forty-Five

Stephen

I count the number of rings I hear on the line "briiiing five, briiiing six" now the familiar phone pickup, I hear his voice and wait for the tone; my frustration is boiling over.

"Peter, this is the fourth time I've called you in the last couple days. Where are you? Are you okay? Please call me back."

I slam the phone down, maybe a little too hard this time. What am I paying this guy for, I wonder? "I haven't heard from him in two days," I exclaim aloud. It's been two weeks since I've seen Samantha. On the bright side, I'm feeling way more comfortable in Hungary. I no longer feel great anxiety going to the store, riding the public transportation, or going to school. When I first arrived, I felt like my heart was going to pound right out of my chest every time someone acted like they might talk to me. Now I'm more comfortable going out. My comfort level seems to coincide with the disappearance of Samantha.

I go back and sit down at the desk in my front room. Today is Sunday. I have school tomorrow, and it's my turn to present on my startup company. This semester, each student is assigned the project of finding a startup business. The company has to be publicly traded and no more than ten years old. We are required to perform a SWOT analysis along with a presentation on what is and isn't working for the business, including a projection of future growth. I have selected an e-commerce company. The company was founded by a former VP of Wall Street. In 1994, the man had been nurturing regrets about his lack of participation in the internet business boom. He decided to leave his Wall Street firm, move to Seattle, and begin his own internet firm. Early on, the company was operated out of his garage.

The founder had read projections of explosive growth in the e-commerce industry and identified twenty different products that could easily be sold online. That list was narrowed to five, including: CDs, computer hardware, computer software, videos, and books. He eventually decided to focus on books because of large worldwide demand for literature, low unit price, and the number of titles available in print. In July 1995, the company sold its first book online and by 1996, announced itself to the public. Its initial public offering of stock went for $18 per share.

What I find fascinating, and ultimately is the reason for selecting this company as my term project, is that the company still hasn't turned a profit. The business started six years ago and is still losing money every fiscal quarter. Yet, the stock value has soared. It doesn't make sense. Wouldn't investors be losing patience? I plan to take the position of recommending the company, but it could be a difficult position to support given the continual loss of money. As I sit pondering how best to sell this position to my fellow students and professor, my phone begins to ring. I look at my watch: it's 10:14 p.m. *Who in the world?* I walk to the phone and pick it up. "Hello?" I'm relieved to hear the voice on the other end of the line.

"Stephen, it's Peter."

"Peter? Where have you been?"

"I'm sorry, Stephen. I've been working another case along with yours and it took me down to Croatia for the weekend."

"Croatia? What kind of case would take you there?"

"It's too long a story to tell you about over the phone. But interestingly enough, the case has intersected with yours. I think I may know what happened to Samantha and the good news is, she's likely still alive."

I'm dumbfounded and suddenly feel a rush of excitement. "What do you mean? How do you know? What happened?"

Peter seems a little more cautious. "I should say it's possible. I won't know for sure until tomorrow. What's your schedule tomorrow? Is it possible for you to meet me and talk about it?"

"I have school in the morning. I'll be done around two in the afternoon. Are you sure you can't just tell me now?"

"No, I'll be able to explain more tomorrow. I owe Tom a visit anyway. I will come by your apartment probably around three or four p.m."

After we hang up, I sit back down at my desk. I pick up the prospectus I had received in the mail, but I can't focus. Is it possible that Samantha might really be found? That she might be, okay?

Chapter Forty-Six

Peter

Peter's alarm clock reads 7:47 a.m. He isn't surprised. He's been lying in bed trying to force himself back to sleep, but it isn't working. After he arrived home from Siófok and spoke with Detective Kovacs, he called Stephen, then crashed. His exhaustion was complete. He went to sleep almost as quickly as he lay down, pulling the covers up to his chin. But, as was too often the case, he woke up around 2:00 a.m. and bounced back and forth between sleep and consciousness. When Andras had cornered him, he was convinced he would die. The adrenaline rush of facing your own mortality isn't easy to push aside.

He finally relents and swings his legs out from beneath his blankets and lowers his feet to the cool wood floor. He's given up on getting more sleep this morning. As he stands, he immediately regrets it, his lower back seizes up and he has to hunch forward, placing his hand back on the mattress. He begins to slowly stretch, pushing his hips forward and back. Normally he does yoga a few times a week and always marvels at how much younger it keeps him feeling, but with the trip to Zagreb and the two whirlwind cases he's working, he has neglected his body and every muscle is letting him know. Finally, he feels up to walking to the kitchen. He picks up his kettle from the stove, pops the top, and fills it to one-third full. He places it back on the stove and turns up the heat. After fetching the lemon from the refrigerator, he sits down and waits.

As he sits listening for the kettle to sing, he thinks back to his conversation with Stephen. *Did I say the wrong thing to him?* Maybe he should have told him simply that he had found a possible lead for Samantha. For all he knew, once he got the pictures of her and compared them to the pictures the police had, she wouldn't match any of the abducted women. Peter hears the familiar whistle of the teapot and stands. As he straightens, he gasps for air, feeling his tight back again. He takes the teapot off the stove and pours steaming water into his mug then adds the tea. Almost immediately, he can smell the fragrance and he begins to feel better. With any luck, today is going to bring some closure to the case. He's not sure how, and he suspects it will be in a way he's not anticipating.

Two hours later, Peter's walking north on Váci utca. He's headed toward the Budapest Police Headquarters after stopping by the photo shop to pick up the pictures Stephen had taken on his outing with Samantha. The woman behind the counter, with just a touch of annoyance, told Peter that the film had been ready on Saturday, but he very politely explained to her he hadn't been in town. As Peter walks north, he's tempted to stop and look at the pictures; he's anxious to see Samantha. Not just because he's been searching for her for a week and it would help him to put a face to the name, but he's also wondering if Stephen's description of her beauty is accurate. It's been his experience that men often exaggerate the beauty of their wives and girlfriends. Peter would normally learn later, when he met them, that they weren't quite what had been described.

Peter finally reaches the tall glass building that serves as the main police station in Budapest. Upon entering, he's asked to pass through a metal detector. Peter places the contents of his pockets in a tray and walks through.

"Can I help you?" a female police officer asks him as he comes through the detector.

"Yes," Peter responds, "I'm here to meet with Detective Kovacs. Will you let him know?"

"Of course, please, take a seat. Can I have your name?"

"Andrassy Peter."

"Thank you."

Peter turns to see there's a row of wooden chairs lined up outside the exterior office door. He sits down.

"Peter! Glad you could make it. Anyone try to throw you off a train today?" Kovacs says.

Peter gives him a sly smile. Kovacs leads him through a large room with multiple workstations set up in cubicles. Peter estimates there must be twenty to twenty-five in total. Kovacs stands to the side and lets Peter enter the room. The office is small, maybe ten feet by twelve feet, but it's an actual office, not just a cubicle. Peter sits in one of the two chairs facing the desk while Kovacs sits behind the desk. Behind Kovacs, on the desk, sits a photograph in a frame. The photo features Kovacs, his wife, and his young daughter.

"Well, were you able to track down a photo of this English girl?" Kovacs asks.

Peter smiles and holds up the bundle of pictures in the white photo envelope. "I just picked them up on my way over here. I haven't had a chance to look at them yet."

As Peter moves to open the envelope, Kovacs holds up his hand to stop him. "Before we look at the pictures, I have something I need to ask you."

"Okay, ask away."

Kovacs sits back in his chair letting it recline and places his hands in a steeple. "Our Director was really impressed by your work on the Dobo Andras case. Even though mistakes were made, we were able to gather important information in determining who is running the human trafficking going on in the city. Some of the information you helped us gather was invaluable. We'll be able to recover many women."

Peter hadn't been expecting to be complimented. Although he has a good relationship with Kovacs, he has always thought Kovacs sees him as more of an irritant than a partner or source of support. Peter wants to respond but isn't sure what to say.

"Anyway," Kovacs waves his hand as if to say forget all that, "the Director has been putting together a special task force to investigate the human trafficking ring going on and he asked me to run it past you."

"What is it that you are running past me?"

Kovacs raises his palms to Peter. "Would you be interested in joining the task force?"

If Peter was surprised before, now he's thunderstruck. After he regains his composure, he formulates a question. "In what capacity do you mean? Join the police here in Budapest?"

"Oh, no, no, you would remain a civilian, but you would work as a consultant for us. You could still work your PI angles when time permits, and we would simply pay you as a contractor."

Peter is flattered but he can't ignore the nervous flutter in his stomach. Kovacs seems to understand that the proposition is coming as a surprise to him. Finally, Peter responds. "First off, I'm flattered you would consider me. I really had no idea this was coming. But, as you know, I wouldn't have taken this case had I known what it would lead to. I had no idea what Andras was mixed up in. I thought it would be a simple infidelity case."

Kovacs nods his head. "I know, Peter. I know you want to stick with lighter cases. But we could really use you in the task force. Your international experience and English skills would be a great benefit to the team. Will you at least think about it? You don't have to decide right now."

"Can you give me a couple days to consider?"

"Of course." Kovacs smiles. "Take a few days then give me a call." Pushing his chair back, Kovacs stands and comes around the desk. "Do you mind if I sit on this side while we look at the photos?" Peter shakes his head and Kovacs sits down next to him.

"Stephen, my client, said there should be several pictures of her on this roll of film. It's from his camera. They took some pictures while on a date. He said there is one for sure of her at Hero's Square." Peter opens the envelope and withdraws the photos. He gives half the stack to Kovacs and keeps the other half to look through himself. The first photo is of Stephen with an older woman, and he can see "Cleveland" on a sign in the background. Must be his grandmother, Peter thinks. There are a few more with other friends and family members at the airport in Cleveland then a couple from the airplane; one that looks like it might be over Paris.

"You said there's a photo with her at Hero's Square here in Budapest?"

Peter looks over at Kovacs. "Yeah, that's what he told me."

Kovacs gives Peter a strange look and places a photo on the desk. Peter leans forward to look at it. It's a photo of Hero's Square, but what he sees in the photo confirms his suspicions.

He immediately looks up at Kovacs and their eyes lock.

"I think you better go talk with this kid," Kovacs says.

Chapter Forty-Seven

Stephen

I look down at my watch, it reads 2:47 p.m. Peter said last night that he would come over around 4:00 p.m. and I don't want to miss him. I've got plenty of time, but I sit here willing the streetcar to speed up. We're coming to my stop, the stop closest to my apartment. To my left runs the Danube River and Petofi Bridge. As I sit looking out at the water, I can't help feeling excited. All and all, it has been a pretty good day so far. My first class of the day was Mr. Hodges's (or Fredrickson's). Since learning the story he told me is true, I no longer believe he had anything to do with Samantha's disappearance. That knowledge has allowed me to be more receptive to his lectures, and today I found myself completely engaged in his teaching style and topic. I suspect, by the end of the semester, his class will end up being my favorite.

But even though I know she won't be there; I can't help missing Samantha in the class. Today, I found myself still looking at her seat, imagining her there. She'd be listening to Hodges and I'd watch her, appreciating her every movement. Her graceful, long hair would be falling softly over her shoulders and her eyes would be intense. She'd sense me looking at her and turn to smile that captivating smile.

The streetcar comes to a stop, and I quickly get up and exit. I look at my watch again, 2:59 p.m. I hope Peter isn't late; it's been two weeks since I last saw her, and I don't think I can bear another minute. As I walk to my apartment building, I force my thoughts back to school. Today, in my Entrepreneurial class, I presented on my startup company. One of the requirements was to state my opinion on whether I would be willing to invest money in the chosen company at its current stock price. Whatever position we supported, we would then defend to the class. I recommended buying the stock. It was certainly a controversial position since, to date, the company had yet to turn a profit in a single quarter. Not only that, but its prospects of doing so next year didn't look likely either. The reason I believed it to be a sound investment was based primarily on the stock appreciation. It had appreciated $6 per share in only a couple years. I made the point to the class, and the professor, that e-commerce was only going to get bigger, and the infrastructure that they had built, and continue to build, would set them up for huge expansion in the future. By the end of the presentation, I felt confident I had convinced most of the class I was right. When the professor called for a vote, those in favor of investing outnumbered those against three to one.

I reach my building, enter the front doors, and call for the elevator. As I step inside and press the button to my floor, I allow my mind to drift back to my conversation with Peter from last night. Peter said he likely knew what happened to Samantha and that she was probably still alive. How could that be, and if so, where is she? The elevator pings and I step out into the hallway. As I do, I'm surprised to find Peter has beaten me here. He's standing outside my door.

"Peter? I'm sorry. I didn't know you were here. I thought you were coming at four?"

He looks at me, and his expression causes a pit in the bottom of my stomach. I'm expecting him to bring me good news, but instead, he has an expression of a reluctant executioner. I'm standing outside the door, looking at him, and he acts as if he never heard a word. "Hi, Stephen. I hope you don't mind that I came early. I wanted to see you."

I fumble for my keys, find them, and put the proper key in the lock. "Of course, I don't mind. I'm happy to see you. It sounds like you might have news for me." Again, it seems as if he's hasn't heard me. He's preoccupied by his own thoughts.

I open the door wide indicating Peter should follow me inside, then shut the door behind him. "Let me just put my backpack down and I'll be with you in a moment. Can I get you anything?" Peter's looking around the apartment, almost like he's searching for something, but not finding it. Again, I see no reaction to my words. It's almost as if I'm not here.

When he finally notices me staring at him, he waves his hand. "No, I'm fine. Thank you." I tell him to make himself comfortable and go back to my bedroom. I throw my backpack on the bed and head toward the kitchen. *What is going on with Peter?* Peter's sitting at the table as I come down the hallway. He looks up and forces a grin and I can't help but feel a rush of nervousness. *What does he know?* I walk past him to the fridge, open it, and lean down. I call out to him, "Are you sure I can't get you a soda or some water?"

Peter seems to hear me now. "No, thank you. I'm fine." Although I'm thirsty, I don't want to be rude and drink in front of him, so I shut the fridge without getting anything for myself. I sit down at the table opposite him. "So, I'm dying to hear what you've learned. Ever since our conversation last night, it's all I can think about."

Peter looks in my eyes, studying me. He seems hesitant, almost like he doesn't know where to begin.

"Why don't I start by telling you about the other case I've been working the last week? That might help you see how the two cases, yours and the other, may intersect." I nod as Peter watches me. "But there are some questions I need to ask you," he holds up his finger and points it sternly at me, "and I need you to be honest with me. Completely honest." He does know something, and I want to leave. Get out of here, but I just swallow and nod.

"At the same time, I took the case with you, I was contacted by a woman who wanted to hire me also. She and I met and she explained that she wanted me to find out if her husband was being unfaithful." Based off his body language, I was expecting him to accuse me of something. Not actually tell me about the other case. I just sit watching him as he stares at me. "I agreed. It was a common case. Most are when it comes to infidelity. She explained that her husband owned a restaurant here in Budapest and I agreed to investigate it for her. I went to his restaurant and met the bartender. She was a nice woman and we hit it off. I also met the husband of the woman who hired me and he seemed like a charismatic man, but something was wrong. I earned the confidence of the bartender and learned that the restaurant owner, my client's husband, was involved in human trafficking. He was stealing women here in Budapest for the mafia and moving them to Croatia where they were sold. This husband also managed a second restaurant in Zagreb, Croatia."

As he says it, I feel the relief wash over me. *Is that what happened to Samantha?* Was she taken and sold? Peter's face is devoid of emotion and I can't understand why. He said she is likely alive. *Why is he so morose?* "I decided I needed to go to Croatia and see if the bartenders' suspicions were accurate."

He's taking forever to get to the point. I want to ask a question but can see he's going to tell me what's going on in his own good time.

"Before I went to Croatia, I had to call his wife and find out how and when he was traveling. When I was on the phone with her, I heard a man's voice and, before I knew it, her husband came on the line. I hung up but not before he heard a car horn from the street below my apartment. He knew she was talking on the phone with someone and lying to him about it." Peter taps on the table with his fingers and for the first time since sitting down at the table, he looks away from me. He looks toward the kitchen as if he's seeing it all again in his mind. "I got on the train, not knowing what happened to my client, and, coincidentally, ended up sharing the same rail car as her husband." Peter turns his head back to me and shrugs. "Anyway, I got to Croatia, got a ride to his restaurant, and learned for a fact that he was definitely involved in human trafficking by way of taking young women from Budapest."

Now I see that look. The look he gave me the first time we met back in the café. The time he accused me of withholding information from him. "When I was there, I learned that an English-speaking red-headed woman had been in the Budapest restaurant around the time Samantha disappeared."

I can't help myself. I smack my hand down on the table then raise my hands to my face. I put a hand to my cheek and feel how hot it is. "There you go," I exclaim, "I knew she had been taken. Did you get her back? Is she in Croatia?" I start to stand from the table and he raises his hand trying to calm me.

"Just wait. Let me finish the story and you'll understand."

I sigh and sit back down. His face is changed now. He's no longer looking at me with suspicious eyes, they've become curious.

"Well," Peter continues, "the restaurant owner ended up trying to kill me twice and the last time was on the train headed back to Budapest. He failed and killed himself in the process." I look at him with surprise but hold my tongue. "The man kept files on the women he abducted, including pictures." I feel myself sit forward at this revelation. That's it, they must have a picture of her. But if they do, where is she now? "So, I talked with the detectives who had those pictures and asked if I could see them. I told them about your case, and they asked me to come and meet with them today and bring pictures of Samantha."

Peter reaches inside his jacket and withdraws a white envelope with red and blue writing on it. I recognize the logo on the front, having seen it in multiple shops around Budapest, "FOTO."

"Luckily, I had turned your roll of film in to be developed and they were ready. Before I even looked at them though, I walked to the police headquarters and met with the detective I was working with." If I was anxious before, I feel myself ready to explode. I want to scream at him to get to the point. "Do you remember what photos you had on that camera roll?"

"I know I had some from when I left Cleveland. I know I had a few I took from the airplane. There were some I took of Budapest when I first got here and then several Samantha and I took when we toured around the city, sightseeing."

The curious look is back. "And why was it that you didn't develop the film?"

How many times have I told him? "I was unsure how to get it developed, and after several days, I just simply forgot. I know that sounds like a weak excuse, but it's the truth."

Peter's looking at me with so much scrutiny that I feel myself squirm in my chair. I imagine he thinks I'm lying, but it's the truth. At least, I think it's the truth.

"That's the truth?" Peter asks, almost as if he's inside my head now. I find the question so disconcerting that I almost stand and get myself a drink of water. My mouth has grown dry and it feels as if it's full of cotton. But, if I was put off balance by that question, the next one rocks me. "Did you have an imaginary friend as a kid?"

"What?" I croak, barely able to get the word out.

"Did you ever play pretend? Or have an imaginary friend as a kid?"

I'm shaking my head at him. "Yeah, I did. Not for very long, just a year or so."

"How old were you?"

"I think I was maybe thirteen or so."

"Did anything big happen in your life when you were thirteen?"

What does this have to do with Samantha? "Yes, my mother died of cancer. A couple weeks later my grandma brought me here to Hungary. While here, I guess I created a friend. His name was Chuck. After I went back home life was much different. My dad was struggling, and I felt alone. Chuck helped me get through it." Peter seems satisfied and begins opening the envelope of photos. He passes the stack over to me.

I turn the photos over and look at the top one, still unsure what is going on. The photo was at the Cleveland airport with Grandma Erzsi. I look up at him, unable to see why he's showing me this. "Keep looking through them. See if you notice anything strange." I begin flipping through them looking carefully. All of the photos are as I would expect. There are pictures of me and my family in the airport in Cleveland, a couple from the airplane, and then several of Samantha and me on our date. I look at the pictures of Samantha closely. Maybe there's something about her that I didn't see before but as I examine her, I see nothing but the beautiful woman I've known. Finally, I look back up at Peter.

"You don't see anything strange about those photos?" Peter asks.

I spread them out on the table and look at them again. I shake my head. "No, what am I missing?"

Peter's brow furrows as he looks back at me. He leans over and points at a picture. "Look at this one with you in Hero's Square. What's wrong with the picture?" Again, I go back to examining the photo and again I see nothing. *Is it something about the statues in the background? Or the people that were far behind us?*

Peter points at the picture. "There you are," he's pointing at me, "but next to you is nobody. Samantha isn't there."

I jerk my head up and stare at him. *What is he saying?! Someone deleted her from the photo?*

"Stephen, Samantha never existed. You imagined her. I'm not entirely sure why or how you did it, but she never existed. There is no missing persons case because there is no Samantha outside of your own head."

I look at him then look back at the picture. As I do, Samantha's image disappears from the photo. I stare at the photo as she slips away from me. My mind retreats back to that first day in school when I hit my head hard on the desk. I think about each time I saw and talked to Samantha. I think about the times we sat side by side on the streetcar or subway as people looked almost fearful of us. I remember the kids laughing at us at Hero's Square. I feel my face grow hot with shame and embarrassment. I imagined the whole thing. Just like when I was thirteen, I imagined a friend to help me deal with my loneliness.

My head's spinning, and I can't help the tears that spring to my eyes unbidden. "How could I have done that? How could I imagine her so vividly then hire someone to chase a ghost? I accused Mr. Hodges."

I look at Peter through tear-filled eyes. "Stephen, I put myself in your position. You are still young, and you come all the way to a foreign country knowing nobody. You go to a school where everyone is a stranger and most of the kids are from other countries as well. Anytime you go in public, you hear Hungarian spoken much faster and different from what you ever have known. And on top of all that, you come back to the place you have only ever visited following the most devastating circumstance a child can deal with. The loss of a parent. Anyone would struggle. It makes sense you would be lonely and invent someone. Don't be too hard on yourself."

Peter sits looking at me, and I look down. I want to be alone and I think he knows it. He stands, pats me on the shoulder, walks across the room, and leaves, closing the door behind him.

Epilogue

I sit looking out the window. It's been a month since Peter came to see me and revealed I imagined Samantha. I'm sitting in Mr. Hodges's Leading and Managing People class. The very class where I first imagined her. Mr. Hodges is up at the front of the class waving his arms around and giving one of his customary lectures. Today, he's talking about a book written many years ago, 1936, by Dale Carnegie called, *How to Win Friends and Influence People*. Ordinarily, I'd like this discussion, but today, I'm only partially listening. I can't quite kick the gloom I'm feeling. For the rest of that night, after Peter left, I sat in my apartment ashamed and humiliated. I went and talked to the school counselor the next day and opened up. I've met with her two or three times a week since. She's helped me deal with things I've carried since my mother died. I'm making progress but I still feel lonely.

As I continue to stare out the window, the same thoughts run over and over in my mind. How could I allow myself to invent a girlfriend? How could I believe it so much that it would consume all my thoughts for over a month? Eventually, I look back to the class. Hodges is no longer speaking, and the class is empty. Hodges stands at the front of the room looking at me, seemingly hesitant to break me from the trance. I feel my embarrassment under his watchful gaze. Hodges starts moving toward me and I contemplate opening the window and jumping out.

"Are you okay, Stephen?"

I consider lying to him. I consider making some excuse about how I had started thinking about something and just lost track of the class. But something in my mind stops me.

"I don't know," I admit. Hodges sits down on the desk in front of me, looking even more worried now. I can hardly stand that look. It's the same look Peter gave me when he told me about Samantha. Something about it feels forced, almost like people assume it's the look they should give to hide their lack of empathy.

"Tell me what's going on," Hodges prompts.

I shrug. "It's probably not anything you would understand." I look back out the window, not meeting his gaze.

"You're right, I probably won't. But then, I could have told you the same thing about my story and my life. I could have given you a quick answer and moved on, but I opened up to you."

He's right, and I know it. I turn back to look at him and the look I see in his eyes transforms from judgmental to sympathetic. *Maybe he does actually care. Maybe he is someone I can trust.*

"You may not believe what I'm going to tell you," I reply.

Hodges raises his eyebrows but responds, "Try me."

I take a deep breath and, before I know it, I'm telling him the whole thing. I'm telling him about how I imagined this ravishing British woman named Samantha; how she had sat right there in the class; how we had gone on multiple dates together and how she had suddenly disappeared; how I had hired a private investigator to find out what happened to her; and how the investigator proved to me that she wasn't real. Through the whole thing, Hodges doesn't even make a comment. At times, he raises an eyebrow or nods, but says nothing.

"And I think I also owe you an apology, Mr. Hodges. For some reason, I invented in my mind that Samantha found you creepy." I inwardly grimace as I say it. "I told the investigator and he followed you and talked to you."

Hodges begins nodding. "The man that followed me?"

I shrug. "I really have no excuse. It wasn't anything against you, I just think you were the teacher we shared. You were impacted by my craziness."

Hodges waves his hand at me. "Oh, come on, that was nothing. It was kind of fun." He laughs and I chuckle.

"No, I want you to know, I'm really sorry. I'm so ashamed and embarrassed."

Hodges shakes his head. "Stephen, I've had way worse than that. No need to apologize. Really! But I am curious about something."

"Okay."

"You said the investigator asked you about an imaginary friend when you were younger. You said you had one for about a year when your mom died."

"Yep."

"Your family is Hungarian, right? Your grandparents and your dad?" I'm not sure why that's relevant but I nod. "Did you ever come over to Hungary when you were a kid?"

"Only once when my grandma brought me after my mom died."

Hodges looks at me solemnly. "I'm not a psychiatrist or trained therapist, but I've had my fair share of counseling and, I must say, I think the two are related."

"What do you mean? What two?"

Hodges stands and starts walking in his trademark way. "I think you have some emotions and things you experienced when you were a kid, and when you came back here, all of that came back to the surface. I think you reverted back to thirteen, or whatever age you were when your mom died, and your grandma brought you here. As a kid, you invented a friend to play with you and keep you company. It's probably what you wanted and or needed most at that time. It makes sense that you would imagine a girlfriend now because that's what you want now at this age."

I absently bring my hand up and start to rub at the back of my neck. "At least my crazy makes some sense."

Hodges rolls his eyes. "You aren't crazy. You definitely have some things you need to deal with, but you aren't crazy. I think you should talk with a professional. Someone that knows way more than me."

"I am. And she says the same thing. I've been meeting with her for about a month now and she says I'm making great progress."

He raises his hands in triumph. "Well, see...there you go."

I chuckle. "You know what actually hurts the most in all this?" Hodges shakes his head and waits expectantly. "I miss her. As crazy and as weird as that might be, I actually miss Samantha. I had a lot of fun with her even though it was absolutely imaginary."

Hodges shrugs. "I don't think that's strange at all. I think that shows you what is missing in your life. You need that companionship. You need that excitement. It's perfectly natural that you should want a girlfriend."

I get up from my desk. "Thank you, Mr. Hodges. Thank you for listening to me and not judging me too harshly. And again, I'm sorry I thought what I did about you."

Hodges waves me away again. "I'm glad you confided in me, Stephen. Promise me you will continue getting some help? Confiding in others is not something to be ashamed of."

I bob my head. "I promise, I will." I turn and start walking out of the classroom when Hodges calls me back.

"Hey, Stephen, a couple other things. We talked about why you imagined Samantha in the first place. But why did she disappear? Have you thought about that?"

"I haven't."

Hodges looks intense now and walks toward me. "She disappeared because you had adjusted. You were used to living in Budapest by then. You were comfortable in this school. You didn't need her anymore."

I consider that and as I let that realization sink in, I begin to feel better about myself. "You said there were a couple things?"

"True I did." Hodges puts a hand on my shoulder. "That girlfriend thing is pretty attainable. You are a good-looking guy and there are plenty of girls right here in this school. You just need to show them you are interested." Hodges smiles as he says the last part and I smile too. He's right.

I begin walking down the hall toward my last class knowing I'm going to be really late. I decide instead to change course and leave the building entirely. I walk across the courtyard and enter the Administration Building. I know exactly what I need and want to do; I just can't believe I'm about to do it. I take a deep breath and open the door to the head office. Just as I hoped and feared, she's sitting behind the desk. I walk right up and lean on the counter.

"Hi."

That's all that comes out at first. Gretchen, the gorgeous blonde who sits at the desk looks up and smiles.

"Hi, can I help you with something?"

My heart is pounding in my chest but I'm committed. "My name is Stephen. You helped me on my first day here." I'm sure she doesn't remember but I don't know what else to say.

"Yes, Stephen, I remember you. How's school going? Do you like it?"

"It's going great. Have you been in Budapest long?" I ask.

"I've been here a little over a year."

I'm stalling and I know it. I tell myself to be bold. "I was thinking I would like to look around the city more to explore all the sightseeing spots. I think you're breathtaking, and I'd like to get to know you better. Would you be interested in coming with me?"

Gretchen grins bigger now. "I have to work right now."

I force a chuckle.

"Oh, I don't mean right now. I mean maybe this weekend?"

"Sure! That sounds fun." Gretchen smiles at me and my knees feel a little weak.

"Great! Maybe Saturday? Can I get your number?"

She happily gets out a Post-it note and writes her number on the yellow paper. She hands it to me with a smile and I feel a spark of electricity as her hand brushes against mine. "I'll call you tonight to work out the details?"

She smiles again and nods.

I turn to exit the head office, but before I do, I wave to her and almost run into the door.

She laughs and smiles even larger.

As I walk down the hallway, I realize I'm now better than ever.

Also By

D.J. Maughan

Pursuit of Demons
Book Two of the Vanished Series

Reenter the shadowy world of Budapest in the year 2000. Join Peter Andrassy, a retired New York City detective and new consultant for the human trafficking task force in Budapest, as he works to uncover the thriving sex traffic in the city. Following the death of Andras, trafficking operations have moved to a nightclub, and Zsuzsa, the intoxicating bartender, is working inside. When a young girl goes missing, followed by Zsuzsa, Peter risks his life chasing their trail to Ukraine.

As obstacles mount, Peter discovers a mole within the Hungarian National Police is feeding the traffickers inside information. Who can Peter trust? Can he save the missing women?

Coming Summer 2023

About Author

Thank you for reading my book. Like you, I'm selective when it comes to books, and I'm humbled you chose mine. I'm an avid reader, event manager, father, public speaker, and author. I lived in Budapest as a younger man and have returned to visit multiple times. I hope you were able to feel my love for the city as you read the book. Hungary gave me the best eduction of my life, and I will always be grateful for the time I spent there. Beyond reading six to eight books a month, I enjoy cooking, DIY projects at home, dinner with my wife, working out, playing basketball with my sons, watching live sports, and traveling. I look for inspiration everywhere especially while studying and visiting diverse places and cultures. Whether jumping from a cliff in Hawaii, or hiking the Plitvice Lakes in Croatia, I'm in heaven as long as my wife and four teenage boys are at my side.

Connect with me at djmaughan.com. Don't forget to subscribe to my newsletter to stay up to date on forthcoming books.

Made in the USA
Coppell, TX
20 December 2022